Darling Jake

Keith Bond

Darling Jake
Keith Bond

All rights reserved. No part of this publication may be reproduced, stored in any retrieval system or transmitted in any form or by any means, electronic, mechanical, photocopying, recording or otherwise, without the prior written permission of the copyright holder for which application should be addressed in the first instance to the publishers. The views expressed herein are those of the author and do not necessarily reflect the opinion or policy of Tricorn Books or the employing organisation, unless specifically stated. No liability shall be attached to the author, the copyright holder or the publishers for loss or damage of any nature suffered as a result of the reliance on the reproduction of any of the contents of this publication or any errors or omissions in the contents.

ISBN 9781914615764
A CIP catalogue record for this
book is available from the British Library.

Published 2023

Tricorn Books,
Treadgolds
1a Bishop Street
Portsmouth
PO1 3HN

Darling Jake

Darling Jake is the sequel to *Jake* by the same author.

This book is dedicated to drag artistes everywhere.
Thank you for your vision, hard work, dedication, fun, frolics, blood, sweat, tears, laughter and entertainment. I feel it is important to mention I am aware not all drag performers are gay, or even male for that matter. Drag has now become a universally accepted and acclaimed form of entertainment thanks to the likes of Danny La Rue, Lily Savage, Dame Edna Everage, RuPaul, to name but a few.

Contents

Chapter 1	9
Chapter 2	19
Chapter 3	28
Chapter 4	36
Chapter 5	40
Chapter 6	48
Chapter 7	53
Chapter 8	59
Chapter 9	69
Chapter 10	73
Chapter 11	79
Chapter 12	85
Chapter 13	95
Chapter 14	107
Chapter 15	114
Chapter 16	122
Chapter 17	129
Chapter 18	141
Chapter 19	148
Chapter 20	153
Chapter 21	160
Chapter 22	164
Chapter 23	168
Chapter 24	178
Chapter 25	188

Chapter 26	190
Chapter 27	195
Chapter 28	203
Chapter 29	208
Chapter 30	213
Chapter 31	219
Chapter 32	222
Chapter 33	229
Chapter 34	238
Chapter 35	242
Chapter 36	245
Chapter 37	250
Chapter 38	256
Chapter 39	261
Chapter 40	263
Chapter 41	270
Chapter 42	276
Chapter 43	281
Chapter 44	288
Chapter 45	296
Chapter 46	304
Chapter 47	308
Epilogue	311

Chapter 1

When Jake had told Pauline and Ned that he was leaving the farm and moving down to London, he had expected them to be a little offhand and disgruntled with him, but they were nothing of the sort. Instead they were encouraging and helpful. He felt a little more guilty for even thinking that they were the kind of people who would behave like he'd imagined, when all they had ever been were the most kind, understanding and generous people he had ever known, apart from his mam and Bridie Maguire of course. His mam had been the one who had voiced concerns when he told her and Ted; she asked him if he thought he was doing the right thing. She had also pointed out that once he'd left and Ned had taken on another worker, he wouldn't be able to come running back to the farm and expect his old job back if things didn't work out in London for him. Jake thought that his mam possibly felt he was letting Ned and Pauline down, somehow betraying their friendship, as well as being slightly overprotective, but he didn't feel that way, he needed to make this important change in his life, get on and live it, be true to himself.

Jake pointed out that he had no intention of doing anything like that; he would love to come back and visit of course, just to see how they were, and look around the old place, but he was determined that he was going to make a go of things and have a new life in London. As much as he loved farm work, he knew that it wasn't going to completely satisfy and fulfil him now. He said goodbye to his mam and Ted, promising to regularly keep in contact.

He had the money that Bridie had left him as well as his own savings. He was hoping to live off his savings and not touch the twenty thousand pounds that was in the bank, until he found a property that he wanted to buy. He wouldn't have to find work straight away, but he certainly didn't see himself lounging around being a man of leisure indefinitely. He had always been a hard worker and kept himself active, so at some point after he had found himself somewhere to live, he would have to decide what he wanted to do for employment. Whatever it was, it was certainly going to be very different from the life he had known on the farm.

That's exactly what he felt he wanted though, something more exciting, more exhilarating, than milking cows, driving a tractor around a field, or lambing sheep. He wanted to meet new people who were like him, he needed to plough a new furrow for himself, so to speak. Pastures new were calling.

Ned was contacted by a man responding to the advert he had placed in *Farmers Weekly*. On the telephone he had said he had a lot of experience in farm work, so Ned asked him to come for an interview. He drove a car and only lived a short distance away in Finckley. Dave Tilsley was thirty-eight; he had a wife called Mary and two children, Paul aged nine and Nina aged seven.

Ned and Pauline found them to be highly suitable applicants, the best out of the four that had applied, so they gave him the job and they moved into the cottage two weeks later. Dave started work with Ned the day after. Thankfully Ned had found someone in time to help him with the harvest.

On the Monday the week before the Tilsleys moved into the cottage, Jake had said a very emotional goodbye to

Pauline before Ned drove him to Hanworth railway station. They shook hands and hugged.

Ned said, "Don't you dare forget to write and let us know how you're doing or Pauline will have my guts for garters. And be careful, life in the city can be dangerous I'm told."

"I won't, and I will be careful," Jake replied. "I'm going to miss you both. Hope all goes well with the Tilsleys. Bye Ned."

Jake bought his ticket and caught the 9.15 train to Euston. As the train pulled out of Hanworth station he thought to himself, *I'm finally on my way, this is the start of a new life and I'm going to make sure it's a good one.*

The journey was very pleasant. The train had stopped at eleven different stations before arriving at Euston. He had read a copy of *Town* magazine that someone had left on the seat next to him, but when the train entered each station Jake enjoyed seeing the people scurrying on and off the train. He could people-watch those on the platform, and the people who came to sit close to him, especially the good-looking men. When he got off the train at Euston, he planned to go by underground train to Kilburn via Baker Street on the Bakerloo line. He was amazed to see so many men wearing bowler hats; he thought it was a very strange sight, but Jake found the hustle and bustle and the noise of the city exhilarating. He was almost swept along by the crowd down onto the underground.

The reason he had chosen to go to Kilburn was that when he had bought a copy of *Daltons Weekly* at home the previous week, he had noticed a lot of bedsits were being advertised in that area so he thought this would provide him with more immediate opportunities to find suitable accommodation. He knew nothing about Kilburn, but that was all part of this new adventure. He was of the mind that if he didn't like the place he would move somewhere else. He left Kilburn station turned right on Kilburn High Road and started to walk along it as the ticket collector had suggested. He had advised him to look in newsagents' windows for flats and bedsits to rent, so that's what he did. Jake spotted one that caught his eye, it sounded promising.

Bed-Sitting Room With Separate Kitchen
Would Suit Professional Man
Rent £80 per Month, Gas/Electricity Provided.
Shared Bathroom & W.C.
One month rent in advance.
References Required
Contact: Landlord, Mr Costa
14 Buckley Road. Kilburn. London NW6

He didn't have a local map so he tried stopping people to ask for directions, but most people were in too much of a hurry, or suspicious of what he wanted of them and wouldn't stop, so he went into the newsagents to ask the shopkeeper. He thought it would be better to buy something as it might make him more predisposed to helping him, so he bought a copy of *Daltons Weekly* magazine and a packet of chewing gum; he could have a look in the paper at houses for sale. The man behind the counter knew Kilburn well and gave him good instructions to get to Buckley Road. It was some distance away, he had to stay on this side of the road, pass under Brondesbury station bridge and look for a Rymans stationers, Buckley Road was just past it on the right. By the time Jake had walked along the busy pavement his case seemed to be getting heavier. He had stopped several times along the way to put it down and have a rest, changing hands countless times to avoid getting blisters. Jake thought Buckley Road was very pleasant, it was lined with pollarded trees and the houses were Victorian with bow-fronted windows. He found number 14 about midway along and walked up the short front path and rang the doorbell hoping that it would be a nice place and that it hadn't already been taken.

A swarthy looking man who looked to be in his late forties opened the door. He looked Jake up and down.

"Yes?"

"Mr Costa?"

"Yes?"

"I've come about the room, is it still available?" Jake asked hopefully.

"Yes, it isa still vacant, rooma three, you lika see a da room?" he said in a foreign accent.

"Yes please," Jake replied.

"Come in, follow me dissa way."

And he led Jake into a large hallway that had bright patterned Victorian tiles on the floor.

The landlord Lorenzo Costa was an immigrant from Palermo. He was friendly but very business-like. He lived alone on the ground floor. He led Jake up the staircase directly in front of them. They reached the top of the first flight, walked along a landing which turned to the left, they went up two more steps and a little further along the landing. Directly in front of them, before the next flight of stairs that continued on the left, was number three.

Mr Costa opened the door which led into a small but adequate kitchen. There was a large square sash window directly opposite that went from waist height almost to the ceiling, which made the room very light. To the left of the window was a stone sink with an immersion heater, a floor-standing cupboard with glass-fronted sliding doors, and a gas cooker with a whistling kettle on one of the rings. There was a kitchen table and two chairs against the opposite wall. Jake put his suitcase down as Mr Costa opened the door by the side of the cooker that led to the bed-sitting room.

"This is it, it isa da good place, yes?"

"Yes," Jake replied.

He looked around. It was a large room with a single bed, a wardrobe, two easy chairs, a coffee table, a bookcase, a gas fire with a real marble surround and a large walk-in bay window that gave a fabulous view of the street. Jake liked it, he thought it would suit him down to the ground. Jake told Mr Costa that he thought the room would be fine and would like to take it.

Mr Costa smiled. "I needa to aska you a few questions. Ara you working?"

"I have just come by train from the Midlands this morning. I intend to look for a job later, but I am of independent means financially. I do not need to work, but I am used to working hard and keeping myself occupied!"

"Do you ava da references?"

"Yes I do." Jake took them out of his inside jacket pocket and gave them to Mr Costa. There was one from Ned, and a character reference from his family doctor Jeremy Carlston.

Mr Costa read both of the references, looked at Jake and smiled.

"Dat isa good, but firsta dee rules of a da ouse, no parties in a da room, and no bringing da ladies in a my ouse, OK?"

"Yes that's fine Mr Costa, but I am allowed to bring my friends back?"

Yes, a you can, but I keep da quiet ouse, understand?"

"Of course, I won't cause you any trouble, Mr Costa."

"Dat is a good, or else you is outa pretty quick."

"You ava da money, that's £80 deposit anda one weeks rent £20, isa £100?"

"Yes I have it." Jake had previously taken the £100 out of his wallet and kept it in his jacket pocket as he didn't want to be having to count it out. "Here you are," Jake said, handing him the money.

"Thank you, you no damage da furniture, you breaka, you pay, OK?" Mr Costa shook him by the hand.

"Yes OK," Jake replied, desperately wanting to get settled in now, nip to the local supermarket for some groceries, come back and make a cup of tea.

"Ere ara da keys, I go bringa da receipt anda da rent book."

Mr Costa went downstairs and Jake walked around the room. The bed was made with clean sheets, a couple of blankets and a pink counterpane. He was making a mental note of the things he would do to make this his temporary home. He went back into the kitchen and looked in the cupboard and the drawers; there was basic crockery, cooking equipment and cutlery, he could manage with them until he bought his own.

Mr Costa came back. "Here isa da receipt anda dee rent book, I hope you will be very appy ere. Any problems, my flat is a downstairs, OK?"

"Yes, thank you Mr Costa."

"Oh I forgeta, the toilet anda da bathroom are justa downa da all, maka sure you cleana da bath."

"Thank you, I'll find them," Jake said.

After the landlord had gone, Jake brought his case into the living room and put it on the bed. He unstrapped the belt from around it, flicked open the flip-up catches and opened the lid. He opened the wardrobe to find there were no coat hangers. He left his case as it was, picked up the keys, went out to the main door and locked it. He would look for coat hangers as he was doing his shopping.

As he walked towards the local Safeway supermarket that he had spotted on his way to look at the bedsit, he was noting what different shops there were close by. He saw that there was a laundrette at the end of the road which would definitely be very handy.

He bought two brown paper bags full of shopping, which included obvious staples like tea, coffee, and milk, but he had also had to buy cleaning materials. His arms were quite tired by the time he had walked back to the house. He was so pleased to be able to unlock his room door, unpack the shopping and put it away in the cupboard, then fill the tin kettle, light the gas and put it on to boil for his well-deserved cup of tea.

He was sitting savouring his cup of tea with a digestive biscuit when there was a tap on the kitchen door. He got up to answer it thinking it would be Mr Costa. He opened the door to see a man around forty-five years old. He was wearing a flamboyant silk kimono with flip-flop sandals which had a flower on the top of each one. Jake gawped at him in amazement.

"Oh hello, I thought I'd come and give you a welcome, love. I'm Ricci and I live on the top floor," he said in an outrageously plummy, camp voice that reminded Jake of the comedian Kenneth Williams.

"Oh, hello, I'm Jake," he replied, still a little bemused and wondering if he should invite him in or not. He didn't really feel like entertaining a stranger, but thankfully Ricci continued.

"I won't stop, I don't want to disturb you love, I know you've only just arrived. I just wanted to say that next Saturday evening I'm having a bit of a get-together with some friends, you'd be very welcome to join us. Just bring a bottle, say seven o'clock?"

Naively and undiplomatically, Jake raised the question, "I thought Mr Costa wasn't keen on his tenants having parties?"

"Oooh, take no notice of her love, so long as she gets an invite she's fine!"

Jake gave a bemused sort of half laugh, he was trying to assess whether Ricci's affectation was put on or just came naturally; he suspected it was the latter. He'd seen a few camp queens in the pub he used to go to in Coventry, they were often loud and outrageous and usually harmless enough, but he'd seen some of them in bitchy mode too and he didn't like that, they could be quite vicious and vitriolic if you got on the wrong side of them.

"Yes, thank you, I'd love to come," Jake said.

"Ooh lovely, don't have anything to eat beforehand love as there'll be plenty to eat."

"Yes, thanks again Ricci, I'll bring a bottle."

"Fab ducks, see you then Jake."

As he went back into his room to finish his tea, he thought that Ricci's little soiree next Saturday would be an ideal opportunity for him to get to know a few people and hopefully there might be a guy there that he liked, as long as they weren't all raving queens.

Later that evening, Jake made himself a simple meal of a cheese omelette and baked beans with bread and butter made from a fresh crusty loaf. He felt like he needed an early night as he'd been on the go since early that morning, he'd found the travelling quite tiring.

After it was dark, he stood in the window of his darkened room looking up and down the street at the lights up on Kilburn High Road, as well as all the lighted windows in the houses opposite. He wondered what sort of people lived in them all. He imagined that there might be a few lonely souls among them, as he guessed that London could be a bit of a cold, impersonal place. He thought to himself, *the last thing I'm going to be is lonely*.

He made himself a cup Horlicks with milk and got himself undressed. He put his pyjamas and dressing gown on, went to the bathroom, came back and climbed into bed. He lay there sipping his nightcap thinking about what he was going to do tomorrow; there were some things that he wanted to buy, one of them being a television and a radiogram, he needed a mop and bucket, some dishcloths, dusters and furniture polish. He must ring his mam, Ted, Pauline and Ned and let them know he was alright and that he had found himself a nice temporary place to stay until he started viewing houses to buy.

Chapter 2

Jake pressed the doorbell to the top flat, number 4. He could hear loud music, voices and laughter coming from inside the flat. A man wearing a black open neck shirt with white trousers, showing a hairy chest with a gold medallion opened the door. Jake thought he must have poured himself into his trousers as they left absolutely nothing to the imagination. Jake thought to himself, *he must have certainly been at the front of the queue when they gave cocks out.*

The man smiled at him and said in a very loud Australian drawl of a voice, "Ah, hello darling, you must be Jake. I'm Toby, Ricci's boyfriend." He shook Jake's hand. "Ricci said you were a looker. Come on in, let me take that bottle from you." He looked at the bottle label with knowledge and admiration. "Thank you, gosh that's class. I'll put that to one side for our cellar, it's much too good for these philistines!" Laughing he asked, "What would you like to drink?"

"I'd love a whisky and dry ginger please, if you have some."

"Oh a man with taste eh. One whisky and dry ginger coming up, would you like ice in that?"

"Yes please," Jake replied.

While he was waiting for Toby to bring his drink, he gazed around the kitchen. It was exactly the same layout as his own but the walls had been decorated in a mid-shade of green and the paintwork a bright white, which gave it a very fresh look. The door to the living room was partially open and Jake could see a few of the other guests' faces, talking animatedly, laughing, enjoying themselves.

"Here's your drink darling. Now, I'll introduce you to everyone and leave you to fend for yourself, so that you can get to know folk. Don't be shy, just enjoy yourself."

Toby pushed open the living room door to reveal it packed with at least twenty people. As he did so, he announced, "Darlings, this is Jake, he's our new neighbour, he moved in earlier this week. Be gentle with him, he's just a shy country boy." He gave a cheeky little laugh and just left him standing there.

Jake felt himself colour up, he thought he would die of embarrassment.

"Hello everyone," was all he could think to say.

"Jake darling!" Ricci shouted across the room waving a gloved hand with several sparkling rings on top. He was in full make-up with pink and green eye shadow, sweeping eyelashes, a pleated turban on his head, and wearing a flowing pink and silver kaftan. Jake thought he looked like a glamorous actress.

He made his way over to Jake, pushing and sweeping through his guests to get to him.

"How lovely of you to come," he said as he kissed him on the cheek. He smelled heavily of expensive perfume. "I have a delightful young man I must introduce you to, before the wolves devour him. Come with me, I'm sure you'll like him."

He took hold of Jake's hand and tugged him into the mêlée. He found the guy he wanted Jake to meet; he was a tall, slim, dark-haired handsome man with a 'Viva Zapata' moustache, deep smouldering brown eyes and thick inviting lips. He looked to be around thirty-five. Jake thought, *Cor, what are you doing the rest of my life, and what do you like for breakfast!* He would have said it out loud but he didn't have the nerve.

"Jake, this is Jim, Jim meet Jake, now you two Js have fun!" Ricci giggled mischievously and flounced off to join two girls who Jake presumed were lesbians as one of them looked very masculine.

A popular hit tune began playing as Jim held out his hand to shake Jake's.

"Hello Jake," he said in a deep manly voice. "It's very nice to meet you. Ricci was telling me you only moved in on Monday, I hope you've settled in."

"It's very nice to meet you too, Jim," Jake replied, feeling an instant frisson between them. "Yes I have settled in thanks, I think I'm going to like it here." He placed his glass on the fireplace surround behind them.

"Where have you moved from? I can't place your accent," Jim asked him.

"A village called Grendore, in Warwickshire. Have you heard of it?"

"No, can't say I have. Where's it near?"

"Addleston."

Jim looked puzzled so he ventured, "Haneaton?"

"Oh yes, Haneaton rings a bell, though I'm not sure why!"

The music changed to a slow romantic ballad, sung by a woman with a soulful, sultry voice, and even though there was hardly room to move, Jim said, "I want to dance with you." He slipped his arm around Jake's waist, gently pulling him closer. Jake put his arm on his shoulder and their other hands' fingers entwined, their bodies closed in and they moved sensuously together, oblivious of anyone else in the room as the haunting words of the song swept over them both.

Come closer to me love

I've been waiting so long,

Come closer and kiss me
This feeling's so strong,
Be mine now, forever
Our hearts are as one
Come closer my darling
Let our kiss linger on.

Jake could feel the warmth of Jim's breathing close to his ear and he so wanted to kiss him, but he didn't want to appear to be too forward or eager and was hoping Jim would make the first move, but he didn't attempt to kiss Jake at all.

When the song had finished playing, Jim still held onto Jake, reluctant to let him go and the beautiful moments they had shared to disappear.

He looked into Jake's eyes and said, "That was lovely, and you're lovely too Jake. I wish we were alone and not in a room full of people."

"Thank you, you're not bad yourself," Jake replied, "but the night is yet young Jim, let's enjoy the party, you haven't got to dash off anywhere soon, have you?"

"No I haven't Jake, I'm not going anywhere," he said pointedly.

Jake picked up his drink and finished it off. "Would you like me to get you a drink? I need another one," he asked Jim.

"Yes please, I'll have a Bacardi and Coke, if you can manage to get into the kitchen to get them."

"Oh I'm sure I'll manage. Don't go away, will you?" Jake said smiling.

"Like I said, I'm not going anywhere, hurry back."

Jake began to ease himself through the people in the room, who he felt sure had grown in number since he arrived. As he moved through them, several pairs of eyes latched on to him, looking longingly at him. He had to ask the people by the door to move aside so that he could get out and he heard one of them say, "Not leaving already I hope darling?" but he didn't see who said it.

Gosh, Jake thought, *I'm in great demand tonight, but I already know who I'm going home with thank you.*

There were quite a few people in the kitchen, including Mr Costa.

Jake said, "Hello Mr Costa, nice to see you."

Mr Costa smiled, "I thinka you ada better calla me Lorenzo now we ava met socially, OK."

"Yes, OK Lorenzo," Jake replied smiling.

It was a struggle to pour drinks, but Toby spotted Jake and asked him what drinks he wanted and as he was pouring them for him he cheekily whispered, "I can see Jim's got the hots for you Jake," handing him the drinks.

Jake thanked him and said, "The feeling's mutual, Toby."

Toby winked at him and smiled. Jake pushed open the door and started to negotiate his way back to where Jim was waiting. He heard a voice say hello but he was concentrating hard not to spill the drinks or get bumped into, so he didn't get to see who it was. Tonight he only had eyes for Jim anyway.

"Here you are Jim, phew, that was fun!" Jake said as he handed him his drink.

"Thanks," Jim said. "I was thinking someone had whisked you away and you weren't coming back!"

"I did have a couple of serious offers worth considering, but I turned them down," Jake said laughing. "What say we grab a bite to eat, finish our drinks then we can make our escape and *you* can whisk me away?"

Jim laughed and replied, "That's the best offer I've had all night, no, all year actually."

"I'm sure that isn't true," Jake replied, smiling.

They managed to move to the buffet table with their drinks to get some food. When they had eaten and finished their drinks, Jim thought that they should find somewhere quieter where they could *talk*. So Jake suggested that they leave separately, not because he was embarrassed in anyway, but he just didn't want everyone knowing his business. Jim agreed, so Jake left first as they'd arranged. Jim was to wait for about five minutes, then join him outside. Jake would wait for him on the landing.

Jake squeezed through the crowd and as he entered the kitchen he saw that Toby was busy serving drinks; he had his back to him, so he quickly slipped out unnoticed.

At least that's what he thought. When the door opened some minutes later Jake expected it to be Jim but it was another older guy.

"Not going yet, are you darling? How about a bit of fun?" He said, slurring his words drunkenly and lurching towards Jake, grabbing hold of his arm, then trying to grope him. Jim realised this was one of the people who had spoken to him as he fetched the drinks.

"Bloody get off!" Jake said, avoiding the claw of his hand aiming for his groin and pushing him away. "I'm not interested."

"I can make you interested," he said in a threatening tone. "You don't know what you're missing." He clutched his own groin and leered at Jake. "You'd love this."

"You're drunk mate. I've told you I'm not interested, I'm waiting for someone."

"Yes me," the man replied as he made another attempt to

grab Jake. "C'mere."

Jake wasn't quick enough to avoid him and with a vice-like grip, the drunk caught hold of his arm, tugged him towards him and started slobbering all over his neck trying to kiss him.

"Bloody let go of me, piss off!" Jake protested, struggling to break free of him. He could smell the vile stench of beer and stale cigarettes from him and he felt sickened by it. Jake was just about to bring his knee up into the man's groin, when the man was suddenly pulled back off him. Jake saw Jim had grabbed him by the scruff of the neck.

"What's your bloody game? Leave him alone," Jim demanded, still holding on to him.

"Mind your own fucking business you!" And the drunk aimed a punch at Jim's chin. He dodged it by stepping aside and pulling the man past him, letting the force of the man's thrown punch propel him into the kitchen door with a loud thump. The man crumpled to the floor with a groan.

Jim looked at Jake. "Are you OK love?" he asked as he put his arms around him and hugged him close.

"Yes, thanks Jim, I'm fine," Jake said as the kitchen door flew open and Toby and some of his guests stood looking at them questioningly.

"What's going on?" Toby asked.

"Oh just a drunk trying it on with Jake," Jim said. "He fell over against the door."

Toby looked at the man sprawled on the floor and said in an exasperated tone, "Brian, not you again, this is the last party of ours you'll be coming to. We had problems with you the last time when you'd had too much to drink. C'mon, get up, I'll call a taxi for you."

"I'm alright. I want another drink."

"Oh no, sonny boy, you're not having any more to drink, you're going home. Jake, you take your friend home, I'll look after this idiot."

"Thanks Toby, it's a lovely party, sorry to leave early!"

"You're not sorry at all," he said smiling and winking. "Have fun you two!"

Jake unlocked the door to his flat, grabbed Jim's hand and walked in leading him through the kitchen into the living room.

"Please sit down Jim, can I get you a cup of coffee or anything?"

"Anything, please," Jim said smiling and raising his eyebrows suggestively.

"OK I won't be a moment; I just need to go to the bathroom."

Jake opened the door a crack to peer out and listen if there was anyone about as he didn't want to run into the drunk or Toby again. It was all quiet so he went along the landing into the bathroom to wash his face and his neck as he felt grubby after the incident with the drunken letch. He had a pee and went back to his room; he opened his wardrobe, took a bottle from the shelf and sprayed a little Jade East cologne on his hands, dabbing the fragrance on his face and neck.

"That's better, I needed to freshen up after that."

Jim stood up, moved close to Jake, put his hands on both sides of his face and gently kissed him.

"You smell lovely," he said. "I think we should go to bed."

Jim kissed him again, this time more urgently, more passionately, his tongue searching for a yielding parting in Jake's lips to push his tongue into. Jake was almost swooning with ecstasy and began to unbutton Jim's denim shirt. He could feel the curly mass of hairs on his chest; he did so love hairy, masculine men.

They continued to undress each other between kisses, both of them searching with their hands and their eyes, savouring the deliciousness of their first loving sexual encounter.

Jake's thoughts were reeling, wondering what kind of lover Jim was going to be. He was hoping he was the kind who would want Jake to take everything he had to give him, and oh boy from what Jake had felt pressed against his leg, he certainly had a lot to give. Jake wasn't small himself, but he thought, *wow, it must be something they put in the London water!*

Chapter 3

Lying in bed lazily one morning Jake thought, *I've actually done it, it's been hard, but I've done it, I'm finally living in London. It was a bit of a culture shock at first, a very stark difference from living in the rural countryside and working on a farm, to being in the hustle and bustle of the capital city, but here I am loving it.* It was the beginning of November and he had been here just over two months.

His thoughts turned to Jim. He began to feel horny thinking about him and his hand went down to caress his growing member and fondle his balls; if only he were here now he thought. Jim would be hard at work though at the theatre, finalising details for the forthcoming variety show at the famous Capital next week, dealing with any issues like artistes going sick, attending meetings with key members of staff and overseeing costumes, stage sets, box office, in fact everything involved with running a leading revue theatre in the West End. He worked unsociable hours so what with work and him having to go home to Hampstead, Jake didn't get to see him as often as he would like. He had been totally honest confiding in Jake that his marriage to Alicia had been a dreadful mistake; he had been denying for years that he was gay and getting married was the ultimate betrayal to his homosexuality. The foolish denial of his true self was a way of appearing to be 'straight' and placating his parents and relatives. It was a loveless marriage, there were no children; they both went their own way, Alicia had a long-standing relationship with another man. Their situation was a silly state of affairs that had gone on for far too many years. Jim had said that if he ever met the right guy he would leave her. It would probably mean losing the house, but finally he would be living the life he deserved. Jake remembered that as a young lad, long before he knew that he was gay, or that homosexuality was illegal, he had hoped and fantasised that one day he would meet a man, they would fall in love and get married. One day perhaps his fantasy would become a reality.

"What about your parents, where do they live?"

"They live in Morden in Surrey. I don't see them as often as I should, I have never told them that I'm gay, I don't think they would accept it. Perhaps they might have put two and two together if I hadn't got married, but we can all say things in hindsight!"

Jake had sworn to himself that he was never going to get involved with a married man, as he didn't see himself as a bit on the side, yet here he was longing for the phone to ring when he wasn't with Jim. The phone would ring in the hall downstairs and Jake would scoot down to answer it in the hope that it would be Jim to say, "I'll be with you in twenty minutes love!"

Jake's reply was always, *don't drive too fast Jim, just because you've got a flashy red Triumph Vitesse with a white flash down the sides doesn't mean you can exceed the speed limit.* Jake knew that Jim drove fast as he had taken him for a drive one afternoon and he had been a bit uneasy about the speed he drove at.

Jim would reply tongue in cheek, *I wouldn't dream of it!*

It had all happened so quickly, he could feel he was falling in love with Jim, but his heart told him it was foolish as there didn't seem to be any long-term future in the relationship because he was married. They were so natural together, Jim was an experienced lover, strong and manly, they had good sex together, he was an attentive and thoughtful lover too with a great fun-loving personality, but what Jake really liked was the fact that Jim only ever wanted to play the masculine role and he wasn't interested in any guy that wanted to fuck him.

Not like a few of the guys Jake had already picked up, who he thought were 'butch' but they had suddenly rolled over in bed and wanted him to fuck them. That was a big turn-off for Jake, he liked to be the passive one.

They were managing to see each other regularly once or twice every week, whenever Jim could get away, and as special as those times with Jim were, they weren't enough for Jake. His sexual appetite was insatiable, it was as though he was addicted to sex, and there was always someone ready and willing to supply him. He was under no illusions about only seeing Jim, he had hinted to Jake that he liked to play the field, but he'd said there was no one special like him who he saw regularly. He had never told Jake that he loved him though. There were four other tenants in the house including Ricci and Toby, one he hardly ever saw who Jake had dubbed The Shadow and who Mr Costa had mentioned was called Mr Montgomery. He was hardly ever seen and when you did see him it was usually a fleeting glimpse in the dark. Jake wondered why he kept himself to himself and didn't seem to want to have any contact with anyone. However, one of the other tenants was a young handsome Arabian guy who he did occasionally see when Jake came in off the street and climbed the stairs to go to his room. He always smiled and said hello, his warm smile showing bright white teeth.

Jake had been here for three months now, it had all been a bit of a whirlwind. He was just about getting used to the frantic pace of city life, everyone seemed in an almighty hurry to get wherever it was they were going to. He soon learned that you had to forge your own path and look determined, or you would get jostled, or worse still, knocked over. This particularly applied to travelling on the underground in the rush hour, which was an experience that Jake usually found he loved.

He was travelling into the city one morning as he wanted to do some sightseeing. The passengers on the train he was on were packed in the carriage like sardines and Jake was penned in against the train door on the far side. All of a sudden he felt himself being groped by a man standing facing him. Jake looked at him totally surprised and the man had the cheek to wink at him. He started feeling for the zip on Jake's trousers as if he was going to take Jake's cock out. He grabbed his hand, moved it away and pushed as hard as he could past him to get away, causing other passengers to give him angry looks.

The sheer bloody audacity of the man. Jake wondered if he had ever done that before; he was probably a serial tube-train groper. When they reached the next station which was Regent's Park, although it wasn't the one he wanted, Jake got out and waited for the next train.

He got off this train at Piccadilly Circus which was only two more stops away. After riding the escalators to get to the platform he exited up some steps past the gents toilets to emerge opposite the Regent Palace Hotel. He walked aimlessly towards names he had only heard of – Leicester Square, Trafalgar Square, Charing Cross – and turned down a little street called Villiers Street which went down to the Thames embankment. He walked up some steps and found himself walking across Hungerford Bridge alongside the trains toing and froing from Charing Cross station. He continued across the river to The Royal Festival Hall and on to Waterloo where he caught the tube back to Kilburn High Road and walked towards home, stopping at Safeway to buy bread, half a pound of bacon and some spaghetti.

He turned the key in the lock quietly as he didn't want Mr Costa to know all his comings and goings; he was a bit of a nosy so-and-so. He was passing the Arab guy's room and heard a moaning sound. Jake wondered if he was alright so he tapped on his door and asked if he was OK.

"Hello, are you OK in there?" Jake asked concerned.

He heard a slight commotion and a voice said, "Er, yes, OK, sorry, just a moment."

After a few moments the guy opened the door in a white vest and white boxer shorts. To Jake he was a golden vision. Before he could say anything, Jake said, "I'm sorry to bother you but I heard a moaning noise and I wondered if you were alright."

"Mm, oh yes I'm fine," he replied looking a little embarrassed.

Jake couldn't help it, his eyes were drawn down to the guy's crotch and he couldn't believe the bulge he saw, he was built like a stallion. It was only a glance but the guy had seen it and he said, "Would you like to come in and have some coffee?"

"That sounds very nice, yes please."

Jake was surprised that the room was a lot smaller than his. It was nicely decorated, though it only had a kitchenette.

He said, "Please sit down" and, giving a lovely smile showing beautiful white teeth, he indicated a chair next to the bed with a little table beside it.

He introduced himself as Amir and asked what Jake's

name was. He went on to say that he had been living here for three months and was at college studying engineering, which explained why Jake didn't see him very often.

He said, "I made Arabic coffee earlier, would you like to try it? It is made with cardamon and cloves."

Jake said he would like some and Amir poured him the light-coloured liquid in a very small cup. When Jake tasted it he found it was spicy and fragrant, very different from the sort of coffee he usually drank.

"It's nice," Jake said.

He thought how hospitable Amir was. He hadn't jumped on him as soon as he entered the room like a lot of the men he'd encountered since he'd been in London, then he thought, *maybe he isn't interested and I've got things all wrong!*

There was more casual conversation about living in London and Amir's studies. He went around to the other side of the bed and placed his coffee cup on the bedside table then lay down on the bed facing Jake with his elbow on the bed and his head resting on his hand.

Jake's eyes honed in on his bulge again, then he looked at Amir's face as he smiled at Jake and said, "You like yes?" Amir put his hand down onto his shorts and cupped it around his cock and balls, Jake's eyes widened in excitement as Amir patted the bed alongside him. Jake quickly took his shirt off, unfastened his trousers, stepped out of them and lay on the bed next to Amir in his underpants.

There was no instant groping or grabbing of each other's cocks, instead it was a beautiful elysian experience with soft gentle kisses, their bodies pressing close to one another as they embraced and looked into each other's eyes; Jake saw that his were deep brown.

Then Amir's hands started to caress Jake's body, working his way down to squeeze his firm buttocks. He then put his hand around to the front and felt Jake's stiff erect prick.

"Mmmm, lovely penis," Amir murmured.

Jake was glad Amir had made the first move. He moved his hand down to take hold of his penis, he could hardly believe the size and thickness of it, it must have been easily nine inches long,

"Wow, you're a big boy," Jake whispered. He had never held one as big as this before!

Amir began to pull Jake's scants down, so Jake helped him by taking them off and dropping them at the side of the bed. Amir took his own shorts off then got on top of Jake and pushed his thick warm cock between his legs, kissing him passionately with breathy kisses and pushing his tongue into Jake's mouth. After doing this for a while he broke off, his body sliding down Jake's until he was kissing and tonguing his cock, then letting his shaft slide into his mouth and taking it deep into his throat. Jake thought it was incredible, he was swooning with delight but he didn't want to come yet, he wanted to make it last, so he tapped Amir's shoulder.

"Let me suck yours now." Amir came up towards him, kissed him, then lay on his back beside Jake. His long erect penis and big hairy balls were a pleasure to behold. Jake's mouth fell on it, taking as much of it into his mouth as he could, but as hard as he tried, he wasn't able to deep throat him.

Their sex session was long and slow, they didn't have intercourse, they mutually masturbated, watching as they climaxed together.

When Jake left to go to his room he told Amir how much

he had enjoyed it; if he ever wanted to do it again he only had to tap on his door and he would be pleased to see him. Amir said that he had enjoyed it too, and he would definitely be coming to his room again soon.

Chapter 4

On Saturday mornings, Jake always liked to have a ritual-like routine. After his second cup of coffee and a croissant and marmalade, he would put the record player on to play his favourite music as he did his housework; his favourite singer was Dusty Springfield. As he hoovered, dusted and polished he would sing along to the songs, emulating her voice, movements and dramatic hand gestures. He was a real fan, he adored her, he had every LP that she had made. Jake wasn't a slave to housework, he didn't particularly enjoy doing it, but the music somehow changed it from being tedious into a pleasure. He had just finished his 'chores' and was singing along to 'Count to Ten' when there was a knock at his door. He quickly turned the music down and answered the door to find Ricci standing there.

"Hello love, I hope I'm not calling at an inconvenient time, but it's been so long since I last saw you, I thought I should come and see how you are."

"Hello Ricci, no you're not disturbing me, it's lovely to see you. I was about to put the kettle on, would you like a coffee?"

"I'd love one, thanks. So how's your love life? Tell Auntie all about it. Are you still seeing the gorgeous Jim?"

Jake smiled and replied, "Yes, I am, he's such a lovely man, a girl would be silly not to, wouldn't she?"

They both laughed as he walked into the kitchen, filled the kettle and put it on the gas.

"Do you take sugar, Ricci?" he shouted from the kitchen.

"I can't remember."

"No, I'm sweet enough love, and I need to watch my figure, or else I'd never get into my frocks!"

Jake knew that Ricci was a drag artiste so his remark didn't surprise him, but he still found it amusing.

"I couldn't help hearing you singing, you've got a great voice darling and a good figure, have you ever thought of doing drag?"

"What me? No."

"I don't know why not, I think you'd be brilliant at it. If ever you feel you'd like to have a go, just to see what it would feel like, just let me know and I'll show you the ropes, darling!"

"Well, it's very kind of you, but I wouldn't have the nerve to do anything like that."

"Let me see your legs."

Jake was rather taken aback. "What, why?"

Ricci became more insistent, flouncing his hands and repeating his request. "Show me your legs, come on don't be shy, take your trousers off. I don't want to see anything else, just your lallies, we're just two girls together anyway, dear, bread and bread."

Jake didn't want to seem pathetic, so he undid his belt, unzipped his trousers and took them off, throwing them over a chair. He could see Ricci scrutinising him, eyeing him up and down.

"Just as I thought, you've got perfect legs, a beautiful eke with a lovely bone structure, and a wonderful singing voice. It makes me sick love, it's enough to turn a girl green with envy. If you'd just listen to your Auntie Ricci and let me help and guide you, you could be a star in the making darling."

Jake put his trousers back on and sat down to drink his cup

of tea. "You're serious aren't you? You can actually see me impersonating a woman on stage."

"You could be fab darling, absolutely bona, people come from miles around to see a good act, but you have to want to do it. It takes a lot of commitment and hard work, I would be happy to help get you started, I've got contacts in the business. I want you to think about it seriously, it could be such fun,"

"I suppose that's how I would have to approach it, Ricci, as a bit of fun, because I'm not convinced that I'd be any good at it. I certainly wouldn't get up on a stage in front of an audience unless I was perfectly confident that I wasn't going to make an absolute fool of myself."

"Jake," Ricci said reassuringly, "there would be absolutely no danger of that happening, I wouldn't let it. After all, I've got my reputation to think of."

"It's a bit late for that, isn't it darling?" Jake quipped, causing them both to laugh.

"Ooooh you cheeky bitch, you see, there's another thing love, you've got a clever, quick wit. You need to have one of those in this game to fend off any hecklers, and some of the jealous bitchy queens!"

"Hecklers, you never mentioned hecklers, bloody hell!"

"Oh don't worry about them love, half the time if you just hold your little finger up and wag it like this, implying that he's only got a little dick, that shuts them up cos the rest of the audience or his mates are laughing at him."

"God, that's so funny, it must be amazing to be able to manipulate an audience like that!"

"After a while it just becomes second nature love, you develop a repertoire of dismissive put-downs and the appropriate ones just spring into your head as you need them, the audience love it. If a drunken guy shouts out something like, 'You're nothing like a woman', you can parry that with, 'That's not what you said last night love'. You've always got the back-up of the barmen or the bouncers anyway, as long as you show them you're not phased by anything!"

They both laughed.

Then surprisingly Jake said, "I think I'd like to give it a go, Ricci. I've always secretly wondered what I would look like as a woman!"

"Ooooh, wonderful, I knew you'd be up for it. You just tell me what evening you're free this week and we can make a start on your transformation."

"I've nothing planned at all, Ricci."

"What about Thursday evening then? I'll need to get a few things organised, in the meantime I'll need to take your chest, waist and height measurements. Have you got a tape measure handy?"

"Yes I have, I'll get it for you." Jake went over to the sideboard and opened a drawer. "I won't have to wear high heels will I? Don't think I could manage those."

"No love, a long gown and comfortable flatties or baby heels will be fine."

Jake gave Ricci the tape measure and he took the measurements he needed to get the right sized frock; it looked like Jake would fit a size 14 frock.

"OK then, I'm done, come up to my flat on Thursday evening at 7pm."

"Yes, I'm really looking forward to it," Jake said excitedly as he showed Ricci out. "Oh by the way, if you need any money for anything just let me know. Bye Ricci, see you Thursday!"

Chapter 5

The next time Jim called to see Jake was on the Wednesday evening, the night before he was going up to Ricci's flat to be dressed up in drag. When Jake told Jim about it, he was amazed and delighted and positively encouraging. He surprised Jake by saying that he would like to come along and see Jake's metamorphosis for himself. He didn't think Ricci would mind him turning up uninvited to be an onlooker and anyway he could always make himself useful in some way, if only to make the tea. He said he would come to Jake's at 6pm.

Later that evening when they made love, Jim was so tender and gently fervent; they had made love slowly for a long time. Afterwards they just lay together in each other's arms enjoying the afterglow of their passion, chatting away about so many different things. When they thought to take note of the time it was 12.30am, not that the time mattered, it was just a surprise at how quickly it had gone by. They realised they were both hungry and thirsty so Jake made them a pot of tea and grilled some cheese on toast which they both sat and relished. They talked about Ricci who was about to initiate Jake that evening into his world of drag. They were both curiously excited about the whole prospect. It was late so at around 1.30am Jim said his lingering romantic goodbyes and left for home saying that it wouldn't be that long before he was back. Jake crawled back into bed and slept soundly until 10am. He yawned and stretched as his mind went back to Jim making love to him and he couldn't help but smile; he felt wonderful, he was so happy.

He got up, made himself a cup of coffee, drew back the living room curtains to let the sun fill the room with light and stood at the window drinking his coffee, watching the comings and goings down in the street – the postman doing his deliveries, a woman looking flustered pushing a pram and holding the hand of another toddler who she was encouraging to walk quicker, a tortoiseshell cat ambling stealthily by the side of a garden wall. He could have stood there for ages watching the world outside of his window but he had things he wanted to get on with today.

The first thing he wanted to do was buy something nice for Ricci as a little thank you for the party invite and for taking the trouble to offer to make him up and dress him in drag. Jake wanted it to be something special and personal for him, probably a bottle of perfume. He would also get a bottle of champagne for Toby, so that he wouldn't feel left out.

He went to take a quick bath and have a shave. When he came back to his room he opened the wardrobe and deliberated over what he was going to wear. He finally decided on a pair of light blue DAKS, a darker blue Campari jacket with red, white and blue trim on the collar and cuffs. He finished the ensemble off with a pair of navy canvas shoes and white socks. He got dressed and admired himself in the mirror, checking out how his tackle looked as the slacks were a fairly tight fit, and they showed him up well. *Not bad, even if I do say so myself,* he thought.

He combed his hair and gave it a spray of hair lacquer to hold it in place, then he picked up his keys and his wallet, came out of his flat, locked the door, descended the stairs and walked out into the morning sunshine. When he reached the high road, he crossed over and just did a short sprint to grab the bar and jump onto the moving platform of a number 16 bus to Marble Arch; he was heading for Selfridges in Oxford Street.

He climbed the stairs to the upper deck and was pleased to find that the front seat on the pavement side was empty so he settled down for the journey. He now loved the hustle and bustle of London, with its exciting atmosphere, the fancy shops, its melting pot of people; he found it all fascinating and he had adjusted extremely well since he had come to live here. It was a far cry from the farm at Grendore.

He suddenly felt a pang of guilt as he realised he hadn't contacted his mum and Ted or Pauline and Ned for ages. He made a mental note to do so first thing tomorrow as there weren't going to be enough hours in today for that.

The conductor came up the stairs. "Fares please," he said as he reached the top. Several other people had got on the bus so it was a while before he stood beside Jake wanting to know where he was getting off so that he could charge him the right fare.

"Where are you going to mate?" he said in a deep cockney brogue.

"Marble Arch please," Jake replied in his softest camp voice as he was quite a dishy looking bloke.

"That'll be one and sixpence then please young man," he said knowingly as he held out his hand for the money.

Jake gave him a florin making a point of gently rubbing the man's palm with his finger as he placed it into his hand and looking up at him to gauge his reaction. The conductor smiled, set the correct fare on his ticket machine, turned the handle and handed him the ticket that came out. He then took a sixpence out of his leather bag, placing it in Jake's palm with an obvious affirming finger movement in reply to Jake's.

"You wanna be careful mate if you're going along Oxford Street. You get a lot of pickpockets on the prowl, so keep your hand on your wallet!"

"Just my wallet?" Jake replied quietly, and the man laughed, putting his hand on Jake's shoulder to steady himself as the bus suddenly juddered.

He leaned toward him whispering, "My name's Terry. Write your name and telephone number down and give it to me when you come downstairs."

"Yes, OK Terry," Jake said, and the man left him and went back downstairs, leaving him feeling an inner glow of excitement at having made such an impromptu and unexpected contact. Yet Jake had found that this sort of thing was happening to him quite often, so why was he surprised, this was London and it was the Swinging Sixties!

Jake didn't have any paper on him that he could write his details on, but he always carried a pen. Luckily there was an empty cigarette packet lying on the floor by his feet so he picked it up and tore it up so that he had a square of card to write on.

He wrote his name and the house phone number on this ready to give to Terry as he left the bus. Jake glanced out of the window and saw that it was passing through the more exclusive Maida Vale district close to Marylebone tube station and would soon be going through Little Venice, a very posh picturesque area at the junction of the Grand Union Canal and the Regent's Canal. Jake knew this because he had looked at some houses in an estate agents and the salesman had told him about it. He hadn't viewed any because he thought they were over his price range.

The bus soon reached the Edgware Road and Jake got up out of his seat, walked the length of the bus and went down the stairs so that he could get off at the Odeon, Marble Arch. Terry was stood on the platform and smiled at him.

"Did you have a smooth ride?" he said cheekily under his breath.

Jake liked the innuendo and replied, "Not bad, but I'm sure the next one will be better" as he slipped the card with his details on into Terry's hand. "Bye, see you soon Terry" as he jumped off the bus and began walking towards Oxford Street.

Jake turned the corner from Edgware Road into Oxford Street, passing the Cumberland Hotel. He continued along the busy thoroughfare, crossing over when he saw the impressive Selfridges building. As he walked in, he marvelled at the vastness of the place and the array of goods on sale. He made his way toward the perfume department and began looking at the famous perfume brands that were on sale – Dior, Chanel, Givenchy, Estée Lauder to name but a few. An attractive female assistant who looked to be in her late forties greeted him; her make-up was flawless and she smelled fragrantly of perfume.

"Good morning sir, can I help you?"

"Yes please," Jake replied. "I'm looking for a gift of perfume for a lady friend."

"Do you know the type of fragrance the lady likes? Does she prefer floral scents, oriental or fresh, and would she wear eau de perfume or eau de toilette? Eau de perfume is the stronger of the two."

"I think she would like both floral and oriental eau de parfum," Jake said, not really having a clue as to Ricci's taste in perfume, but then he added, "I think it should be something ultra-feminine!"

"Ah, yes, I know several she might like then." She reached for a bottle on the counter.

"This one is a classic called Shalimar by Guerlain." She sprayed some on a piece of card and wafted it under Jake's nose.

"Yes, that's really nice," he said, at the same time thinking to himself, *definitely pure essence of Ricci*.

"She proceeded to show him several more and in the end he couldn't decide between Shalimar by Guerlain and Diorissimo by Christian Dior.

"I can't decide so I'll take both of them," Jake said.

"Certainly sir, she's a very lucky lady. That will be seventy-five pounds please. Would you like them gift wrapped?"

"That would be lovely," Jake said, as he began to write out the cheque. "Do I make it out to Selfridge and Company Ltd?"

"Yes please, sir'.

Jake finished writing the cheque and stood watching the assistant deftly wrapping his purchases in a beautiful pastel pink paper with a lime green ribbon.

"Will those be alright for you sir?" she asked.

"They're absolutely lovely," Jake replied, "Very pretty."

Jake handed her the cheque and the woman gave him a receipt.

"I hope the lady will like those, sir," she said, smiling and placing them in a large Selfridges paper bag and handing the bag to Jake. "Thank you for shopping with us today, good morning."

"Good morning and thanks very much for your help, I'm sure she will love them." Jake thought to himself *she's not getting both of them, one of them's for me.*

He was thinking that he would probably give Ricci the Diorissimo as he had just adored the smell of Shalimar and thought it would really suit him. He made his way to the wine department next to the food hall and purchased a bottle of Dom Perignon champagne to give to Toby. It was put in another bag for him so as not to damage the perfume he had bought. He had a good look around the whole store, especially ladies' fashions. He saw the most beautiful floral kimono style dressing gown in a soft glazed cotton fabric and he just knew that he had to have it. Jake asked a young lady assistant to help him find the right size to fit him. She was so kind and helpful and didn't even bat an eyelid. He began to get excited at the thought of wearing this while Ricci was making him up and of being dressed up as a woman this evening. He wondered what clothes Ricci had procured for him, and where he had got them from.

As he left Selfridges he thought he might like to go for a pot of tea at Lyons Corner House in Marble Arch but then he remembered what Terry had jokingly said, *keep your hand on your wallet, there are pickpockets about.* Jake wasn't so worried about his wallet as he had put it in his inside pocket and zipped it up – he would surely feel it if anyone tried to steal that – *but,* he thought to himself, *if there are pickpockets there could also be bag snatchers about,* so he thought better of it and decided to hail a taxi and go home. He held his bags with a firm grip in his left hand, went to the kerb and flagged a black cab that had its yellow for hire light on.

It pulled up in front of him, he opened the door, got in and as he sat down said to the driver.

"Buckley Road, Kilburn please."

"OK mate," the driver replied.

On the way back home, Jake tried to pass the time of day with the driver, commenting on the weather and such like, but it was hard work. OK, he was civil in bothering to reply but that was about it. Jake thought that perhaps he either needed to concentrate on his driving or he simply wasn't Mr Personality of the Year, so he just enjoyed looking out of the window, checking out the sights. He was glad he had decided to hail a cab rather than return home by bus.

Chapter 6

He paid the driver and tipped him, though not for his scintillating conversation. Once he had got inside the front door, he felt so relieved to be home; for some reason he had felt quite vulnerable on his own in the centre of town carrying expensive-looking bags from Selfridges. He walked up the stairs to his own front door and couldn't wait to get inside and make himself a cup tea, he felt really parched, he was ready for a bite to eat as well.

He put his bags down under the table and filled the kettle, putting it on before taking his jacket off and hanging it in the wardrobe. He returned to the bags, picking them up and carrying them into the bed-sitting room and placing them on the coffee table. He thought how much he had enjoyed his shopping trip as he delved into the bag with the two gift-wrapped bottles of perfume in it, lifting them out carefully one by one to put them in an exalted position on the shelf of the marble fireplace and slightly titivating the bows on each one and standing back to admire them. He was absolutely delighted with his choices, and he was sure now that he would give Ricci the Diorissimo. The kettle whistled so he went back to the kitchen and made himself a pot of tea, one cup was not going to slake his thirst.

After preparing the tea and a ham sandwich, he brought it and put it on the coffee table. He quickly took off his slacks and his shoes to be more comfortable. He deliberated about putting on his dressing gown but decided to keep that pleasure for the evening and slipped on a loose pair of shorts and his flip-flops instead. He put his favourite album onto the turntable of the radiogram, then he sat down to enjoy his lunch. He planned on having a bit of a rest afterwards as he wasn't going to Ricci's until 7pm, which meant it was probably going to be a late night and he didn't want to be yawning and feeling tired. It was one o'clock now. Around 5pm he would follow Ricci's instructions and have a very close wet shave, making sure that he moisturised well afterwards to create a barrier for the theatrical make-up that Ricci would be applying on his face. Thinking about it, Jake began to get a twinge of excitement, he was really looking forward to the evening, especially as Jim was coming to watch his transformation.

Lunch over with, he went into the kitchen, washed and dried his plate, cup and saucer, then he lay on top of his bed to rest and very easily drifted off to sleep. Something outside woke him up as he had left the window open. He thought he had heard the sound of a car horn tooting. He looked at the clock and was amazed to see that it was three thirty. Getting up he went over to the window and looked out to see a black cab parked outside of the gate and Ricci was just getting into it. Jake wondered where he was off to and hoped that everything was going to be alright for later on!

He went into the kitchen, opened the fridge and poured himself a glass of cold orange juice, drinking it down in one go; it tasted good, so tangy and fresh, it helped him to wake up.

The rest of the afternoon passed so quickly and before Jake knew it, it was time for him to have a bath and a shave. He went to the toilet first, then came back and undressed, wrapped a towel around his waist, grabbed his toilet bag and went back along the landing to the bathroom. He rinsed around the bath to make sure it was clean before he started to run a bath for himself. While the bath was filling up he had a really close shave. He tested the water with his hand to see that it wasn't too hot, poured a capful of Radox into it, then he took his towel off, hanging it on the rail, and stepped into the bath, lowering himself slowly down through the foam into the silky warm water.

He luxuriated in the herbal-smelling liquid for some twenty minutes or more before washing himself all over and shampooing his hair. Then he stood up, stepped out, reached for the towel and dried himself off. His skin, glowing clean and pink, felt velvety soft and smooth. He cleaned around the bath then, wrapping his towel around him and picking up his toilet bag, he unbolted the door and went back to his room.

The next half an hour or so was spent drying his hair, moisturising his face, making himself a cup of coffee, putting his favourite pair of black scants on, then he took the cotton kimono out of the bag, removed the label and slipped it on. It felt so soft and feminine on his skin, he adored the pinks, reds and greens on the black background. When he looked in the mirror, he mentally congratulated himself on making such a good choice, it really suited him. He looked at the clock and it was ten to six. He thought to himself, *my lovely Jim will be here shortly* as he went over to the mantel shelf, picked up the box of Shalimar and opened it. Caressing the contours of the bottle and undoing the stopper, he sprayed a modest amount behind each ear, swooning with pleasure at the delightful fragrance.

Jake had been watching the time from six o'clock, wondering where Jim had got to, so when the doorbell rang at quarter past six he rushed down to let him in.

Jim took one look at Jake and whispered quietly, "You look

lovely, I can't wait to get you upstairs and kiss you!"

Jake shut the front door and, pulling Jim to him, said, "Why bother waiting then, no one will see." They kissed passionately then Jake walked ahead up the stairs. Once in the privacy of Jake's room, Jim embraced him, kissing him again and again, saying how much he had missed him and how he longed to make love to him. Jake was flattered and would have liked to jump into bed with him there and then but he diplomatically said, "I want you too, Jim, but we will have to wait until later. I'm all bathed and ready to go upstairs to Ricci's. We have all the time in the world, darling."

"Of course we do love," Jim replied. "I have been so looking forward to this evening, I can't wait to see what Ricci has in store for you."

"No neither can I, I'm getting quite excited about it now, and I'm looking forward to what you have in store for me later on too."

Jim laughed and gave him another kiss.

Jake told him all about his shopping trip that morning and showed him what he had bought for Ricci and Toby. Jim said he felt they would both be very pleased with his thoughtful gifts as he was thinking, *you wait until you see the present that I have for you, darling.*

"Gosh, I need a drink," Jake said, walking over to the drinks cupboard and grabbing the bottle of whisky. "Would you like one Jim?"

"Yes please," he replied. "Is that a bit of Dutch courage?"

"It is actually, I admit to having a few butterflies in the tummy. I'm not used to being the centre of attention."

He poured two whiskies.

"Did you want ice in it?" Jake asked.

"Yes please."

Jake walked into the kitchen, opened the fridge and took some ice from the freezer compartment and dropped several cubes into Jim's glass, taking it back and handing it to him. They said cheers and clinked glasses; Jake knocked his straight back.

"I really needed that."

"Here's to a great evening," Jim said. "I'll bet you're going to look great."

"I hope so. We'd better get going, it's gone seven."

Jim hurriedly finished his drink. Jake put the glasses on the kitchen drainer and they left the flat, locked the door and started to go upstairs.

"I'll either give them their presents later on or leave it until tomorrow," Jake said. "Oh, hang on though, I'd better get the champagne, it looks bad going in with nothing."

He ran back down the few steps, opened the door, dashing in and quickly scooping up the bottle of champagne inside its bag. He came out, fumbled with locking the door and hurried up the stairs to join Jim who was waiting outside their door. Jim pressed the bell and they both stood waiting for someone to open it.

Chapter 7

"Hello darlings, do come on in, we're all ready for you. Nice to see you both."

"Hi Toby," they both replied as they stepped in.

"Here's a little something as a thank you for you Toby, I hope you'll like it."

"A thank you for what?"

"Inviting me to a party where I met the most wonderful man," Jake said, putting his arm around Jim's shoulders.

"Aaaawww, that's so sweet," Toby said. He looked in the bag. "Oh Jake, you really shouldn't have, but thank you, I'm impressed. He leaned towards Jake and gave him a little peck on the cheek. "Now we had better take you in to see madame!"

Toby opened the inner door where Ricci could be seen throwing a cover over something. He exclaimed with delight as he came over, "Jake darling, love the kimono darling. Oh and you've brought Jim too, splendid, why am I not surprised to see you Jim?" Ricci gave them both a little kiss and chuckled. "You realise of course that you two men are going to have to disappear off to the pub for a couple of hours, which of course will be no hardship to you at all. I can't have you seeing my beautiful creation until her transformation is complete."

"Anything to oblige, honey bunch. C'mon Jim, let's get going before she changes her mind."

Jim looked at Jake questioningly. Ricci saw his reaction and said, "Don't worry Jim, I promise no lovely young country farm workers will be harmed in the making of a glamorous drag queen. I'll keep him warm till you get back. Go on, shoo!"

Jim laughed, gave Jake a peck on the cheek, and said, "See you later, love."

"Yes bye, Jim, don't have too much to drink will you love." And looking at Toby said, "I'd like him back relatively sober please Toby."

"Bye, see you later," Toby said, as he ushered Jim out of the door.

"Now, that's got rid of the boys for a while, would you like a little drink to sip as we're going along?"

"I wouldn't say," Jake replied.

"What would you like?"

"Can I have a whisky please, with a little soda?"

"Yes of course, one whisky coming up."

Ricci went over to a large sideboard, opened a door and, bringing out a bottle of whisky, poured Jake a drink, putting a splash of soda into it. He came back and handed it to Jake.

"There you are sweetie, now you come and sit over here next to the table. T first thing we have to do is get rid of your eyebrows by concealing them. I see you've had a lovely close shave, did you remember to moisturise?"

"Yes," Jake replied.

"That's good, theatrical make-up can play havoc with a girl's complexion. You have such lovely skin, we need to take care of it."

Ricci began to apply some sort of paste over Jake's eyebrows and was pressing hard as he did so.

"I hope I'm not being too rough, but I have to put pressure on them to make sure they stick down before I put your foundation on."

"No, it's fine," Jake said as he looked with curiosity at the table which was covered with different types of make-up, brushes, sponges, etc.

Ricci finished pressing and dabbing at his eyebrows and said, "There, we'll leave that to dry for a while. I'm not going to let you see your face until I've finished and you have your wig on. I need to know which you see yourself as, a blonde or a brunette, as this has a bearing on what face colouring I give you and which frock you will wear."

"Well, being naturally dark, I'd kind of like to be a very feminine blonde bombshell."

"Darling, you won't have any trouble with the feminine part, by the time I've finished with you, you won't know whether you're Arthur or Martha dear!"

They both laughed out loud and Jake took a sip of his whisky. He thought Ricci was so wonderfully camp and funny.

"Now honey, while we're waiting I want you to tell your Auntie Ricci how things are progressing with you and Jim. I have to say you seem to light up when you're with him and Jim certainly looks a happy man."

"I'm so glad you introduced me to Jim, Ricci, we hit it off right from the start, we seem perfect together. I'm doing my best to keep

level-headed over him and not get completely carried way. There you are, you did ask!"

"So what on earth's wrong with getting completely carried away sweetie? Don't you think he feels the same way about you?"

"I'm not sure if he does. There is just the little complication of him being married!"

"Oh I wouldn't worry your little head about that Jake, she can look after herself. From what Jim has told me, she can't wait to get her greedy hands on the house and he's only waiting for 'Mr Right' to come along then it'll be the big heave ho. From what I can make out, I think you're definitely 'Mr Right' so whatever you do girl, don't let him slip through your fingers. He's a real catch!"

"Do you really think I am his 'Mr Right'? If I am, I wish he would tell me."

"I know so, you trust your Auntie Ricci. Be patient, you'll see, I'm never wrong." She touched his eyebrows gently with slim fingers. "The brows are dry so I can put your foundation on now."

"How long have you and Toby been together?"

"Why, an absolute age darling. I met Toby just after I'd left college, bllbblmm, years ago!"

"Did you fall for him straightaway too?"

"Hook, line and sinker sweetie, we were meant for each other."

"Have you always lived here? Sorry, I'm asking too many questions."

"I don't mind love. No, we've only been here about ten years, we had our own house before that. Look sweetie, I may as well tell you." Lowering his voice, he went on. "We had to sell our house to pay off Toby's debts."

"Oh, I'm sorry Ricci, I don't want to pry into your personal affairs."

"It's alright sweetie, I don't mind telling you, it isn't as though you're going to go round yelling it from the rooftops, is it? You see Toby has a gambling problem, we almost lost the house in a poker game he was involved in, but thankfully he came to his senses at the last minute. He did lose his beautiful car though unfortunately. He sobbed and poured his heart out to me that night, he said he needed help as it had gotten out of control. Well, to cut a long story short, as I said we sold up, paid off his debtors and I took charge of the finances. He has no contact with money at all now, we moved here and we're perfectly happy. We'd be happy anywhere as long as we have each other."

"Oh Ricci, I'm so glad you've come through all that together. That's true love for sure!"

"Bless you darling, now let me get your foundation on or we'll be here all night."

Ricci began applying Max Factor Pan Stick on Jake's face and neck, he then darkened the hollows on the sides of his face to accentuate his high cheek bones, he set the foundation using Leichner face powder. Jake was watching him intently as he picked up a stencil with a curved shape cut out of it. Holding it to his face, he used a small brush to make him new brows.

Taking a step back, he said, "They're just you."

He then produced a thick pair of false eyelashes and put a line of glue on one, asked Jake to close his eyes and placed it deftly on his lid; he did the same with the other one. Jake fluttered his eyelashes a few times, they felt slightly strange and heavy, but he guessed he would soon get used to wearing them.

Picking up a bottle of eyeliner and a small brush, he moved it along Jake's eyelid and swept it up at the side. He used a pencil under the lower lash to make a line, balancing the make-up on each eye, he then applied mascara on his lashes. Once that had dried, he worked on the eyelids with a combination of blue and green eye shadow, blending the two colours together, leaning back every so often to see the overall effect.

When he was satisfied with his handiwork he said, "Mmm,

good, I just have your lips to do, and then we can give you hair. I've got the most gorgeous wig for you sweetie!"

Jake took another sip of his whisky. He was dying to have a look at what Ricci had done, but he knew he had to be patient and wait.

"You're so kind to do this for me Ricci, I feel so lucky."

"Oh it's my pleasure love, I enjoy doing it, besides it's not entirely altruistic on my part. I do have something up my sleeve, but I'm not going to tell you about it yet, it's Auntie Ricci's little secret!"

"Mmmm, sounds very intriguing, I hope I'm going to like whatever it is."

"I hope you will too, I'm sure you will!"

Chapter 8

"I'll just get your wig for you, sweetie." Ricci walked over to the sheet that was draped over a portable metal hanging rail on wheels. He disappeared behind it and came out carrying a mannequin head with a beautiful light blonde coloured wig on it.

Jake gasped.

"What do you think of this then, sweetie?" Ricci said, removing the wig from its stand. "Isn't it adorable?"

"Oh Ricci, it's fabulous, it looks just like the one that Dusty Springfield wore when she appeared on TV last week!"

"That's what I thought, I know how much you idolise her, so I just had to go for this one."

"Thank you Ricci, it's absolutely gorgeous."

"OK, I'm so pleased you like it," he said as he approached closer. "Tilt your head forward and I'll help you get it on."

With a little tug and a few tweaks, Jake was wearing it.

"How does it feel?"

"It feels wonderful, I love these flicks on the side of my face."

Ricci walked over to the clothes rail again.

"It was just made for you darling, now, let's get your tits on then I'll show you the frock." He fetched a bra from behind the sheet that already had falsies in it. "Stand up sweetie and turn around."

Ricci swung the bra around Jake's chest, grabbing the other strap then bringing it behind him and fastening it.

"Jake, I want you to close your eyes while I get your frock, no peeking, keep them closed until I tell you to open them, OK?"

"OK Ricci, what colour is it?"

"Wait and see!"

There was a lot of movement and rustling; it seemed like an age to Jake before Ricci finally said, "You can open them now, ta da!"

Jake's mouth gaped open, he couldn't believe what he was seeing. Ricci stood there holding the most glamorous and expensive looking full-length gown he had ever seen. It was an ice-blue colour with shimmering crystal droplets all over it, with a slit from the hem up to the knee. Ricci was struggling to take the weight of it.

"Well, say something sweetie!"

"Mm, I ... I'm overwhelmed Ricci, have I died and gone to heaven or what? It is beyond divine." Jake rushed to him and kissed him on the cheek.

"Right darling, I won't look while you tuck that big thing Jim likes to hold between your legs."

Jake turned around, put his hands inside his scants and, grabbing hold of his cock, he pushed it between his legs. He turned around and saw that Ricci had ruched the frock up as best he could so that Jake could step carefully into it, he had bent down nearer the floor. Jake put one hand on Ricci's back to steady himself, lifted one leg inside the dress, then the other, Ricci then slowly pulled it up and over his bra, fastening it at the back and pulling the broad straps onto his shoulders to hide the bra straps.

Ricci stood back and gave a worried frown. It hadn't gone unnoticed, a concerned Jake asked, "What is it Ricci, what's wrong?"

"I'm sorry Jake, you'd better take it off, I can't possibly let you see yourself in it, it's just awful. Hahaha!"

"Oooh, that was so wicked Ricci, you certainly had me fooled for a minute."

Ricci went to the wardrobe and opened it to reveal a large mirror. "Sorry sweetie, I couldn't resist that, but you can take a look now, c'mon!"

Jake moved so that he could see his reflection. There was a vision of loveliness looking back at him and he was totally amazed.

"Oh my God, I don't believe it Ricci, you've made me look beautiful. I don't know what to say except thank you so much. I wonder what Jim will say when he sees me looking like this?"

"I shouldn't think you'll have to wait long to find out, I would think they'll be here soon. Now let me just say to you that this isn't the complete look you would normally wear, you are missing a necklace, long gloves, flashy rings, tights and glitzy sandals with baby heels, but this will do for a first effort."

"I'm just flabbergasted. Look at me, you've made me look absolutely gorgeous!" Jake couldn't take his eyes from the vision in the mirror. He felt he had found his alter ego, the person that had always been somewhere inside him trying to get out was standing there looking at him. He couldn't get over how much he looked like his mother. He thought to himself, *I wonder what she would say if she could see me now!*

They heard Toby and Jim coming up the stairs so Ricci said, "Stand in the middle of the room so they will see you as soon as they walk in."

They walked into the kitchen and Jake waited nervously for them to reach the doorway to see their reaction. Toby was the first to see him, or should I say her, then Jim, *but who was the other man with them?* he thought.

"Oh wow, I can't believe it, just look at Jake, Jim!"

"Oh Jake darling, you look incredible, you're beautiful," he gushed as he walked towards him and hugged him.

"Yes I am, all thanks to the miracle worker Ricci of course."

Ricci came and put his arm around Jake and said, "Jake, let me introduce you to my little secret. This is Mr Sharman, he is the owner of the Black Orchid. I invited him to come and see you because he is always looking for new acts!"

Jake couldn't believe that Ricci had set this meeting up and the guys were obviously in on it.

The stocky well-dressed man beamed a pleasant smile, extended his arm and shook Jake's hand.

"I am very pleased to meet you, Jake, Ricci has told me so much about you, and I must say he was right about your potential to be a sensational drag act. If you can sing as good as you look then we can certainly do business. I'm going to put you on the spot and ask you to sing me your favourite song!"

"What, here, now?"

Jake's knees went wobbly and he must have looked scared stiff.

Mr Sharman touched Jake's arm to steady him as he looked as if he might faint "Yes, here and now, why not?"

Ricci then said, "Go on Jake, imagine you're on your own in your flat singing along to your records."

"OK," Jake said, "just give me a minute."

Jake closed his eyes, trying to think of a song that was right for the moment and would do him justice, and then it came to him. He took a deep breath and began to sing; it was a poignant ballad.

Friends tried to tell me you would walk away
But I never imagined I would see that day,
Now I'm here alone, crying bitter tears,
For the love I've lost and the wasted years.

He lost himself in the song, gesturing dramatically with his arms at appropriate moments, he sang the whole five verses of the song with its catchy chorus.

Come on home to me my love
My eager arms are open wide
Love me the way you used to love
Together we can turn the tide.

When he'd finished, they were all applauding and congratulating him, Jim was dabbing his eyes and looked as if he'd been crying, the others all looked elated. Mr Sharman insisted on taking photographs of Jake, moving him to a suitable part of the room where there was a plain background and taking quite a few pictures using the flash attachment. He said he would let Jake have copies, and then he asked, "I've never heard that song before, which artist sang that?"

"I just did, it's my own song, I wrote it, I've never sung it to anyone before."

"Well, I would like you to sing it again next week at the Black Orchid. Ricci can bring you for a rehearsal so that you can get used to singing with a microphone, do you have the music for that song?"

"I'm afraid not Mr Sharman, I can't write music."

"That's alright Jake," Ricci interjected, "we can put it on the tape recorder, the pianist can notate it from that."

"Good, shall we say rehearsal on Friday afternoon then at two?"

"That's fine by me, is it OK for you Jake?"

"Yeah, great."

"OK that's settled. It's been a pleasure Jake. I think you will do well. What will you be calling yourself by the way?"

"I like the name 'Rusty L'amour', Rusty is my way of paying respectful homage to my favourite singer Dusty Springfield and the L'amour is to give her some love as well."

"I like that, I like that a lot, it's catchy and memorable. Bye everyone." He went to Ricci and kissed 'her' *mmoir mmoir* on both cheeks, then to Jake's surprise he did the same to him.

"You did very well tonight, Jake, I'm looking forward to hearing you again on Friday."

Everyone said goodbye and Toby showed Mr Sharman downstairs and out of the house.

While Toby was gone, Ricci, Jake and Jim excitedly talked about Jake's impromptu audition, congratulating him on how he sang so well.

Jim said, "I didn't know you wrote songs Jake, you sang it beautifully, I'm so proud of you love."

"Thank you, Jim, that means such a lot, did I really do well? I was so nervous."

"You were superb Jake, I could see Mr Sharman was impressed, and who wouldn't be!"

"Thank you so much for all your time and effort in making this evening happen, Ricci, providing everything, doing Jake's make-up and dressing him up, you've done wonders for him."

"Oh that reminds me," Jake said, "I've just got to pop downstairs." He grabbed his keys. "I'll be back in a moment." He left to go to his flat.

As he was unlocking the door, Toby came back upstairs. As he reached Jake, he said, "I think this calls for champagne Jake, the man was blown away by you, and so was I!"

"Oh thank you Toby, I'll be up in a moment, I've just come to get something."

"I'll get the glasses out, the champagne is already chilled, see you in a minute."

"Yeah."

Jake went into his flat to get Ricci's present; he was so glad he'd thought of buying it, he had done a superb job. As he came out of his flat, who should come out of his room but Amir. He stood there looking at the glamorous woman standing there, wondering who she was.

Jake said, "It's alright Amir, it's only me, Jake."

Amir came walking towards him to get a closer look. "I don't believe it, why are you dressed as a woman, where are you going?"

"It's a long story Amir and I can't stay to talk at the moment, but I promise I'll tell you all about it. Come and see me on Monday morning."

"OK Jake," he said chuckling, "about ten, alright?"

"Yes that's fine, see you then sweet boy." Jake put his hand on Amir's face and caressed his cheek. "Must dash!"

He left Amir on the landing still staring up at him in disbelief. When he got back upstairs, Toby was already pouring the champagne. He went to hand a glass to Jake, but saw that he had his hands full.

Jake went over to Ricci and said, "Here's a little something for all your hard work, Ricci love."

"Oh darling, you really shouldn't have!" Ricci exclaimed with excitement. "I wonder what it can be?"

"Only one way to find out," Jake replied.

Ricci began to take the bow from around the box and tear the paper away. When he saw the name on the box he was ecstatic – Diorisimo by Christian Dior. He opened the box, took the bottle out and undid the stopper, spraying a little on his wrist and sniffing it.

"Ooh it's heavenly Jake, thank you so much, it's so sweet of you."

"No, thank you Ricci for what you've done. I'm glad you like it."

Ricci kissed Jake on the cheek and said, "It was so worth it, you were in your elements earlier darling, you have such remarkable talent, I knew I was right about you."

"Thank you," Jake said humbly.

"Come on, come on," Toby said, handing everyone a glass of champagne. "Let's have a toast. Here's to 'Rusty L'amour', may she go on to much greater things."

Everyone raised their glasses and said in unison, "Rusty L'amour." Jim added proudly, "God bless her and all who sail in her!"

They all laughed and clinked their glasses together.

"Oh by the way, Jim Hartnell, I haven't forgotten how sneaky you and your co-conspirators were keeping Mr Sharman's visit a secret from me, but I'm very glad you did. I would have been nervous all evening, as it was, I didn't have time to think about it."

"That's what we all thought," Jim replied, smiling.

"When I said it wasn't entirely altruistic on my part to dress you in drag, I knew we needed new blood at the club so I wanted Mr Sharman to see you."

After they had chatted and had another glass of champagne, Ricci said, "We had better get you out of your finery sweetie, and get the slap off your face."

"By the way Ricci, please forgive me for asking but I'm

very curious, where did you get this beautiful gown?"

"Oh I know the senior costumier at Burmans, sweetie, he lets me loan anything I want. Such a dear man, would you like to wear this on Saturday for your debut performance?"

"Yes please Ricci, do I need to buy make-up or anything?"

"Nooo, you're OK Jake, I've got a good supply, there's no point buying any until you're absolutely sure about things. Turn around, let me unzip you sweetie!"

"Oooh, I've met men like you before." They both laughed hilariously.

Jake stepped out of the dress and Ricci caught it up in his arms, putting it back onto the hanger with its own zip-up bag. Ricci pulled off Jake's false eyelashes and gave Jake some cleansing wipes and make-up remover. After he had taken most of it off, he went down to the bathroom to wash his face. Jake was drying his face with the towel, wiping his eyes he looked into the mirror and, smiling, said aloud to himself, "You did well tonight darling, they loved you!"

He left the bathroom and went back upstairs. He was putting on his kimono as Jim came over to him, wrapped his arms around him and kissed his neck, making him go all weak and shivery inside.

"I think we should thank Ricci and Toby for everything and say goodnight love."

"Yes I do too, thank you both of you, it's been a fabulous evening, we'll say goodnight now."

"It's been such a pleasure darling," Ricci said, kissing Jake on both cheeks. "I'll pop down and see you on Wednesday evening if that's OK. We can have a good chat about things."

"That'll be good Ricci, see you about seven shall we say?"

"Yes, great."

Toby gave Jake and Jim a big hug each; he wasn't the kissy kissy type like Ricci.

"Goodnight both, sleep well, be good!"

"I'm sure we'll be very good," Jim replied. "We usually are," and laughed. "Goodnight, or should I say good morning, it's a quarter to one!"

Chapter 9

They were lying in bed together, both spent with passion after making love for a long time, wrapped in each other's arms. Jim began giving Jake little affectionate pecks of kisses and running his finger down the side of his face as he began to murmur softly, "Jake darling, I've been meaning to tell you something since I first met you, but I wanted to be sure about us before I said anything. You probably know what I'm going to say, but please don't say anything until I've finished speaking."

Jake was listening intently, wondering what on earth Jim was going to say, gazing at the earnest expression on his face.

"Jake you are the nicest, most genuine man I have ever met, I am hopelessly, deeply in love with you, and I hate it when I'm away from you, it makes me miserable. I want to be with you all of the time, my love. If I could have my way we would be living together tomorrow, we are perfect together. I am of course speaking on the premise that you feel the same about me too?"

"Oh Jim darling, I've been waiting for you to tell me that you love me, because, yes, I am very much in love with you, you must know that, but I was scared that I might make a fool of myself and end up getting hurt, so I didn't say anything. Each time you leave me, I long for the next time I'll see you again. So you see I feel exactly the same way about you as you do about me, so why can't we live together? What is there to stop us if it's what we really want to do? We need to think seriously about how we can make it happen."

"Oh my love," Jim sighed, kissing Jake passionately. "We will make it happen and very soon, I promise!"

Jake said, "You don't know this Jim, but it was always my intention to buy a property of my own when I came down to London. I only came to live here temporarily so that I would have a base to use to do property searches. I guess I kind of lost sight of that with all the excitement of being in a new place and meeting new interesting people, especially you love. It was meant to be, why did I choose Kilburn to live out of all the different places I could have picked, then decide to take this bedsit where your friends Ricci and Toby lived? Well, it all seems a bit like fate really."

"Yes darling, we were destined to meet, because I nearly didn't come to Ricci and Toby's party at all. I'd told them I couldn't make it as I was working that Saturday, but my assistant asked if I would swap weekends with him because he wanted the next weekend off to go somewhere. So I was able to go in the end, amazing really, it was meant to be my love."

"It will take some time for me to sort things out, I've got some personal savings, but the bulk of my money is tied up in the house. So firstly, I will have to tell Alicia that I'm selling up. I'm not sure how she will take it, but it's got to be done. Secondly, we will need to get a valuation done and put it on the market. Thirdly, on the basis of that valuation we can decide what kind of property we want, which area of the city we would like to live in, then my love, we can start looking at properties. I will tell Alicia when I get back to the house."

"That's wonderful Jim, but we could start looking at properties straightaway. We don't have to be reliant on selling your house, we can be cash buyers as soon as we find something we like. I've already got the money to pay for it!"

"Jake, I had no idea, forgive me love, I presumed that because you had been a farm labourer you're renting this bedsit because that was all you could afford. What must you think of me, how could I be so presumptuous?"

"You weren't to know that I had been left a substantial legacy by my godmother, how could you? So tell me, where would you like to buy a house Jim?"

"Let me see now, I think the best thing to do would be for me to take some time out and drive you around the areas I think you would like. I'm thinking maybe, West Hampstead, Highgate, Clapham Common, Holland Park, Notting Hill to name but a few, that way you would get a feel for the places and have a better idea of what you're looking for."

"*We're* looking for darling. I'm so excited Jim, I feel like opening the window and shouting, *he loves me and we're going to live together.* Isn't it wonderful?"

Jim said, "Don't you dare," and kissed him, then added, "Yes Jake, it is the most wonderful thing ever, I know exactly how you feel."

Jim jumped out of bed and went over to his clothes. Picking something from his pocket and concealing it from Jake, he came back to bed.

"I want you to have this, Jake. As soon as I saw it I knew it was right for you, give me your left hand."

Jake held out his hand and Jim placed a ring on his pinky.

"There you are my love, I hope you like it."

Jake was completely surprised. He lifted his hand to look at the beautiful gold and opal ring that Jim had placed on his little finger.

"Like it? It's absolutely gorgeous Jim, thank you so much

darling, amazing, it's a perfect fit!"

"Just like we are sweetheart," Jim said as he kissed Jake tenderly.

"Oh darling I love you so much. Can I tell Ricci and Toby, or should we tell them together?"

"What time is it? My God, it's half past two in the morning, we should get some sleep, we can tell them tomorrow, but I think they already know anyway. Talking of telling people about us Jake, at some point I need to tell my parents, it's going to come as a shock to them to find out I'm gay. Anyway, we'll sort that out later, let's get to sleep."

"I don't think I can sleep Jim, I'm too excited. I'm going to make a cup of tea, and I'm hungry/ I fancy a piece of toast with cheese on, do you want some?"

Jim looked at Jake and smiled. "I'll have a cup of tea please, but I'm not at all hungry."

Jake went into the kitchen to make a pot of tea. He poured a cup for both of them and then came into the bedroom.

"Here you are lo …" He let his words tail off because Jim was sound asleep, so he took his cup back into the kitchen and made himself a slice of toast. After he had made it he wanted to go for a pee so he quietly unlocked the door and went outside onto the landing. He didn't bother to switch the light on, he never did, as he could see quite well without it. He went to the loo, returned to the kitchen and quietly gorged on his cheese on toast, washed down with his cup of tea, then he gently climbed into bed beside Jim without waking him up.

Chapter 10

Jake and Jim were startled awake by an alarming thunderous crash with sounds of breaking glass, splintering wood and voices shouting. They heard the word 'police' several times. Looking at the clock he saw that it was 3.30am. They jumped out of bed, Jake threw his dressing gown on, Jim quickly put on his scants and trousers. They walked through the kitchen, unlocked the door and went out onto the landing. Walking cautiously forward a few steps allowed them to peer over the banister rails to try to see what was going on. They could hear the commotion of raised voices and loud protestations of innocence which were coming from Mr Montgomery's room. Amir came out of his room asking Jake what was going on, and glanced inquisitively at Jim.

Jake said, "We don't know Amir, but the police have broken in, they are in Mr Montgomery's room."

Lorenzo's voice suddenly screamed out, "Whadda da hell isa goin ona ere?" He was standing in his pyjamas shouting at the policeman standing by the front door. "You ava broken a my fronta door, my beautiful staineda glass isa gone." The poor man was almost crying. "I cannota replace a dis, where isa your boss?"

The policeman indicated that his boss, Detective Inspector Dunwoody, was in the room with a wanted suspect who was about to be arrested. Lorenzo said that he would wait until they came out. He didn't have long to wait, a few minutes later the door opened and Mr Montgomery was led out in handcuffs by two uniformed constables, looking very sorry for himself. D.I. Dunwoody came following them out of the room and Lorenzo said to him, "Who isa gonna repair anda pay fora the damage to my door? If you had runga my bell I woulda let you in anda there would ava beena no damage. My beautiful Victorian glass isa broken ina pieces."

"And you are?" D.I. Dunwoody queried.

"I ama da owner of a da ouse, Lorenzo Costa," he replied angrily. "What ara you gonna do abouta this anda why ara you arresting Mr Montgomery?"

"We are very sorry for any damage caused to your property Mr Costa, we didn't ring the bell to gain access as we did not want to alert our suspect to the fact that we were onto him. We couldn't take the chance that he might escape, and we weren't sure whether he had accomplices or not. I need to ask you how you know this man and what you know about him. Mr Montgomery you called him, is that the name he gave you?"

"Yes he cama ere looking for a da room that wasa vacant, he showda identification saying he was Mr Montgomery, he paida a months rent ina advance."

"Were you suspicious of him in any way?"

"No, he seemed OK to me anda he never giva me any trouble. Wot as he dona wrong?"

"Well his name certainly isn't Montgomery, it's Harry McFarlane and he's wanted in connection for a very serious crime, that of murder."

Lorenzo Costa's face showed utter amazement and disbelief at the thought that there had been a murderer hiding out in his house and in the room next door to his flat as well. All he could do was say, "Murder, *mio dio!*"

"Later today I will send some people round to repair your

door so that it is secure, meanwhile, I will leave a uniformed officer on guard. We obviously will not be able to replace your glass like for like, you will need to come to the police station, give a statement and put in a claim for compensation regarding that."

"Thanka you, I will coma later today, er how dida you know whicha room he was in?"

"We had been watching the house and had seen him come in and put the front room light on. Did anyone else in the house have anything to do with McFarlane?"

"No, he kepta himself toa himself, can I go insida da room anda clean it?"

"I'll bet he did. Oh yes, that's alright we've done all our checks. Thank you for your help Mr Costa, goodbye."

"Goodbye."

Jake, Jim and Amir looked at each other in total surprise at hearing the detective say that 'The Shadow' was a murderer. No wonder he kept to the shadows and didn't get to know anybody. Jake was very pleased he'd never knocked on his door.

Lorenzo walked past the door with its broken lock into 'Mr Montgomery's' room, room 1. It was in a bit of a state, looking as though it had been ransacked; there were clothes strewn all over the floor, a chair was lying on its side with a broken backrest and the curtain pole had been pulled down. Lorenzo wasn't sure if all this had been done when the police broke in or not, perhaps 'Mr Montgomery' had put up a struggle but it certainly was a mess. He opened the wardrobe door and had a look inside. There was very little by way of belongings there, just an old black jacket, a wool cap, a scruffy old pair of shoes with some socks shoved into them. There was a case on top of the wardrobe that he lifted down and opened. It was empty apart from some dirty, well-thumbed girlie magazines.

Jake tapped on the door and put his head around the door. "Hello Lorenzo, are you alright?" he asked, concerned at having heard all the commotion earlier and seen the extent of the damage done to the front door. "Can I help you clean up or anything?"

"Oh hello Jake, what a horrible business, looka at alla diss mess."

Jake could see he looked a bit shocked. "Would you like me to make you a nice cup of tea? Then later I can help you clean it up."

"Yesa please Jake, you ara very kind, I coma to youra flat."

"Come on then, I'll put the kettle on." Jake put a comforting arm around his shoulder and led him out. "This lot can wait," he said.

As they went into the hallway, Jake asked Jim to ask the constable on duty at the front door if he would like a cup of tea and whether he wanted sugar and milk in it; he couldn't have been more thankful as he looked really cold.

Jake and Jim took Lorenzo to his room, told him to make himself comfortable and Jim put the kettle on. As Jake sat beside Lorenzo to talk with him, Amir said "cheerio" and returned to his room.

"I'm so sorry this has happened Lorenzo, but in a way we might have had a lucky escape, no one has been harmed. It's sad about the damage and the loss of your lovely Victorian glass, but you can put something else in their place. If there's any way that Jim and I can help, you only have to say."

"You arra right Jake, things coulda beena mucha worse, soma one coulda beena hurt, and I woulda felta really bad about that."

"We'll soon have all the mess cleaned up," Jim said as he brought the tea in and handed Lorenzo his cup. "Here you are Lorenzo, I've put plenty of sugar in it for you." Jim had heard somewhere that sweet tea was good for people who were recovering from a shock.

Jake told Jim to keep Lorenzo talking while he went downstairs to get rid of the broken glass in case anyone came in or out. He carried a dustpan and brush in one hand, a cup of tea for the police constable in the other.

The constable thanked Jake for the tea and apologised for the mess. Jake said it wasn't his fault and they would soon have it cleaned up. Jake then started picking up the bigger pieces of glass; he had an idea to salvage as many decent pieces as he could to take to a local glazier to see if he could make a smaller mosaic window as a surprise memento for Lorenzo. He quickly ran back upstairs, grabbed last Sunday's copy of the *Observer*, ran back downstairs and wrapped the chosen pieces carefully in it, then he fetched the broom and swept up the debris, gathering it up with the dustpan and brush to put in the refuse bin. Taking the pieces of glass wrapped in newspaper up to his flat, he laid it on the kitchen table.

"How are you feeling now, Lorenzo?" He could see that he had drunk his tea and looked a bit brighter.

"I ama ok now thanka you Jake, you ara botha very kind."

"We're only doing what anyone would do," Jake replied, and Jim agreed.

"Well, I ama very grateful toa you both."

"Shall we make a start on the room then?" Jake urged.

"Yesa we go nowa eh?"

They all went downstairs and began the process of tidying

up the room, first bagging up the clothing for the refuse bin, getting rid of the broken chair, throwing the suitcase with its pornographic magazines in the rubbish bin, putting the curtain pole back up then thoroughly cleaning up. When they had finished, the room was back in a lettable state again, so Lorenzo would be able to advertise for another tenant when he was ready and not lose money by having an empty room on his hands indefinitely.

"Youa boys hava beena so good, I ama very grateful fora alla youra elp, Lorenzo willa nota forgeta this!"

It was beginning to get light, the milkman's float was trundling down the street. They said goodbye to Lorenzo and returned to Jake's flat. Jake made coffee and toast and they both sat and talked as they ate and drank, Jake saying how lucky it was that no one in the house had been a victim of Mr McFarlane, 'The Shadow', and how he now felt more than ever that they should look for a house of their own.

Jim agreed and kissed him and said, "That's settled it, I'm booking a week's holiday next week, and we are officially house hunting."

Jake squeezed his hand and said, "I'm really excited about that, Jim. By the way, are you going into work today?"

"Yes, I'd better get home, have a shower and shave then go in later. I'll give you a bell to tell you when I'm coming to see you again."

"Alright darling, don't leave it too long!"

Chapter 11

Later that morning, Jake heard the telephone ringing and dashed down the stairs to answer it. Picking up the receiver, he heard the butch voice at the other end saying, "Hello, is that Jake?"

"Yes it is, who's that?"

"It's Terry." Jake was at a loss, he couldn't think if he even knew anyone called Terry!

"Terry?"

"The bus conductor, I've got the day off, I wondered if we could get it together?"

"Oh Terry, I'm so sorry, I'm all at sixes and sevens, the police are here at the moment, we've had a murderer in the house!"

"What, ooer, oh don't worry then, I'll call some other time, take care, see ya!" and the line went dead.

Because of how abruptly Terry ended the call, Jake presumed that he had misheard what he'd said, perhaps hearing, *we've had a murder in the house,* or it could have been when he'd told him, *the police are here at the moment,* that frightened him. Whichever it was, he was never to receive a phone call from him again. Years later, Jake would still often recall that telephone conversation, chuckling inwardly to himself and thinking, *what a shame, poor Terry, it might have been fun!*

As Jake reached his flat door, he heard Ricci calling softly, "Jake is that you?"

"Yes, Ricci."

"Can you come up a minute love?"

"Yes," Jake said as he made his way upstairs.

When he reached the top, Ricci was stood in his sarong-style dressing gown, clutching it at one side to keep it wrapped around him.

"Did you hear any strange noises in the night darling?"

"I'll say, you don't mean to tell me you and Toby slept through all of the kerfuffle?"

"What kerfuffle? You'd better come in and tell Auntie Ricci all about it."

After Jake had finished relating the events of the early morning, Ricci exclaimed, "Oh my God, a girl could have been raped, debauched or murdered in her bed darling!"

Toby who had been lying in bed listening, opened one eye wearily and said, "In your case, probably the latter!"

Ricci retorted playfully, "Oooh, such a bitch," and they all laughed.

"No seriously though, poor Lorenzo, I expect he feels dreadful, not just because of the damage, but what could possibly have happened in the house!"

"I think he will be alright, Jim and I helped him clear up the mess, but he was very upset about the Victorian glass."

"Well I would be too. Now then, what about you and Jim, how are things progressing on that front darling?"

"Jim told me he loved me last night, I told him I felt the same, he gave me this beautiful ring, look!"

"Sore arse day today then eh Jake?"

Ricci glowered at Toby, "Ignore him Jake. Toby, do behave, don't bring noble feelings down to your subterranean level, go and take a bath while I talk to Jake, there's a love!"

Toby was out of bed in a flash. "I'll leave you girls to talk then, see you later."

"That's wonderful, it's a beautiful ring, so when's the wedding? I'll have to buy a new hat if I'm going to be matron of honour!"

"Oh stop it, be sensible, we're serious, Jim is going to book a week's holiday next week so that we can go house hunting!"

"That's wonderful darling, I'm so pleased for you. Now you are still up for Friday afternoon rehearsal, aren't you?"

"Of course, I wouldn't let you down Ricci. I'm so excited about it all, my life just seems to be one euphoric whirl at the moment!"

"Just how it should be, darling. Can you sing your song again for me now so that I can record it and get it to Adrian the pianist?"

"Now? Sure, OK."

"And Jake, I really am so pleased for you and Jim, you make a lovely couple."

"Thanks Ricci," Jake said, giving him a kiss on the cheek.

The recording of the song took all of ten minutes to do.

"Thank you for doing that, Jake, I'll get it to Adrian, he's the guy that will be playing for you at rehearsal this afternoon and for your debut performance tomorrow. You can have a chat with him about any other songs you could do on the night, he's very good."

"I am so grateful to you for doing all this for me Ricci, it's taking up a lot of your time."

"It's worth it darling, I can't bear to see good talent go to waste, just you remember your Auntie Ricci when you're rich and famous!"

"Some chance of that happening love."

"There's every chance, you've just got to believe in yourself, and take whatever good opportunities come along, they will darling. you'll see!"

They talked for a while over a pot of tea and butter croissant with strawberry jam which were absolutely delicious. Jake was curious about Ricci's background so he asked him when he had done drag?

Ricci's reply, "Oh some years ago, I did it for a while, I was good at it too, but I had a nervous breakdown and couldn't do it anymore sweetie, so I decided to use my talents for backstage work. I loved doing make-up!"

"I'm sorry to hear that Ricci. Do I need to buy jewellery for tomorrow's performance?" Jake replied,

"Don't worry, I've got all that sorted, all you need to do is get yourself a nice comfortable pair of light blue or white cotton slip-on shoes, they'll be fine for tomorrow. Mademoiselle Modes in the high street do a good line in them." Then Ricci glanced at the clock and exclaimed, "Oh my, look at the time, I'd better get going so that Adrian will have time to sort the music out."

Jake said his goodbyes and went back to his own flat. It was about fifteen minutes later that he heard Ricci saying goodbye to Toby then run downstairs and out of the front door, past the tradesmen who had arrived to mend it and make the house secure once again. Jake decided to write an apologetic overdue letter to Vera and Ted telling them about everything – well, nearly everything – that had happened, including the dreadful goings on with 'The Shadow'. He would have to reassure them that he was perfectly safe though. He didn't want to say too much about him and Jim yet, he just said that he was seeing someone called Jim and they seemed to be getting along like a house on fire. He went into great detail about dressing in drag for the first time, doing his audition which resulted in him rehearsing for his debut as a drag artiste on Saturday evening at a club called the Black Orchid. He was so glad he had decided to call himself Rusty L'amour as he thought it sounded really sophisticated. He promised that he would ring to tell them how the evening went.

When he had finished the letter, he put a stamp on it and went out to post it on the corner of the High Road. He then walked further up the street looking for the shop that Ricci had recommended. He found it, went in, and was able to buy the exact shoes he wanted.

When he was back home, Jake made himself a light tuna salad lunch with a thin slice of sourdough bread to go with it. He thought it wise not to overeat as he didn't want to feel bloated through rehearsal; he was also thinking about fitting into his frock again tomorrow evening. He was just about to sit down and eat when he heard the telephone ringing. He scooted downstairs to answer it; it was Jim.

"Hello darling, I just wanted to tell you that I love you so much, enjoy the rehearsal. I'll be over to see you this evening as soon as I can get away and you can tell me all about it."

"Thank you sweetheart, I love you too. I'm looking forward to it but I'm a little nervous!"

"You'll be fine love, most of my professional acts would tell you that it's natural to have a few nerves, because you want everything to go right, so you have to channel those nerves positively to give your best. I know you will, just let yourself go and enjoy it!"

"Oooh, I've met men like you before who've said that," Jake laughed, and so did Jim on the other end of the line. "I can't wait to see you tonight love."

"I can't either, the audience will wonder what's hit them

tomorrow. You'll knock em dead. I must go now love, someone's waiting to see me. I love you, see you soon, bye!"

"Thank you darling, I love you too, thanks for ringing, bye for now."

Jake replaced the receiver and started to walk back upstairs. He had such a warm glow inside him knowing how Jim and he felt about each other. Over lunch he could think of nothing else but the two of them living in their own place together, he couldn't imagine anything more wonderful.

He came back upstairs to grab his jacket and wallet, locked up and went upstairs to knock on Ricci's door.

He answered it looking very flushed, he said, "We'll be with you in a jiffy darling. Come on Toby, we don't want you making us late."

Jake was surprised to hear that Toby was coming along too, but he thought *what the heck, the more the merrier!*

"You would prefer it if I was actually wearing trousers, Ric?"

"Yes of course."

"Well give me time to get the buggers on now that you've had your wicked way with me!"

"Oh shush, come on, Jake doesn't want to know you've managed to get it up and have your yearly playtime!"

Toby shouted, "Bloody cheek!"

Jake was amused by the conversation but he tried to keep a straight face when they came out.

Toby looked at him, gave a wry smile and said, "Nearly stopped me in mid flow there Jake," and laughed.

"Ignore him Jake, crude Aussie that he is!"

Jake thought it best to just say, "Have you two got everything? We'll be there on time if I grab us a taxi."

Chapter 12

When the taxi pulled up in front of the pub/nightclub, Jake paid the driver and tipped him. He looked at the place and was very impressed, the brick walls of the building were painted black, the windows though were painted in a glossy fuchsia pink and there was a large fluorescent neon sign that had big letters saying 'The Black Orchid' with a neon flower motif angled on the side of it. Jake thought how marvellous it must look at night when it was lit up and he looked forward to seeing it. As they walked in up the steps, he saw that there was a large wood-framed glass-fronted notice case which was empty apart from a banner with the words 'Coming Soon' in bright lettering inside. Once they had entered the thick deep-blue carpeted foyer, you were greeted by a reception desk either side of which were two sets of double doors with signs saying 'Bar' over one, the other, 'The Black Orchid Club'.

As they veered towards the latter, Ricci asked Jake, "What do you think of the place darling?"

"It's fabulous Ricci, I don't really know what I expected but it's far better than what I imagined!"

"Wait until you see inside the club, honey!"

Toby had gone on ahead, he pushed both of the double doors back until they clicked and held on automatic catches. When Jake saw inside the club his mouth gaped open and for a few minutes he was speechless. The doors had opened onto a small stone semi-circular dais with ornamental metal banister rails that descended down four curved steps onto the club floor.

Revealed was an expansive room with a burgundy carpet, numerous small circular tables covered with pink cotton cloths filled the room up to where the carpeted area was punctuated with a brass metal edging denoting the beginning of the sprung wooden dance floor. Beyond this was the stage which was curtained in burgundy velvet with two swags across the top, separated by an orchid motif in the middle. Jake couldn't believe the size of the stage, it looked to be about fourteen feet across with a three or four foot drop to the main floor. It had a little staircase of five steps on the side. On the left of the stage was a baby grand piano and in front of the stage, up on a gantry, was a bank of spotlights, and at the back of the stage was a shimmering curtain of metallic strands. Mr Sharman certainly hadn't skimped when he'd kitted the place out.

"Ricci, it's gorgeous, wow, what a stage, the place is just bona, it's so camp!"

"I'm so glad you like it darling, I helped Monty design the place!"

They walked down the steps and arced their way past the tables to the stage. Jake was overwhelmed, he had butterflies in his tummy but he was keen to get started with the rehearsal now so that he could get the feel of what it would be like to perform here. Ricci took him backstage and showed him his dressing room. He was pleased to learn that it was exclusively his, there was another communal one for the other acts. They were walking back on stage as Adrian came in, he came up to where they were standing.

Ricci greeted him with, "Hello Adrian darling, how are you? Let me introduce you to Jake Wiggins, or should I say Rusty L'amour."

"Hello Jake, I'm pleased to meet you at last, I've heard such a lot about you!" They shook hands, his grip was strong and warm.

"Oh, all good I hope, I'm pleased to meet you too and I hope I haven't given you too much of a headache in fitting music to my words?"

"Yes of course, glowing in fact, however, it would have been nice to have a little more time for the task, but that isn't your fault Jake, it's a great song, I'm looking forward to working with you."

Jake liked the look and sound of Adrian; he thought him to be in his mid-fifties, he was quite tall and slim with dark hair thinning on top and a trimmed beard and moustache revealing plump sensuous lips. His voice was deep and soft and he had large brown puppy-dog eyes. He was dressed casually, but smart, in a cream open-necked shirt which showed a few curly chest hairs protruding out over the top button, he wore a pair of beige trousers and canvas shoes. Not that Jake had taken any real notice of course!

"Well, would anyone like a drink before we get started, Adrian?"

"I wouldn't say no to a small G&T with ice and a slice please sweetie."

"Jake, what would you like to drink?"

"I would love a whisky and dry ginger, but I insist on buying these Ricci." As Jake said that he reached for his wallet from his back pocket and gave Ricci a twenty-pound note. "There you are, please get them out of that love."

"OK, thanks Jake."

Adrian put his hand in the middle of Jake's back and said, "Come up on stage and get the feel of being here. We'll run through your song 'Wanting You' first, just to make sure I transcribed it correctly, and then you can sing it through if that's OK? I have added a short intro to it."

"Yes that will be fine," Jake replied, standing centre stage and looking out at the full expanse of the club. "This is incredible, I can't believe I'm here."

Adrian began to play the notes to Jake's song. Hearing the tune being played was surreal to him, surreal and beautiful, he began to hum along.

"You've got it perfectly!" Jake said enthusiastically. "That's so clever of you!"

Adrian smiled and continued playing. "It's a great song Jake, you're the clever one really!"

"Here you are darlings, dwinky poos, Toby and I will sit quietly and listen."

Jake picked up the tray with their drinks on, placed Adrian's on the small table next to the piano, took a gulp of his whisky and said, "Right Adrian, let's give it a shot, shall we, from the top, that's what they say isn't it?" he said with a smile as he switched on the microphone and took a deep breath.

Adrian smiled as he started to play the introduction. Jake came in on cue.

"Friends tried to tell me you would walk away …" His voice was clear and melodic and he used the microphone as if he had used one all his life, like it was the most natural thing in the world, moving it away as he sang louder, bringing it up close to his mouth for breathy quieter parts. Hardly surprising really as he had studied Dusty's stagecraft and just emulated her.

When he had finished, he was poised like a consummate professional with his head bowed waiting for applause, only looking up when Ricci shouted as he was clapping his hands furiously,

"That was brilliant darling! What did you think, Adrian?"

Jake then saw that Mr Sharman was sitting at the table with Ricci and Toby. He wondered what he thought of his rendition.

Adrian replied, "It was superb, considering it's the first time Jake has sung it to music. Just one little suggestion Jake, if you leave dropping your head until the last tinkling notes of the piano end, I think it would look better, have a greater effect. How do you think it felt?"

"It felt amazing singing with your piano accompaniment and using a real microphone, instead of my old hairbrush!"

They all laughed and Jake picked up his drink and took a gulp as Adrian continued. "I also think you will do it even more justice when you have an audience, hanging on every note you sing. I don't think we need to run through it again, unless you want to."

"No, I'm happy with it, Adrian."

Adrian looked over to Mr Sharman and said, "What did you think, boss?"

"I didn't like it." He paused. Jake looked crestfallen. "No, I absolutely loved it!"

Jake gasped with relief and there were smiles all round.

Adrian took some sheet music from his bag. "Shall we look at some other possible songs now then?" He invited Jake to come over to the piano.

Jake began sifting through the music. "I feel I need to do some up-tempo numbers, and perhaps we should leave 'Wanting You' until last. How many numbers will I be doing by the way?"

"We can fit four into the show between the other comedy

drag acts. You're the guy providing the glamour, Jake."

"Ooh, thank you Adrian, what about 'Bobby's Girl' by Susan Maughan. I know it's a favourite for drag artistes to mime to, but I'll be singing it, which will give me an edge. I can also invite them to sing along for the chorus."

"That sounds great Jake, let's have a go at it then."

Jake took a sip of his drink to moisten his lips as Adrian played the intro for him to come in. Jake sang it very coyly, almost with a Marilyn Monroe pout, in certain strategic places he made suggestive movements with his hips, that would make the crowd laugh but wouldn't lower the tone of his act.

"Wonderful, you must do that one Jake!" Mr Sharman shouted excitedly.

They rehearsed until five o'clock, going through loads of songs, they had managed to come up with five they all really liked. Adrian asked him if he would be able to learn them in time. Jake looked at the list written in the order they were to be sung.

"If I take the music and lyrics home with me I will," Jake replied confidently, smiling reassuringly at him, but privately thinking, *I bloody well hope so!*

'Walking Back To Happiness' by Helen Shapiro

'Everybody's Somebody's Fool' by Connie Francis

'I Couldn't Live Without Your Love' by Petula Clark

'Bobby's Girl' by Susan Maughan

'Wanting You' by Jake Wiggins

Mr Sharman had approved them, he bought drinks for everyone and left with a cheery, "See you all tomorrow."

Ricci said later that it was very unusual for Monty Sharman to buy a round of drinks, so he must have been pleased. Adrian suggested that they should all go to a local restaurant for a meal, which everyone thought was a great idea. He recommended The Rendevous in Camden High Street saying it was popular with the gay community as well as serving delicious food at reasonable prices. They had an excellent meal which Adrian insisted on paying the bill for, Jake had ordered spaghetti Bolognese which he thoroughly enjoyed. They all said how well the rehearsal had gone, he and Ricci discussed the arrangements for tomorrow evening, Jake suggesting that he help Ricci with carrying the gear that he would need for his act. This reminded him of things that he had to remember to take like his shoes, Aristoc tights, wet wipes, deodorant, perfume, etc. He had made an appointment at a local beauty salon called The Studio that Ricci had put him on to, where he said all of the girls were lovely and one of them would fit him with false nails as well as wax his arms and legs. All this felt like another world to Jake, a world that he was happy to fully embrace and enjoy.

When Ricci, Toby and Jake finally got home it was half past nine. They said goodnight, Jake walked into his flat and immediately got undressed ready to have a good hot soak in the bath and prepare himself for when Jim would arrive later.

He slipped his dressing gown on, picked up his soap and towel and went along the landing to the bathroom, placing them on a chair. He swilled around the bath making sure it was clean, put the plug in the hole and turned on the taps; he intended to luxuriate in deep hot foamy perfumed water until his skin had gone all wrinkly.

When he was coming out of the bathroom Lorenzo called out to him from halfway up the stairs, "Hello Jake, ina case I don'ta see you tomorrow beforra youa go, breaka da leg eh!"

"Thank you Lorenzo, that's very thoughtful of you, will

you be there?"

"Willa I bea there, you try toa stoppa me!"

"Oh lovely, see you tomorrow then, goodnight."

"Gooda nighta Jake."

Jake thought how sweet it was of Lorenzo to take the time to wish him well. He had been meaning to ask him how things were progressing with his dealings with the police but he just hadn't had the time, he would get around to it at some point.

He made himself a whisky and dry ginger and put the television on. He tuned into a late-night film, they were showing *Rear Window*, one of Jake's favourites, with James Stewart, the lovely Grace Kelly and Thelma Ritter; he loved Hitchcock films.

The doorbell rang at eleven thirty, it woke Jake from a doze, the television was still on, the film had finished, now there was a chat show host interviewing some obscure celebrity that Jake didn't recognise. He went down to let Jim in,

"Hi darling, you look tired, did I wake you?"

"I must have dozed off watching a film, probably a combination of a long day's hot bath and the glass of whisky I drank, but it's so lovely to see you." He kissed Jim, adding, "I've got so much to tell you."

"I've got something to tell you too, but it can wait. I want to hear all your news first!"

Once they were in the flat, they kissed each other passionately, long and lingering kisses that were usually a prelude to a passionate love session, but they both wanted to talk and hear about the other's news more than anything. Jake asked Jim if he wanted something to drink,

Jim replied, "No thanks love, I'm fine. C'mon then don't keep me in suspense, how did it go, start at the beginning, I want to know everything."

Jake began to relate everything that had happened, Jim listened intently, loving seeing Jake so excited and hearing every aspect of how the rehearsal went.

When he had finished, Jim said, "I told you everything would go well, I knew the first time I saw you in drag and you sang your song to Mr Sharman that you were a natural. I'm so pleased for you, well done love." He gave him a peck of a kiss.

"Thank you, Jim. Now what was the news that you wanted to tell me?"

"You know that we said we were going to start house hunting?"

"Yes."

"Well, we don't need to if you like what I'm going to tell you!"

"What's that, c'mon spit it out, I'm all ears!"

"I told Alicia that I was intending to sell our house and move out, so that we could buy a property together. I was so surprised at her reaction, I thought she would be angry and put out, but what she said I thought made absolute sense. She said, why sell a perfectly good house that you love, I would prefer it if you gave me half the value of the house so that I can get myself a decent flat, and you and Jake could move in here."

Jim was watching Jake's face to try to gauge his reaction to what he was telling him, wondering if he would like the proposal.

"I've been thinking about the pros and cons and I think she might be right. It's in a lovely area, it's convenient for me getting to work, we could make any alterations you wanted to, and in the long run I think it would work out cheaper for us. What do you think?"

Jake was quiet for a few moments, obviously mulling over what Jim had just told him. He had been looking forward to the prospect of them searching for a place together, in one way he was disappointed, but he saw the reasoning and practicality of what Jim and Alicia were advocating.

"In theory what you are both saying could be absolutely right Jim, but considering that I've never even seen your house, it would be impossible for me to make an informed decision. I'm not against the idea, I just need to see it before I make my mind up!"

"Well of course you do darling, and you shall as soon as we can arrange it, but I want you to understand that I will accept whatever decision you make and not be offended if you say no. It will just take a little longer for us to find somewhere suitable that we both like if you decide that you don't like it."

"OK my love, I can't wait to see it, arrange it as quickly as you can. I just want to be with you, wherever it is!"

"You're a darling. Now, I can see you're really tired and it would be selfish of me to stay. You've got a big day ahead of you tomorrow and you need your sleep, so I'll say goodnight. I'll be there cheering you on tomorrow evening. Tell Ricci to reserve a place for me!"

"Yes I will Jim, you're so thoughtful, I love you very much."

"I love you too darling," Jim said, giving him a hug and kiss. "Now get some rest, I'll see myself out."

As Jim left, Jake walked over to the window and watched him drive away. He set his alarm for nine, his appointment to get waxed and have his nails done wasn't until ten fifteen, that would give him plenty of time to have a wash, clean his teeth, have some breakfast, dress and get to The Studio. He turned out the light and climbed into bed; he was asleep almost as soon as his head hit the pillow.

Chapter 13

The claaaang, claaaang, claaaang, of the clock alarm startled Jake out of a deep slumber. He hit the off button with a lazy thud, almost knocking it off the bedside table. He wanted to turn over and go back to sleep but, as tired as he felt, he knew he couldn't have a lie in, he needed to get out of bed and get cracking. Today was a really big day in his life; he knew that it was going to be filled with a mixture of nerves, anticipation, excitement and hopefully success!

The girls at the beauty salon were charming and lovely, although he didn't enjoy the waxing, it bloody well hurt! They wanted to know all about Jake's forthcoming debut as a drag artiste, how he came to be doing it, and what he did before he came to London. They were amazed when he told them he used to work as a farm labourer. Sharon, the woman who did his nails, said that she and two of the other girls were going to come along and watch his performance, they wouldn't miss it for the world. Ricci had told them it was going to be such a fun evening! But the best thing was Sharon had said that if Jake ever needed a make-up artist she would be very interested.

Jake came out of the salon on a real high, resplendent with gorgeous new long nails that were a tasteful pale glossy pink; they would contrast beautifully against the ice blue frock. He had worn a jacket with deep pockets, that would hide his feminine talons as he walked home along Kilburn High Road although part of him wanted to show them off by emulating Shirley Bassey-style hand movements. He thought it best to resist the idea, especially as he was just passing The Lord Palmerstone pub where a group of rough looking Irishmen were standing outside.

By midday he was home, packing a small bag containing the things he needed, revising the words to the songs as he did so and mentally affirming positive facts to himself, ***you know your words, you know the musical arrangements, have you packed everything? YOU CAN DO THIS … YOU'VE GOT TO FUCKING DO THIS.***

The telephone rang down in the hall, but before Jake could get downstairs Amir had answered it. He lingered on the staircase and heard Amir say, "Yes OK I'll get him." He turned to see Jake standing on the stairs. "Jake, it's for you."

"Thank you Amir," Jake said as he took the receiver from him.

"Hello."

"Hello Jake, it's Adrian. I just wondered what you thought about having more rehearsal time this afternoon, just to make sure you feel one hundred per cent OK with everything?"

"Adrian, that would be marvellous, it would make me feel more confident about things."

"OK, are you free from two o'clock? I could pick you up from home."

"Yes that would be great. Are you sure it's not too much trouble, I could get a taxi."

"I only live in Brondesbury Place, just around the corner from you. I'll see you at two then?"

"Yes, thank you Adrian, see you later."

Jake replaced the receiver and went back upstairs to finish putting things together. He suddenly remembered that he had offered to help Ricci with any help he needed carrying stuff.

He went upstairs and rang his bell.

Toby answered, "Hello gorgeous, what's up mate? You look in a tizz."

"Hi Toby love, is Ricci in?"

"Yeah, come on in."

Ricci was sat drinking a cup of coffee at the table in the window alcove. "Hello darling, is everything alright?"

"Yes it is, Ricci, I just wanted to tell you that I'm going to the club this afternoon to have more rehearsal time with Adrian and I wondered if you wanted me to take anything for you as I said I would help."

Toby gave a knowing smile. "More rehearsal time eh? Adrian's keen!"

"Yes, it's very kind of him isn't it?"

"Oh yeah, very, but oid keep me hand on me hapenny, if I were you Jake!"

"Why do you say that?"

"I think he's got the hots for ya!"

Ricci frowned at Toby. "Shut up Toby, you've got a one-track mind."

"You mark my words Jake, he'll have the knickers off you in a flash if you let him!"

"I won't bloody let him, I'm sure he won't try anything like that!"

Ricci touched Jake's arm and said, "Take no notice of him love, you could take your gown, then I can manage all the other stuff, if that's alright."

"Yes that's fine, do you want me to take it now?"

"You may as well darling, you can take it from the rail, I've dressed your wig, you'll look gorgeous."

"Thanks Ricci. What time will you be coming to the club?"

"I'll be there for six thirty to start getting you ready. We don't need to rush things, your first spot will probably be around nine."

Jake lifted the weighty gown from the rail and moved towards the door. "Great, I'll see you both later, I'll put my cast-iron knickers on then Toby!"

"Yeah, Ricci's got some like that!"

Jake lay his dress on the bed next to the bag with everything else in, he took a look at himself in the mirror and thought, *you're not wearing those trousers, they're too tight and revealing.* He found an old baggy pair of slacks in the wardrobe and put them on; they were extremely comfortable but certainly not flattering, definitely passion killers.

When Adrian arrived, Jake was already standing with the door open. He had locked up and brought his frock and case downstairs.

"Hello Jake," Adrian gave broad smile. "Can I help you with anything?"

"Hello Adrian, yes please, if you could just carry my case, I'll bring my frock."

"Have you got everything? I'm parked just up the street."

"Yes, that's all, Ricci's bringing the rest."

They arrived at the club and as they walked inside Jake couldn't believe his eyes, there in the glass notice case was a large promotional poster showing a picture of him, with the name Rusty L'amour above it in big letters. He stood looking at it, thrilled and stupefied at the same time.

Adrian said, "Monty has done you proud Jake, what a beautiful photograph, you look stunning."

"Gosh, is that really me, I can't believe it!"

"You'd better believe it, my boy. In approximately seven

hours from now you'll be on that stage singing your heart out!"

Jake gave a deep sigh and said, "We'd better get some more rehearsing done then, hadn't we?"

"Definitely."

Jake took his frock to his dressing room and hung it up, leaving his case by the dressing table. He walked on the stage where Adrian was looking through his music. They had engaged in pleasant conversation in the car on the way, just general conversation with each of them asking one another questions about their backgrounds.

Jake was surprised to learn that Adrian's full-time job was a florist and that he had his own shop in Notting Hill Gate with a flat above, which he used to run with his partner Stewart, but they split up two years ago, after Stewart met someone else, Adrian had bought him out. He hired a manageress to run it for him and let the flat to a lesbian couple he knew.

He said, "I pop in occasionally and help out when Siobhan is particularly busy, say with a wedding, around Valentine's Day or at Christmas time. I like to keep my hand in. How about you? I hear you used to work on a farm."

"That's right I did, I'm currently unemployed, I don't really know what I would like to do now, I'm in between positions!" Jake thought, *oh shit, I wish I hadn't said that, he'll think it's a come on!*

"There's certainly a big difference between working on the land driving a tractor and being a drag artiste in a club. How did that come about?"

"Serendipity really, Ricci heard me singing, saw my potential and got me a surprise audition with Mr Sharman. I wanted to do it for a bit of fun, a new experience, but Ricci had other ideas."

"Yeah, nice that you can have a bit of fun as well though, eh?"

Ugh Ugh, Jake thought, *here we go, perhaps Toby was right after all!*

"Come and sit on the stool beside me and we'll go through the first number," Adrian said, patting the seat.

"I prefer to stand thanks Adrian, it helps the breathing." He put some distance between them by walking to the front of the stage and saying, "Shall we make a start?"

"OK we don't need an intro to 'Walking Back To Happiness' if I give you the first note and you can come straight in, if you're looking over at me, I'll give you a nod and hit it. Just try the first line as you are, then we'll do the whole number with the mic, OK?"

It worked like a dream.

They did all five numbers straight off. Except for a stumble with the words of 'I Couldn't Live Without Your Love', Jake had done everything perfectly.

Adrian congratulated him and suggested that they take a well-earned break. It was during this break that Jake learned something he didn't know. The recent party that Ricci and Toby had given cropped up in conversation and Jake was surprised when Adrian said that he was there, he thought Jake looked nice, he had spoken to him, he'd said something like, "Hello darling" but Jake hadn't responded.

Jake thought he should make light of it and let him know the reason he hadn't responded was because he had just met Jim.

"Oh that was you, was it? I wasn't really taking that much notice, I was intent on getting drinks for myself and a lovely guy I'd just met called Jim. We've been seeing each other ever since, we've fallen in love and are about to live together!"

"Oh, it's serious then, I was thinking I might be in with a chance until you told me that!"

'I'm sorry Adrian, we really are head over heels in love, there's no chance for us but I'm sure someone will come along for you soon." Jake wondered how he would take what he had said, whether he would accept it or still try it on with him.

Surprisingly he said, "He's a very lucky man, Jake. We can still be good friends though, I hope?"

"Of course we can Adrian, I think we are already. C'mon, I'm gagging for a cup of tea!"

After this conversation it was as though they had been friends forever and there was no tension between them anymore. They made use of the kitchen facilities, and were laughing and joking, thoroughly enjoying each other's company. Jake thought to himself, *thank goodness Toby warned me so that I was prepared, otherwise the outcome might have been very different. Adrian is a nice guy though; hope he finds someone special soon.*

Ricci and Toby arrived and found Jake sitting in the dressing room. He had obviously been crying.

"Jake, whatever's the matter darling? Why are you upset?"

Before Jake could answer Toby exclaimed, "I bladdy knew it, don't tell me, ragtime piano Joe has tried it on with you, I'll kill the lecherous bastard!"

Ricci tutted at Toby and Jake immediately said, "No Toby, it's nothing like that, Adrian hasn't done anything. I don't know why I got upset, I think it must be nerves and emotions coming out."

"Nothing to worry about, first night nerves affect different people in different ways, darling. You'll be absolutely fine once we start getting your slap on and we have a little dwinky poos." He began placing out all his make-up. "Now, tell me, how did your rehearsal go? Oh by the way, did you see your photo in the foyer darling, isn't it divine?"

Jake smiled, he felt cheered up already. He began telling Ricci all about the rehearsal and how he was so grateful to Adrian for suggesting they have another one, even if he may have had an ulterior motive.

Later Ricci told Jake about his three fellow artistes and took him into their communal dressing room to introduce him to them. Their names were comedic in their own right. Folly Berserk, who does a comedy can-can dance which ends with her attempting to do the splits that always goes horribly wrong; she has to be hauled off on a stretcher by two strapping male hunks who are stripped off to the waist, showing their muscles. Rita Reject who does a very funny act dressed as an ugly, lank-haired, love-starved woman who proceeds to take sex toys, vibrators and such out of her handbag, making rude jokes and sharing smutty banter with the audience. Lastly, Kitty Kaboom who does a mock burlesque strip routine wearing a basque which has tits that open up and squirt the audience, the crutch opens and she pulls out flags of the world all strung together, finally turning round and bending over as she tears off a velcro panel to reveal the word kaboom!

"Girls, this is Jake, shortly to become Rusty L'amour." They all stopped what they were doing and greeted Jake with spontaneous enthusiasm, each saying something complimentary or encouraging.

Kitty said, "We've seen your photo, you look gorgeous in drag, and not bad out of it either. I can't wait to see your act."

Rita and Molly smiled and Molly said, "Ricci tells me you have the most amazing voice, I look forward to hearing you sing."

Rita said, "They're going to love you, Jake."

Jake thanked them as Ricci led him out to the foyer and introduced him to a very burly man wearing evening dress.

"This is Harry, Jake, he is our compere for the evening, he introduces all the acts and keeps the crowd under control.

Then it was time to go and get ready, Ricci working his magic transformation on Jake. Later there was a growing buzz of voices and laughter as people began to fill the club. Molly was first on as she was considered a warm up act, then it was …

SHOWTIME!

Jake couldn't believe the reaction from the audience after he had sung what he thought was to be his last number; the thunderous applause, the whistling and cheering with loud shouts for more. He had such feelings of elation and excitement surging through him, the response was incredible, the adrenalin was giving him a tremendous high. He stood on the stage looking out at the crowd of faces in the packed club, he wasn't nervous anymore he was being buoyed up with the sheer adulation that was flowing out from them, completely enveloping him. Then he realised that he would need to say something to them, thank them for being such a wonderful audience and let them know that he would sing one final number as an encore to finish his performance.

Although he hadn't thought about it previously, he knew exactly what song it would be. He raised and lowered both his hands several times to indicate to them that he wanted to say something and gradually a hush came over them.

Jake lifted the microphone from the stand and said, "You have been such a wonderful audience, I thank you all so much for your appreciation and I would like to sing one final number for you."

He began to sing the opening words and notes of his favourite Jacques Brel song, 'Ne Me Quitte Pas'. Jake had learned the words by listening to Dusty Springfield's version on one of her LPs. There was a frisson in the air as he sang the poignant French words without any accompaniment. It didn't matter that he didn't fully understand the words, the feelings he conveyed were coming over loud and clear. After he finished singing there was a silence for a second or two, in which you could have heard a pin drop. Then the audience erupted again, they roared, whooped, whistled and clapped their hands in rapturous pleasure. Jake blew them kisses, bowed to them. Ricci walked on stage and handed him a massive bouquet of red roses which were from Jim. Jake walked off stage feeling on cloud nine.

Jim was waiting for him in the wings and he threw his arms around him, kissed him and said, "You were amazing, an absolute star, I love you so much!"

Jake said, "I love you too Jim. Wow, did I really just do that or is it a dream?"

"A dream come true for you, darling."

Jake looked at the card attached to the flowers and read the words,

To Darling Jake, The Love Of My Life, For All Of My Life, Fondest Love, Jim.

Jake, embraced him and whispered in his ear, "You're my dream come true, Jim."

Then Ricci hugged and kissed him as well. "They haven't seen the last of you, darling. Mr Sharman the manager is waiting to see you in his office. You knocked em dead sweetie!"

Jake caught Ricci's arm. "Thank you Ricci, none of this would have happened without you." He kissed him on the cheek. "You're an absolute angel."

When Jake and Jim walked into Monty Sharman's office he was beaming. "You were superb Jake, absolutely tremendous, you're the best this club has seen for a long time. How would you like to work for me permanently?"

"Well, Mr Sharman." Jake was flabbergasted. "I hadn't thought about it." He looked at Jim who smiled knowingly at him.

"Well I'll give you time to think about it, I'll draw up a contract, you talk it over with your manager. You do have a manager, don't you?"

Jake didn't even hesitate, "Yes I do, Jim here, he's my manager."

"Good, leave me your contact details, Jim, what's your surname?"

"Erm, Hartnell," Jim replied, a little taken aback at the suddenness of being given such an important role. "Jim Hartnell, 0HA2 9476, 34 Highgate Road, Hampstead, NW3."

Monty Sharman wrote the details down and said, "I'll send the contract to you for your approval. I hope we can do business, Jim." He stretched out his hand to shake Jim's, then he shook Jake's hand too. "Now how about a drink in the bar?"

Walking into the bar created quite a buzz. People were smiling at Jake, congratulating him, saying how much they had enjoyed his performance, complete strangers raised their glasses to him as he passed. He felt as though he had arrived at a place in his life where he had always wanted to be, it seemed as though the whole club wanted to buy him a drink. Mr Sharman led them to a table in the corner. Almost as soon as they had sat down, a waiter brought champagne to the table and popped the cork. There was a chorus of 'Ooooos' from the people in the bar. Lorenzo came over and hugged Jake excitedly, forgetting himself and speaking in Sicilian.

"*Sei la donna piū bella, sei stata magnifica, oh scusami, dico in inglese.* You arra the mosta beautiful woman, you wera magnificent Jake," and he did no more than lift his hand and kiss it, then walked off to join his friends. Jake thought it was so sweet of him!

"Let me propose a toast in advance of you signing that contract. I'm not buying champagne twice," they laughed. "Here's to Rusty L'amour, the toast of Camden Town!"

They chinked glasses and said in unison, "Rusty L'amour!"

Chapter 14

They had all left the club together. Jim had offered Ricci and Toby a lift and they ended up in their flat having picked up a Chinese from the takeaway on Willesden Road, eating, talking, laughter, drinking. The celebration went on until after one in the morning when Jake and Jim finally said their goodbyes and went downstairs to bed.

Once in the privacy of Jake's flat Jim said, "After a long lie-in, how about we go over to my house? Alicia is away for the week, you can take a look at the place, stay for a few days, get the feel of the place and see if you want to move in!"

"Yes, that sounds good Jim, I'd love to. Now we must get some sleep."

"I've got something else to tell you as well, but it can wait until the morning."

"It's morning already darling, so you can tell me now."

"It's nothing really important, you might not be interested." He paused.

"What is it Jim? I won't sleep now if you don't tell me."

"I've got the week off work!"

"Oh, that's fantastic, a whole week to ourselves!"

"You see, I knew you wouldn't be interested!"

"Oh silly."

"Oh the other thing I wanted to say to you is, yes I'd love to be your manager darling, how nice of you to ask me!"

Jake chuckled saying, "Well it was the only thing I could think of to say at the time, but you are the best person for the job, darling!"

They fell asleep in each other's arms. For Jake it had been a long, beautiful, exhausting day, one that he would remember for the rest of his life and one that had already begun to shape his future.

Jim was the first to wake up. He looked at the clock which showed ten twenty, climbed over Jake trying not to wake him up and went out to the bathroom. He came back and put the kettle on to make coffee. Looking in the bread bin he found the half remains of a white bloomer loaf, he sliced four slices from it and popped them in the toaster, poking his head around the door to find Jake sitting up wide awake.

"Good morning darling, do I smell coffee and toast?"

"Yes, want some?"

"Oooh yes please, I'll have some coffee and toast as well!" Jim replied laughing,

"You're on good form this morning sweetie, did you sleep well?"

"I certainly did, must have been all the alcohol we had last night, but I don't have the hint of a hangover, thank goodness, just an almighty appetite. Is the toast done?"

"It's on its way, do you want it there or in the kitchen?"

"Oooh, there's a novelty, I've never had it on the kitchen table before!"

"Oh c'mon, you must have done!"

The whole house must have heard them laughing. Jim climbed back into bed and they relaxed together eating their breakfast.

It was inevitable that they would want to make love, their close proximity and desire for each other dictated it. They vented their passion until they both lay, blissfully contented in each other's arms.

After they had both bathed and dressed and Jake had packed a few things in a bag, while Jim was in the bathroom he quietly went and tapped on Amir's door to tell him he was sorry he wouldn't be able to see him tomorrow. He also told him that they couldn't make love anymore as he was in love with Jim. Amir said he was pleased for him and wished them both well. Jake gave him a loving kiss and went back to his flat before Jim came out of the bathroom. They left to drive over to Jim's house at Hampstead. The house was on a tree-lined road close to the heath and was set back behind a lush green lawn. It was a four-bedroom semi-detached grade 2 listed Georgian house that Jim said looked very pretty in May to June as the frontage was covered in lilac-coloured wisteria. There was a large, shuttered bay window on the left-hand side, the top of which provided a wrought-iron railed balcony for the bedroom above. There was a front door and a large garage with another door to the side of it, which Jim said was the one they mostly used. It was an impressive house in a very desirable peaceful area. Jake was excited.

As Jim steered the car onto the gravelled driveway, Jake said, "Jim it's adorable, I can't wait to see inside!"

"I'm glad you like it darling, I hope the inside meets with your approval too. I'll leave the car on the drive for now. I'll take you in through the front door, as I said we usually use the door through the garage, but I want you to see the best part first."

As Jim opened the front door he motioned for Jake to go inside. He stepped into a large hallway with cream marble tiles that had a sweeping staircase on the left, curving into a railed galleried landing, this extended the whole width of it.

Beyond that, underneath the gallery, was a wall with a door which Jake presumed led into a reception room.

They stood in the hall for some time, Jim explaining some of the things they had altered as a result of obtaining planning permission from the local authority. One major job was having a wall knocked out upstairs to create a larger bathroom with a walk-in shower.

Jim continued the guided tour through the house showing Jake everything, but drawing attention to those special features that had made him fall in love with the house and want to buy it in the first place. He explained that these were the key things they needed to consider in deciding whether or not to sell and move, or keep it, as well as practical considerations such as location, house prices, etc.

The downstairs rooms were large and attractive, comfortably furnished. The kitchen, Jake exclaimed, was to die for, he could just imagine cooking meals in it to entertain guests for dinner parties, or enjoying baking, which he loved. He used to bake his own bread when he lived with Pauline and Ted on the farm, they loved his rustic loaves.

Jim said, "I'll show you the upstairs and you will be able to see a great view of the rear garden from the window. We'll walk around it after we've finished looking around the house."

"That's fine Jim, what I've seen so far is just gorgeous, it's a grand house."

"That sounds promising, but don't tell me your final verdict until you've seen absolutely everything, OK love?"

The bedrooms were out of this world as far as Jake was concerned. They were spacious and beautifully decorated, all the time he was mentally asking himself the big question, *could I live in this house?* as well as other significant questions like, *would the ghost of Alicia spoil things, would I resent not being able to buy my first property with Jim?* He put them to the back of his mind for now as Jim opened the French windows to lead him out onto a veranda with decorative wrought-iron railings that stretched the whole width of the house to overlook a large charming lawned garden and terrace. The view continued beyond the substantive garden, onto the heath.

"Wow, Jim, I can see why you love this house so much. How long did you say you've lived here?"

"Nearly fourteen years. You should see it in the summer, Jake. Come on love, we'll take a stroll through the garden!"

Jake didn't say anything, he'd noted the serious wistful look on Jim's face.

They went back down the beautiful, curved staircase. Jake felt slightly regal as he descended it, holding on to the banister rail and imagining calling out *darlings, how lovely to see you* to arriving guests.

Walking out onto the flagstone terrace, Jake noticed the cute metal table and chairs and thought to himself how wonderful it would be to sit there with Jim on a lovely sunny morning drinking fresh brewed coffee and eating some of his home-baked scones or croissants.

The whole garden was full of trees and shrubs, south facing with high hedges on both sides, a veritable haven of seclusion.

They descended the steps into the garden and began to wander; Jim's hand slipped naturally into Jake's and they looked at each other and smiled.

"I'll go and make us a pot of tea, you stay and explore. I'll call you when it's ready."

"OK love."

Jim thought to himself as he walked back up the garden towards the house, *I hope he likes the place, I'd be sad to leave it.*

Jake heard the tinkling sound of a spoon being clinked against the edge of a teacup and he guessed that was his call to join Jim for tea.

"The garden is very well-established Jim, do you look after it, or do you have a gardener come in?"

"Alicia looks after the planting, we get a gardener in to cut shrubs and what have you. I'm not really much of a gardener myself, Jake."

"I love it. I can just see myself out here in my sunhat and summer frock, looking like Susan Hampshire, gathering flowers to make an arrangement, camp as arseholes!" Jake was laughing at himself and Jim was laughing too, he thought the imagery was very funny,

"No, but seriously Jim, I'll come straight to the point." He paused. Jake's expression was so serious.

Jim was thinking, *oh no, he's going to tell me he doesn't want to come and live here.*

Jake continued, "I'd be a fool if I turned down your offer to come and live in this beautiful house with such a gorgeous man as you, but we need to sort out the financial side of things legally with a solicitor so that we are joint owners."

Jim jumped up out of his seat and threw his arms around Jake. "You won't regret it Jake, I love you so much." Jim kissed him passionately. "I can't wait for it to happen now!"

"You don't need to wait very long love, it isn't as though I've got a houseful of furniture and a load of goods and shackles to move. I can pack a suitcase, you can get what stuff I have in your car to bring over here. Lorenzo can have a couple of weeks' rent in lieu of notice, so as and when you're ready darling."

"I'll talk to Alicia when she comes back. It will depend on how long it will take her to move out, but it's so wonderful, I've already thought of a way we might celebrate."

"How darling?"

"I'm taking you out for a lovely meal this evening."

"Oh that's nice, but it's not anywhere posh is it?"

"Why?"

"I haven't really brought anything suitable to wear!"

"That isn't a problem Jake, I'm sure you can find something of mine to wear. We're the same size and build, you can take your pick from my wardrobe, I even think we're the same shoe size. I'm a size nine, what are you?"

"Nine."

"There you are then, no problem, I'll book us a table. What would you prefer, English, French, Italian? There's even a Vietnamese restaurant in the village."

"I think I'd like Italian please. I fancy antipasti, followed by a juicy steak with creamy tagliatelle!"

"Gosh, sounds like you know your way around an Italian menu!"

"I used to go regularly to one called Marco Polo in Coventry, I really fancied one of the waiters there. I never pushed it with him though, I think he would have told me to you know what, *vaffanculo*!"

"You'll never know now, will you?"

"No, aah, the missed opportunities I've had. I'm glad I didn't miss out on you darling. I knew the moment I saw you at Ricci and Toby's party that you were the one for me, it was like an electric shock had run through me!"

"Same for me love, it was overpowering, I knew I had to have you."

"Well, you've got me darling, and like you told me that first evening when we'd just met, I'm not going anywhere."

Chapter 15

On the Sunday evening as they were enjoying their meal at the Venezia, Jim came up with the marvellous idea that they should drive down to Brighton the next day so that Jake could see his mum and Ted. Jake was ecstatic about the idea, thanking Jim for thinking of it.

"It will be marvellous for them to meet you, and I'm dying to tell them everything that's been happening, but I wish I had a photo of myself in drag to take to show them. It won't be the same just telling them about it."

"That's easily remedied. When we've finished our meal, we'll shoot over to the club and see if we can get hold of one, shall we?"

"You're wonderful, Jim, you think of everything."

"I know I am," he said, and they laughed.

Luckily Harry had access to Monty Sharman's office and knew exactly where the promotional photos were, as he'd been the person who had displayed the one of Rusty in the notice case. He gave them a copy of the same one, they thanked him and returned to Hampstead.

They awoke early, despite having made love until it was quite late, they both showered and dressed. Jake looked smart in a pair of chinos and a checked shirt of Jim's. Jim made a cooked breakfast, bacon, egg, a grilled tomato and toast, washed down with a cup of delicious percolated Kenyan coffee, and by nine thirty they were in the car, driving down the road towards Saltdean to surprise Vera and Ted. Jim reckoned on the journey taking about an hour, he hoped if he kept him talking, that Jake wouldn't notice how fast he was driving!

"I can't wait for them to meet you," Jake said excitedly.

"I'm dying to meet them too, but what if they don't like me?" Jim replied, half joking.

Speaking in a refined 'queenie' voice, Jake said, "Then I'll have to completely disown them." He paused, then continued in his ordinary voice to say, "They can't possibly fail to like you, Jim!"

Jim's arm stretched over to Jake. He squeezed his hand without saying a word.

Ted was watching a car that had pulled up outside the bungalow with what looked like two men inside it. He was a little wary as there had been a few burglaries in the area lately and he wondered if they were sussing the place out. He didn't recognise the car or the driver, and he didn't have a clear view of the passenger either. He called to Vera who was in the kitchen.

"Vera, can you come here a minute!"

Vera came in from the kitchen drying her hands on a towel.

"Do you recognise this car that's parked outside, love?"

Vera looked out of the window. "No, Ted, I don't. They're probably going to be on a leaflet drop, or cold call selling. Did you get the numberplate?"

"No, I didn't spot the car until it was parked. Oh hang on, they're both getting out, it looks like J …"

"Ooooh it's Jake! It's our Jake, Ted, oh my goodness!"

The doorbell rang.

"Well go and open the door for them gal, don't leave em standing there!"

Vera recovered from her initial shock at seeing Jake outside and rushed to the door, throwing the towel to Ted for him to get rid of.

"Jake darling, what a lovely surprise!" Vera exclaimed, flinging her arms around him and giving him a kiss. "What brings you here?"

"Hello Mam, why you do of course, I thought a visit was long overdue. I've got such a lot to tell you. This is my friend Jim by the way."

"You're right Jake, long overdue." She turned and smiled. "Hello Jim, pleased to meet you." Vera thought, *what a good-looking man*. She was about to shake Jim's hand but before she knew it he'd planted a kiss on both of her cheeks.

"Hello Mrs Beavis, I'm very pleased to meet you too."

"Come through and meet Ted." She led the way into the lounge.

"Jake's come to visit and brought his friend Jim, Ted."

"It's great to see you again Jake, my you're looking well lad, the London air must agree with you." He hugged him. "So this is Jim is it?" he said, shaking his hand warmly. "I'm very pleased to meet you. At first when we saw your car pull up, we thought you might be burglars looking the place over!"

Jake and Jim looked a bit puzzled.

"There've been a few burglaries in the area, so we keep our eyes open. You never know do you?"

"No, I guess not," Jim agreed.

"Sit yourselves down," Vera said. "I'll make us all a cup of tea, unless you'd prefer coffee of course?"

"A cup of tea would be lovely, Mam."

"OK, won't be a tick, don't start telling us your news yet, I won't hear you from the kitchen."

"Such a lovely bungalow you have here Ted, and Saltdean

seems a nice place."

"Thank you it is, we both love it here, it's so quiet and peaceful. We've got good neighbours and we've made a lot of friends in the area."

The three of them were talking pleasantries when Vera came back in with a tray of tea and biscuits.

"We're just dying to hear all your news Jake, but your letter worried us, hearing about this man you had in your house that had done a murder, and what with the police breaking in and everything, we were concerned about what sort of house it was you were living in and whether you were safe or not."

"Well as you can see Mam, I've been perfectly safe, it was just unfortunate that the landlord took him in without asking for any references. Unfortunately these people don't have **'Murderer'** tattooed on their foreheads, so it's impossible to tell!"

"It's natural for a mother to worry though. Still, enough about that, I want to hear all about what happened after your audition and how your first performance went!"

Jake proceeded over tea to tell them all about his debut into the world of drag, describing everything from the moment he walked into the club on the Saturday and saw his picture in the showcase with the heading: **Tonight: Rusty L'amour.**

Then how in the dressing room later before his friend Ricci started making him up, how he was so nervous he very nearly didn't go through with it, but once Ricci had given him a stiff whisky and a good talking to he went on stage to do his act. When he began to sing he could feel the people were with him, then afterwards hearing the applause, cheers and whistles from the audience he knew this was what he was born to do. Luckily, he told them, the manager liked his act so much that he asked him to work at the club on a permanent basis. What that actually entailed, he and Jim wouldn't know until they received the contract and had a good look through it.

"I know it's not the big time or anything, it's not Sunday night at the London Palladium in the West End, just a provincial club in Camden, but it's a start."

"Don't put yourself down Jake, it's a great start. There are some drag queens working their socks off – *he nearly said tits* – performing in spit and sawdust pubs who would give their high teeth to be appearing in the Black Orchid." He looked at Vera and Ted. "Honestly, you should have seen him, he was so professional, he had them eating out of his hand. Anyway, with me as his manager, the West End is certainly worth aiming for."

"Oh Jake, how marvellous, I would have loved to have seen you."

"So would I," Ted echoed.

"Well, I have brought a photograph to show you." He pulled the large promo photograph out of the envelope and handed it to Vera. "What do you think?"

Vera's mouth gaped open and she stared at Jake, then at Ted, struck speechless for a few moments.

"Noooo, I'd never have believed it, you look like a film star, Jake!"

"Oh, which one, Rin Tin Tin?"

They all laughed.

"No silly, you're beautiful, if anything I'd say Elizabeth Taylor, you should have been a woman, Jake!"

"I'm perfectly happy being a man, Mam, this way I've got the best of both worlds!"

"It certainly looks like it," Ted said. "Blimey, I wouldn't

have been able to tell you weren't a woman, it's amazing!"

Vera asked, "Where on earth did you get such a beautiful dress, it must have cost a small fortune?"

"It didn't cost me anything. Ricci knows a man that works at a costumiers, he lets him have what he wants. Mind you, I think it's in return for Ricci letting him have what *he* wants, if you know what I mean!"

"Jake, really, you are naughty," Vera said, giggling.

"So what do you anticipate the contract might look like Jim?"

"I won't know until I see it of course, but judging how Monty Sharman raved about Jake's act, I would think he's going to want to use him as often as he can, which will probably be every weekend, Saturday and Sunday performances, plus bank holidays as and when they arise. If he does, it's going to cost him, he's not going to get Jake on the cheap, and I want star billing for him as well. There might even be 'specials' like private hen or stag parties for which we'll have to negotiate a percentage of the takings. All in all, his wallet's going to get fatter, and ours is too!"

"Oh by the way this isn't rude question Jake, but how long are you staying?"

"Mam, do you want to get rid of us already?"

"No silly, I was just thinking about meals for us, but I suppose we could go a walk along the front later, there's a nice restaurant there that does wonderful cod and chips."

"That sounds nice Mam, what do you think Jim?"

"Yeah, great."

"It's only ten minutes' walk away," Ted said. "Before we go, I'll show you the garden."

Ted had done wonders with the back garden. He described

what it was like when they first moved into the bungalow, all the changes he had made to it, now it looked a picture with the crop of different vegetables that he had grown. He had worked hard, they hardly had to buy any fresh vegetables at all he told them.

The walk along the seafront was good exercise, it gave them the opportunity to help digest the very large portion of cod and chips that they had eaten in the seafront chippy. Jake couldn't believe it when he saw the size of the piece of cod the waiter had served him, it hung over the sides of his plate. Jake thought to himself, *by the look of him he must go in for dishing out big portions!* When they got back to Vera and Ted's place and they were all sitting chatting, Jake thought it was a good time to tell them that he was going to move in with Jim.

"That's wonderful," Vera said. "I'm really glad about that. I didn't like the idea of you living on your own in that house with god knows who living there. It's good news, isn't it Ted?"

"Yes it is," Ted replied, looking directly at Jim. "Tell us all about the house then, what's it like?"

Jim went into great detail explaining what the house looked like, describing all its rooms and features, what the area was like, how long he had lived there, etc.

"It sounds so lovely Jim," Vera said tearfully. "I'm so happy that you want Jake to come and live with you, I know you will both be happy together."

"We will be Vera," Jim replied, as he reached and squeezed her hand. "Once he's settled in, you and Ted will have to come and stay with us for a while. If you'd like to, we'll introduce you to London, perhaps even take you to a show."

"Ooo yes, we'd love to, wouldn't we Ted?"

"Absolutely, you try stopping us," Ted replied, patting Jim

appreciatively on his arm.

Vera rose from her chair, went over to Jim and gave him a kiss on the cheek, then she gave Jake a hug and a kiss and said, "I'm thrilled for you both and your godmother Bridie would have been too. You both look after one another, do you hear?"

Chapter 16

On the drive home, Jake and Jim talked about how nice the visit to see Vera and Ted had been. During one conversation, Vera mentioned Pauline and Ned as she kept regularly in touch with them. She said they often asked how Jake was doing as they worried how he was coping after all the things that had happened before he left the farm. She realised that she had said too much as soon as she saw Jake's face and Jim's curious, questioning look, but Jake covered it well saying casually that he would telephone them soon as unfortunately he hadn't kept in touch. Jake could see that Jim had picked up on what Vera had said, *worried how he was coping after all the things that had happened before he left the farm!* He hadn't ever told Jim about all the events that had taken place in Grendore, his abduction when he was eleven, how his dad assaulted his mam and went to prison for it, how when he was released he came to the farm to try to get revenge and ended up dead after being shot by Jake as he was protecting himself, Pauline and Ned. He had never told Jim because he was worried how he would react, but he was going to have to tell him now.

"You've been very quiet for most of the journey home, Jake, are you alright?" Jim asked as they pulled up outside the house.

"Yes, I'm fine thanks Jim, I'm just feeling a bit tired."

Jake's F.I.N.E could easily have been interpreted as a mnemonic standing for Fragile, Insecure, Neurotic and Emotional. The last thing he wanted was for anything to ruin his relationship with Jim.

They both needed to relax after the journey. Jim put their favourite LP on and asked Jake if he wanted a nightcap, Jake said he would love a whisky. While he made the drinks, Jake went upstairs, undressed and put his dressing gown on; he would have a shower after he'd had a drink. He came back downstairs to find Jim sitting enjoying his on the sofa. He looked up at Jake and patted the space next to him.

"Come and sit here by me, love."

Jake sat beside him, taking a gulp of the delicious brown smoky liquid, swishing it around his palate, savouring the warm stinging sensation.

Jim put his arm around behind Jake's neck and leaned in to kiss him on the cheek.

"Now, c'mon love, tell me what's troubling you, you know you can tell me anything, I'm not going anywhere, remember?"

"I always intended telling you about some things that happened in my past, but I confess that I've been putting it off because I didn't know how you would react. Anyway, I guess now is as good a time as any. I think Mam gave you an idea that there was something you didn't know." Jake looked at Jim for confirmation.

"Yes she did, but listen Jake, you don't have to tell me anything if you don't want to, we've all got things in our past that we might not be particularly proud of and don't really want to talk about."

"I know, I appreciate that, but this is something bigger and I want you to know about it. It's a long story but I'll condense it as much as I can." Jake began by talking about the poor relationship he'd had with his father, how he physically abused him and also his mother.

He talked about when he was eleven, recalling the camp he had built in the woods where he used to go to when things were bad at home; to avoid a good hiding, or at least to put off the inevitable for a while.

He went on to tell Jim how a stranger came to his camp who Jake thought wanted to do similar sexual things with him that his uncle and another man had done before, not anal intercourse, just kissing fondling in a loving way and oral sex. Jake liked those things so when the man invited him to go back to his farm, he went with him, he was called Arthur. Jake told Jim that he didn't know it at the time, but Arthur had lost his son in an unfortunate accident on the farm, he was psychologically all mixed up and imagined Jake to be his son, as they were about the same age, he even called him by his son's name, Danny. Arthur had never tried to do anything of an inappropriate nature with Jake. Once when Jake had tried to touch *him* inappropriately, Arthur had told him in no uncertain terms that he was out of order and was never trying to do anything like that again. He had loved him like a real father, the only sin he'd committed was lying to Jake that his parents had said he could stay with him while they attended to important business, and taking him away from his home. Because he had gone missing there was a big police search for him and eventually after a few weeks they found him at the farm. Unfortunately, Arthur had tried to escape and fell to his death over a high precipice. Unbeknown to Jake, while he was staying on the farm, Arthur's ex-wife returned. She put two and two together because Jake's disappearance was in all the newspapers. She must have asked where the real Danny was and challenged Arthur that the boy she had seen in the bedroom was the missing boy Jake. Arthur had apparently strangled her; her body was found some time later in an old ice house in a wood nearby.

Jake then skipped a few years to when he was fifteen and working on Pauline and Ned's farm. Bridie Maguire, his mother's friend and also Jake's godmother, had died and left Vera a substantial amount of money. Vera's relationship with Jake's father had deteriorated until one evening after he came back from the pub drunk, he seriously assaulted Vera, causing her to be hospitalised. Jake's father was arrested and ended up getting five years in prison. On his release he returned to the farm in the dead of night with a shotgun, looking for Vera who was no longer living at the farm. He threatened Pauline and Ned with the gun and, on seeing Jake, fired a shot at him and missed. Jake fired his own gun in self-defence and shot his father, fatally wounding him.

Recounting all of this to Jim had somehow triggered a lot of pent-up emotions for Jake, he was shaking and tears were rolling down his face. Jim held him close and kissed his cheek.

"Oh Jake, my poor love, you've certainly been through some horrendous experiences, but listen to me my love." He cradled Jake's face in his hands. "If you think any of what you've told me is going to make me feel any differently towards you, I can assure you it isn't. You are the loveliest, gentlest and most honest soul I have ever met. That is why I fell in love with you and why I always will love you. Now, I'm going to pour you a brandy, you look as though you could do with one, in fact I think I'll join you."

"Thanks Jim, yes I could."

"You just sit there quietly and relax, I'll be back in a jiffy." Jim went over to the cocktail cabinet and poured out two generous brandies, bringing them back and handing Jake's to him. "There you are darling, you drink that, it will make you feel better."

"Thank you," Jake said, taking a good mouthful of the brandy and swallowing it down. "I didn't know what you would think of me after I told you those things, I was so afraid you might not want to have anything more to do with me, but now I know you are the most beautiful understanding man I have ever met."

"You haven't done anything wrong darling, you were a hapless victim of what your father and those other people did to you. Hopefully now that you have talked about it, you can consign it to the past where it rightfully belongs. None of those things define who you are now Jake."

"I know that's true Jim, so now I can just get on with my life, my new life with you, and forget all about it."

"That's right love, now shall we go up to bed and get some sleep?"

"Yes let's," replied Jake, going on to bat his eyelids and mimic Vivien Leigh's famous line in *Gone With The Wind*, "After all, tomorrow is another day!"

"Oh Jake love, you are so adorably funny, come on."

Jim made a snap decision to visit his parents a couple of days later as he had been mentally rehearsing and rehearsing how he would actually tell them that he was gay, let them know about Jake and the fact that Alicia was moving out and at some point he would be living with Jake as a couple. He was dreading their reaction, not knowing how they would take the news. When he had sat them down and they were having coffee together he took the bull by the horns and said his piece. His father looked shocked, looking at his wife as he held her hand. She patted his and said, "Are you alright dear, didn't you know? I've known for years that his marriage to Alicia was a convenient one for keeping up appearances."

"No, I didn't know Mary, why didn't you tell me?"

Mary gave a little chuckle, "I just assumed you knew. Anyway, it's no big deal Howard, we want our son to be happy and if this is what Jim wants then all we can do is support him. I never really liked Alicia anyway, she was far too aloof and precious for my liking. How did she take the news, Jim?"

"Really well, I was surprised. Alicia and I have shared a house, but we have lived our separate lives for years. She can now buy herself a flat and have her long-term boyfriend all to herself at last."

Howard looked dismayed and said, "Do you mean you've been unhappy and living a lie all these years Jim? Why ever didn't you tell us before and do something about it? Surely you didn't think we'd turn against you, son?"

"I wasn't prepared to take that chance back then, but it was really a combination of things that made me get married. I didn't set out to deceive anyone, but there's something very important I have to tell you."

"What's that son?"

"I've met a man, his name is Jake. I met him some time ago, he now lives with me in the Hampstead house. I would really like you both to meet him and I'm really sorry for not letting you know sooner. He very much wants to meet both of you, I have a photograph to show you if you'd like to see it?"

"Of course we'd like to see it," Jim's mum said, reaching out her hand. "His face seems familiar, I've seen him somewhere before. Look Howard, where have we seen him? You're better at these things than I am." She passed the photograph to her husband.

"If I'm not mistaken, he's the guy that was on the TV on the Marty Lennox Show, he was talking about the film he's just made, he's a female impersonator, isn't he?"

"You've got him Dad, spot on, that's my Jake!"

"Well I never, who'd have guessed it, we've got someone famous in the family!"

Jim found his dad's reaction both surprising and somewhat amusing in the light of his revelation that he was gay.

"You don't mind about what I've told you then, Dad?"

"Look son, why should I mind, it's your life, and you're the one that's got to live it. If I was upset about anything it's you not telling us about it before and not being true to yourself. Nothing has changed as far as we're concerned, eh dear?"

"Silly, of course it has, we've got a celebrity film star in the family. I can't wait to meet him Jim, when can you both come and see us, we appreciate you are busy people."

"Jake has Sundays off, so that's really the best day."

"You must come to lunch with us next Sunday, if that's OK?"

"Oh lovely, thanks Mum, Jake will be so pleased to be meeting you at last."

Chapter 17

They lay in bed, playfully fighting verbally over who was going to get up first and make the coffee, Jim knowing full well that it would be him as he loved bringing Jake his coffee in bed. They had slept until quite a lot later than usual; it was nine thirty.

"Oh alright I'll go, I make the best coffee anyway, but you'll have to make it up to me somehow!"

"You cheeky thing, and what did you have in mind?"

"You'll find out soon enough!" Jim shouted as he was going downstairs.

"I can't wait!" Jake yelled.

As Jim was making the coffee, the postman pushed an envelope through the door which landed with a loud plop on the floor. He went to have a look and was surprised to see a large brown envelope that had been folded over so as to get it through the letter box. *I wonder what this is,* he thought, picking it up and taking it through into the kitchen, then it dawned on him it was probably a copy of Jake's contract that Monty Sharman had sent. *Gosh, he's keen,* Jim thought, *I'll open it with Jake over our coffee.*

He extended the legs on the tray, loaded it with the fresh coffee, croissants and jam, checking to see if he had forgotten anything, then he took it upstairs. Jake was sitting up in bed waiting. Jim placed the tray over Jake's legs.

"Here you are your highness, your morning coffee, and I think the postman has brought us something interesting."

"Has he indeed, well don't leave him waiting downstairs, tell him to come up!"

"You bad boy, I think it's the contract from Monty Sharman."

"Open it please darling, while I pour the coffee, you can read it out to me."

Jim skim read through the pages hastily until he came to the financial details he was interested in.

"He's not offering you a bad deal actually love, but I think we can hold out for a better one. He quotes a flat figure of thirty-five pounds a week. I think we should ask for fifty-five, that's an extra twenty to cover all the expenses you'll have, such as buying make-up, wigs, gowns, jewellery, etc. He either agrees to that or the other possible alternative is for him to buy a fairly extensive wardrobe of gowns for the club so that you won't have to lay out cash for them. I personally think he'll pay you the extra."

"I think you're absolutely right about the money, Jim, but what's he proposing regarding the length of the contract?"

"I'm just coming to that bit. He's saying it's for one year initially, to be renewed by mutual agreement after the contracted time. He points out that for the length of the contract, you will be working solely for him at the Black Orchid Club."

"That sounds reasonable, doesn't it Jim? Drink some of your coffee, it's getting cold, but don't have a croissant, you'll mess the contract up!"

"Ugh, OK." He took a slurp of his coffee and carried on reading. "Aargh! this is interesting, it goes on, should you at any time wish to end the contract, or should you renege on the contract by walking out, you would be liable to pay the sum of one thousand pounds as compensation for terminating his goodwill!"

"I certainly wouldn't do that anyway," Jake said indignantly.

"Oh you might love, if something better came along and it was an opportunity you couldn't afford to miss, that's why it's down here in black and white. These things do happen."

"Now come on Jim, put it down while you eat your breakfast, you can look at it later."

"OK love, I'll make a few amendment notes later, then I'll give him a ring and arrange for us to go in and see him to discuss and finalise the deal."

"Sounds good to me, gosh, it's all happening at the moment isn't it. I'm soon to move house, start my nightclub act, what I must do is let Ricci know I'm moving out and ask him if he will be available to do my make-up and loan me gowns until I get on my feet. If she can't, I don't know what I'll do."

"I have absolutely no doubt that Ricci will help you out, if he can't, I'm sure he knows someone who will, love."

"I hope so. Do you want to shower first love, or shall I?"

"You go ahead, I'll have another cup of coffee while I mull over this contract."

"OK."

Jake went off to the bathroom to do his toilet and shower. He couldn't ever remember a time in his life when he was this happy and carefree. He stepped into the shower, letting the warm rivulets of water cascade all over his young firm body, he closed his eyes and began to shampoo his hair, humming to himself contentedly. Just as he was rinsing the suds away, making sure not to get soap in his eyes, he felt Jim get into the shower behind him. Jim started kissing him all over his back, at the same time reaching his hand around him, taking hold of Jake's prick which had already begun to swell and get hard. Jake murmured deliriously, turning around to face Jim. They kissed fervently as Jim soaped his own bulbous erect member, pushing it smoothly between Jake's legs. He then began playing with his nipples, squeezing and caressing them between his thumbs and forefingers.

"I want you like this," Jim murmured in Jake's ear. He didn't hear any objection as he kissed him again, placed his hands on his slim waist and manoeuvred him gently into position, then soaping Jake's arse he let his fingers probe into him before soaping himself and slowly sliding into Jake's eager hole. The water played on both their impassioned bodies as Jake's moans of erotic delight when he was coming, sounded in rhythm to Jim's more urgent thrusts, and deep murmuring groans of blissful simultaneous climax. They washed and towelled each other before they shaved and dressed, telling one another what their lovemaking had been like for them, before going downstairs for more much needed coffee.

The morning was spent with Jake reading the paper while Jim scrutinised and read through the contract, at the same time making notes of points that he would raise with Monty Sharman when they met to discuss the details of Jake's employment. He hoped to be able to arrange a meeting with him for some time tomorrow; he picked up the telephone to dial his number.

"Hello Mr Sharman, Jim Hartnell here, we received the draft copy of the contract this morning. I've had a look at it, I wondered if we could meet to discuss a few details, perhaps some time tomorrow?"

Jim looked over at Jake and made a gesture of crossing his fingers.

"Ten thirty, that's fine. We'll see you tomorrow then Mr Sharman."

"Oh well done love, hopefully he'll agree to everything we want there and then so that we're not waiting on tenterhooks for days on end for a decision."

"I would think he will, he'll be thinking about all the potential extra revenue he can make having a glamour puss like you pulling the punters in!"

"Oh thank you, darling."

"Well it's true love, if you think about it, all his other acts do comedy routines, you'll be providing the classy glamour and you sing rather than lip-syncing like all the others."

"That's right, I knew I'd picked the right man to be my manager. By the way love, how about we go over to Buckley Road today so that I can pick up a few things and while we're there we can pop up and see if Ricci and Toby are in."

"Yes, fine by me. When, after lunch?"

"Great, what would you like for lunch, a sandwich?"

"That will be very nice, thanks. Talking of lunch, don't make any arrangements for next Sunday, we've been invited over to my mum and dad's, they're dying to meet you."

"That's marvellous Jim, I'll look forward to that very much."

Jim pulled up right outside the house. As they got out, Jake looked up to the top-floor window and saw Ricci standing in the window waving. Jake waved back and indicated that they would come up and see them.

"Hello darling, where have you been? I've been down to knock a couple of times thinking you might be ill or something, then I realised you were staying with Jim. Anyway, it's lovely to see you both, come on in."

"Yes Ricci, sorry we should have mentioned it, but we got up around ten-ish on Sunday and didn't want to disturb you. I guess if I'd have used my head I would have slipped a note under your door telling you I was staying with Jim."

"Don't worry, sweetie, there's no harm done, would you both like tea or coffee?"

"I'd love a cup tea please," Jim said.

"Me too, please Ricci, then we can tell you all our news."

"Sounds interesting, I'll be quick then."

Jim raised his voice so that Ricci would hear him. "Where's Toby?"

"He's just popped to the off-licence to get a bottle of wine, he'll be back shortly."

Jake was studying Jim without him realising it and he was thinking to himself, *you are such a gorgeous looking man, I can't believe you are mine!*

"Here we are then, a lovely cup tea." Jake came back from his deep thoughts. "Oh, where were you, daydreaming away, that's a sure sign you're in love sweetie. Shall I be mother?"

"You must be psychic, Ricci, that's the reason we're here. We have something to tell you."

"If it's that you're both in love and you are going to live together, you don't have to be a clairvoyant to see that darling, it's obvious you're both besotted with one another. Anyway, naughty me, I've stolen your thunder, you tell me what you were going to say!"

Jake said, "I'll let Jim tell you."

Jim looked at Jake and then at Ricci. "I have fallen madly, hopelessly in love with Jake. I want him with me as much as possible, so it makes perfect sense for us to move in together."

"And what does the wicked witch of the west think about

this idea? I presume it's your place you want Jake to move into."

"I've told Alicia and surprisingly she's all for me getting a valuation on the house and giving her a half share. Jake is prepared to buy into that. I'll get all the necessary legal aspects drawn up with my solicitor, just so that everything is up and above board."

"I've told him it's not necessary to go to all that trouble but he insists."

"Darling, in my experience anything concerning money is worth having in black and white. Jim's absolutely right. So when are you thinking of moving out? We're both really going to miss having you around."

"It won't be straightaway," Jim said, "but as soon as I can get things sorted out with my solicitor so that it's on paper that Alicia has been given her dues, she's signed to say she has received it, then Jake will need to sign the document to say that half of the house belongs to him. I'll try to speed things up as much as I can. Just in case someone changes his mind."

"No chance of that happening darling, look at the beautiful ring Jim bought me, Ricci."

"Ooo, it's lovely, you lucky girl, I can just feel a new hat and frock coming on. I'll make a lovely matron of honour!"

There was raucous laughter.

"There'll be a big party that's for sure, eh Jim?"

"Definitely!"

"Ah, here's Toby."

"What's all this jollification about then?"

"Congratulations are in order Toby, these two darlings are going to move in together."

"Aaw that is good news." He shook Jim's hand vigorously,

gave him a hug, then he kissed Jake on both cheeks. "Congratulations, both of you, best news I've heard in a long time. We'll have a drink or two later."

"Have you heard from Monty Sharman?" Ricci asked.

"Yes," Jim replied, "he sent us a draft of Jake's contract, we're seeing him tomorrow morning to try to finalise things."

"I do hope so, the sooner Jake starts the better, the club needs some new blood to breathe new life into the place. Just lately I've heard takings have been down and Monty wasn't sure of the club's future."

"Oh have they now, I wasn't aware of that. Well that certainly gives me some good bargaining power if he isn't keen on what I propose to him!"

"You didn't hear it from me, of course darling."

"Of course not Ricci."

"Ricci, I wanted to ask you if you will still be able to do my make-up for me and get me some frocks on loan until I can buy a wardrobe of my own? I'd happily pay you what you think is a fair price for your services, if you're agreeable."

"I can always borrow frocks, that's no problem sweetie, and I would love to do your make-up at weekends. There may even be an opportunity to buy some gowns from Burmans as they occasionally have a clear out. I'll speak to my friend Michael."

"We have to agree some kind of terms though, Ricci, I can't let you keep doing it out of the goodness of your heart."

"OK sweetie, what about a tenner for a weekend, is that alright?"

"Fine by me Ricci, if you're happy with that, and I insist on having my own make-up. I can't keep using yours, it's not fair. Would you write me a list of the things that I need and tell me where I can get them?"

"Sure, honey, no problem, shall we do it now?" Ricci stood up and went to get a pen and paper. "Right, first of all you'll need a good dark foundation, dusting powder, two pairs of eyelashes – you stick them together to make them look really lush – mascara, a selection of eyeshadows, eyeliner, eyebrow pencil, some cleaning pads, make-up remover, I think that's everything. You could invest in a nice carrying case for all your slap. Oh, how could I possibly have forgotten lipstick, you'll need a good selection of those, and some lipgloss and brushes, you will be able to get all of these from Swan and Edgars in Piccadilly, darling!"

"That's marvellous, thanks Ricci love, I don't know how I'd manage without you."

"Have you two made any arrangements for lunch?" Jim asked.

"No, not as far as I know, have we Ricci?"

"Not unless you count leftover chicken in a sandwich an arrangement?"

"How about we walk down to The Old Prague? They do a nice lunch there."

"What a lovely idea, Jim," Jake said, looking at Ricci and Toby. "Yes, say you'll come?"

"How could we possibly say no, we'd love to darlings, give me time to spruce myself up and powder my nose," Ricci replied.

"That's an hour then!" Toby jibed.

Jake and Jim looked at each other and smiled.

"I'll just pop upstairs to the flat and throw a few things in a bag," Jake said. "I won't be long."

He gave Jim a peck on the lips and left them getting ready. As soon as he walked in, the package on the kitchen table reminded him that he was going to find a glazier to have him make a small memento out of the broken stained glass for Lorenzo. He walked into the living room, went to the wardrobe, reached up and lifted down his small overnight case, threw it on the bed, opened the lid hastily packing a couple of pairs of trousers, some shirts, clean underwear and some socks. He thought, *that should do until I come back at the weekend, before Alicia comes home.* He closed the lid and took it back into the kitchen, putting it on the table next to the glass. He decided that he would nip downstairs to see Lorenzo and break the news to him that he would be leaving soon. As he turned the curve on the staircase to pass Amir's room he could hear a radio playing softly. *He would have to say goodbye to Amir too,* he thought.

There was a strong smell of garlic emanating from Lorenzo's flat as Jake tapped on his door.

Lorenzo opened the door and gave Jake a broad smile. "Jake what a surprisa, it isa so nice to see you, come ona in."

"Hello Lorenzo, how are you?"

"I ama fine thank you Jake, how isa Jim?"

"He's very well, thank you."

"So when ara you moving out to liva youra lives together eh!"

Jake was really surprised to hear Lorenzo state the reason he had come to see him, and replied, "How on earth did you know I'd come to see you about that, Lorenzo?"

"I ama nota stupid Jake, two people meet, they falla in love, they wanta to liva together, simple!"

"I suppose put like that, it is, so yes I came to tell you that I will be moving out soon. I'm going to live with Jim, in his house in Hampstead, but I have been really happy here. In some ways I will be sad to leave, will two weeks' notice be enough?"

"Two weeks willa be fina Jake, I willa be sorry to see youa go, you ava been a good tenant, give me no trouble and I ama glad you ava meta youra sweetheart."

Jake thought this was such a sweet thing for Lorenzo to say.

"Thank you Lorenzo, I will let you know as soon as I know when I am actually going and settle up then, OK?"

Jake moved towards the door and opened it.

"That willa be fina Jake, I'll see youa then, OK. Goodbye."

"Goodbye Lorenzo, thank you."

Jake left and started to climb the stairs, stopping outside of Amir's room and gently knocking his door. He heard movement as Amir opened the door, giving a beaming smile.

"Hello my friend, please come in."

"Hello Amir, I've only come to tell you that I will be leaving soon and to ask you if you would like my television or my radiogram. You can have both of them if you like, they are both almost new. I no longer need them and I don't want anything for them, you are welcome to come and see them. I won't be offended if you don't want them."

"That is very kind of you, I would like to see."

"Do you want to look now?"

"Yes OK, I will come with you."

He opened the door for Jake to go on ahead and he followed him. Jake unlocked the door and walked through to his living room, showing Amir the TV and radiogram. He switched the TV on to show him it was in good working order. Amir looked impressed. Jake had noticed that the TV in his room was a lot smaller. He slid the door open on the radiogram to let him see the record deck, switching the radio on and turning up the volume.

"What do you think, Amir?"

"They are fantastic, are you sure, can I have them both?"

"You are very welcome to have them, they will be something to remember me by!"

"I will remember everything very well, even if I don't have these,' he said genuinely with a sad wistful look in his eyes.

"Oh bless you, Amir, I won't forget you either." He gave him a loving kiss and a hug for old times' sake, hoping that Amir wouldn't misread it and want something more.

"I hope you will be very happy with your man Jake, he is very lucky."

"Thank you Amir, I don't know exactly when I'm leaving yet but I'll let you have them before I go."

"Thank you, Jake."

"You have a good day then Amir."

"Thank you, you too, bye."

"Bye."

As soon as Amir had gone, Jake picked up his case and the glass, locked up and went back upstairs.

"You were a long time love, is everything alright?"

"Yes, fine, I had a few things I needed to do. Would it be OK if we called at a glaziers on the way to the restaurant? There's one on the High Road."

"Yes of course, but why do you need a glazier? The flats OK, isn't it?"

"Oh yes, I just want to arrange a little surprise for Lorenzo, that's all."

"What surprise?"

"You'll see later, darling."

"We're both ready, if you are," Ricci said.

"Yes, shall we go then?" Jim replied.

Chapter 18

The Sunday that Jim took Jake over to meet his parents turned out to be the most lovely occasion. Jake was slightly nervous but his parents put him at his ease right away, the conversation was easy and relaxed. They were offered a sherry on arrival and the lunch that Mary had cooked was delicious, it was good old-fashioned homely cooking; it was Jake's favourite, roast beef and Yorkshire puddings with roast potatoes, carrots, cabbage and parsnips and lovely thick gravy, it was followed by a creamy rice pudding. They wanted to hear all about Jake's life, so he told them the abridged version, including how he and Jim met and how he first got into show business.

Jake couldn't have been happier, here he was with the mother and father of his darling Jim, they had both made him feel so welcome and accepted, they had shared so much warmth and laughter together it felt like he had known them all his life. When it was time to leave he was quite sad to be going, but they had made promises that it would not be long before they would see them again.

It had been three months now since they had called to see Monty Sharman at his office and they had gone through the contract together. For a while, during negotiations there were a couple of sticking points that Monty wasn't happy with, but Jim was absolutely marvellous, he pointed out to him all the benefits of having Jake working for him and how he was certain the people would come flocking in to see him, bringing lots of new revenue to the club. It was a strong hint to Monty that Jim had heard things had not been good recently, without being obvious. He agreed to all conditions, even the one that Jake had raised which he felt was very important, he wanted to be billed as a female impersonator and not a drag artiste.

So many positive things had happened, for one thing he had learned to drive a car. He had done so more or less on Jim's insistence who had said, "You need to be self-reliant and able to go where you want, when you want, without having to bother with buses or taxis. If you learn and pass your test, I'll buy you your first car!"

That was all the encouragement Jake needed. After all, he had driven for years on the farm, but he could hardly drive a tractor around the streets of London, could he! Jim had given him a lot of private tuition in quieter areas as well as helping him with his Highway Code, so after a few lessons, when his driving test came up, he was able to pass first time with flying colours! Jim was true to his word, he and Jake toured around the car showrooms where Jake fell in love with a red MGB GT. He said it was a corker and he was going to call it 'Diana' after his favourite actress, Diana Dors.

Jim's feeling about Jake's impact on the club were spot on as well, the shows were going tremendously well and every time Jake was appearing the club was packed to the gunnels. He had already attracted a regular fan base who clamoured expectantly to see him perform.

There had been other positive changes in Jake's life too. At the beginning of December he had been able to move in with Jim, Alicia having left to live with her long-term boyfriend. Jake had said a tearful goodbye to Ricci and Tobyl even though he knew he would be seeing Ricci at the club, somehow leaving the house was bit of a wrench. He had also said a very awkward goodbye to Amir as he made it obvious he was desirous to say goodbye in a 'for old times' sake' way. Jake somehow manoeuvred his way out of the situation, gave him his TV and radiogram and left hurriedly. He went down to see Lorenzo, settling his notice with him, handing over the keys to his flat and presenting him with a neatly wrapped package.

"What isa this Jake?' Lorenzo said looking at him puzzled.

"Open it and see," Jake replied smiling, "but do it carefully, it's fragile!"

Lorenzo carefully began to unwrap Jake's present. When he saw what it was he became so emotional, tears flooded his eyes.

"Isa da beautiful surprise Jake. You ara so kind, I willa treasure this, mya beautiful Victorian glass, I can hang it ina the light ofa my window and allaways remember you, blessa you!" Lorenzo placed the package on his table, grabbed Jake's shoulders and kissed him firmly on both cheeks.

Jake left the house with a feeling of immense gratitude for everything it had brought him; it had given him independence, it had given him friendships, but most of all it had brought him love.

Jake couldn't have been happier, here he was with the mother and father of his darling Jim, they had both made him feel so welcome and accepted, they had shared so much warmth and laughter together it felt like he had known them all his life, when it came to time to leave he was quite sad to be going, but they had made promises that it would not be long before they would see them again.

Jim and Jake's new lifestyle together couldn't have been more perfect. They spent their first blissful Christmas together, Jake had a performance on Christmas Eve but they were able to spend Christmas Day all to themselves, which began with Jake making breakfast, after which they gave each other their presents as they sat on the floor in their dressing gowns, alongside the Christmas tree. Jake had bought Jim a gold pinky ring with an oblong onyx stone set with a small diamond in one corner. The jeweller who sold it had remarked that it was an unusual shape that he had not seen before. Jake bought it for that very reason that it was different. When Jim opened the box he was delighted with it, it was the only one he would wear now as he had removed his wedding ring.

"Darling, it's beautiful, thank you, I was hoping you would buy me one." As he kissed Jake he added, "Now we both have one."

"I'm so glad you like it, I picked it because the shape was unusual. It will be a memory of our first Christmas together."

"It's lovely, you open mine now please."

Jim handed him his present which was wrapped in gold shiny paper, it looked very classy. Jake read the label, *To the love of my life, thank you for making me so blissfully happy.* Jake was so moved he started to cry. Jim put his arms around him.

"Hey, hey, darling don't cry, it's supposed to be a happy time."

"I know my love, it is, these are happy tears, it's just that your words were so beautiful they overwhelmed me, and I never ever dreamed I would find a man like you. Please don't ever leave me!"

"Don't be silly, I could never leave you, remember what I told you the first time I met you? *I'm not going anywhere.* Now come on, open your present and put me out of my misery. I hope you like it!"

Jake began to carefully unwrap the gift as he didn't want to tear such lovely paper; Jim waited expectantly. Inside, Jake found a dark royal-blue box with gold writing embossed on it, saying Rotary, Swiss. Lifting the lid there inside was the most stunning watch with an oyster-coloured dial and black leather strap.

Jake gasped. "Oh Jim, it's gorgeous, put it on for me," he said, as he stretched forward his wrist. "It's just what I wanted, my other old thing is so scratched you can hardly read the time, but then it's the one I used to wear when I was working on the farm, so it's hardly surprising."

"Yes I know," Jim replied, "that was the reason I bought you this one!"

Jim took the watch from its box, placed it around Jake's wrist and fastened the buckle.

"There, how does that feel?"

"Wonderful, and it looks perfect," Jake replied as he held his arm out, turning his wrist one way and another to admire it. "Thank you ever so much darling!"

Jake kissed him and said, "I'll have the other present you've got for me, later, you don't need to gift wrap it"

Jim looked at Jake and he smiled, he reached under the tree and brought out the present that Vera and Ted had sent them.

"You open this one Jake, it's from your mum and Ted." It was a large box, it was fairly heavy.

"OK, I wonder what it is?" Jake tore off the paper wrapping and opened it up. "How lovely." He was quite surprised to see a photograph album, a silver photo frame along with a letter, a collection of snaps of Vera and Ted, some childhood snaps of Jake and two photographs that Vera and Ted had taken when they'd visited, one showing Vera arm in arm with Jim and Jake, the other with Ted with his arms around the two of them. Both Jake and Jim thought that this was a most welcome and thoughtful gift.

Jake read the letter out loud to Jim:

> **Dear Jake and Jim,**
>
> **We both wish you a very Happy Christmas and a wonderful New Year. This being your first Christmas as a couple, it is the start of you making many beautiful memories together. There will be many happy Christmases to come so we thought you might like to start recording all your happy times together so we bought you this album. The silver frame is for a really special one of the two of you that you can put on display. We have sent a few photos that you might like to include in your collection, including the ones we took when you came to see us, we kept copies of these as they are very precious to us. We will be spending the holiday relaxing, as we hope you will too, because you are such busy people. Anyway, whatever you are doing enjoy yourselves and we hope to take up your kind invitation to come up to London and see you sometime in the new year.**
>
> **All our fondest love,**
> **Vera and Ted xx**

Jake's voice was beginning to crack as he finished reading it out and there were tears in his eyes.

"What a lovely letter," Jim said, putting his arms around Jake and pulling him close. "Come here love, don't cry, we can have Mum and Ted up for a visit as soon as we can arrange a suitable time. I do love you, you big soppy thing."

"Yes I know you do, I love you too."

Chapter 19

Jake could not believe how the two years had just flown by. He was well established as a female impersonator at the Black Orchid, so much so that most people associated the club with him, or rather Rusty L'amour. It seemed she was the Black Orchid to them! After the first year, Jim had negotiated a much better contract for him as it was Jake who was largely responsible for drawing the crowds to the club. Now it was the month of November 1969, and it was drawing close to the renewal of his contract again. As far as Jake was concerned, he was perfectly happy to sign up for another term, that is if something very unexpected, exciting and advantageous hadn't happened.

Jim came home in the early hours of Thursday morning after the show at The Capital. Jake had stayed up waiting for him to come home as he usually did, unless he was tired and had to go to bed, but in his line of work you quickly became a night owl. This particular evening Jim seemed to be particularly pleased with himself, his eyes had an excited twinkle in them, and he was almost grinning; he looked as though he was about to burst with whatever it was he had on his mind. Jake gave him a kiss, poured him his usual Bacardi and Coke, putting it on the coffee table in front of where he usually sat.

"Hello love, you look happy, how did the show go?"

Jim didn't answer, or sit down, it was almost as though something was bubbling inside him and he couldn't relax. It wasn't like him at all, usually he flopped down in his chair, picked up his drink, gulped some down and they would talk about their respective days until they decided it was time to go to bed.

"Are you alright my love? You look as though you've something on your mind. Why don't you sit down, have a drink and tell me about it?"

"I've got something on my mind alright, have had all day. My top act, Selena Dreyton, has only gone and quit the show, she's left me right in the lurch!"

"Well surely that's nothing to look so pleased about, you'll need to find a replacement for her and pretty quick!"

"I already have, love."

"Oh great, that was quick, well done, who is it?"

"Why, you of course darling!" Jake gave a little guffaw.

"What? You can't be serious, that's silly, how could I replace a top household name like Selena Dreyton?"

"Because *you're* going to be a top household name yourself love, that's how. You look better than she does, your voice is better than hers, and you've got novelty on your side, you're a bloke in a frock that becomes a stunningly glamorous woman. I'm not having you giving your all for peanuts at the Black Orchid forever, you're destined for greater things Jake, it's the bright lights of the West End for you, darling."

"But Jim."

Jim said calmly but firmly, "No buts, listen to me my love." He took Jake gently by the shoulders and positioned him by his chair. "Sit yourself down, I'll get you a drink, then once you've got over the shock, we'll talk about it calmly. I've got everything under control, trust me darling!"

For once Jake was stunned into silence, but his mind was

whirling with uncontrollable thoughts. *Could this proposition really be possible? It's something you've always dreamed of, surely Jim wasn't losing his marbles? He seems pretty sure of himself, you're just going to have to do what he says and trust him, after all you made him your manager, he must think you're perfectly capable of doing it!*

Jake sat there for a while not speaking, just rationalising his thoughts. *Jim loves you, he wouldn't want anything bad for you, he wouldn't set you up to fail, remember how you doubted yourself when you first started out, just hear what he has to say!*

"Are you feeling more relaxed now darling? I left you wrestling with your thoughts, I didn't want to deluge you with too much information all at once, or make you think that you have no say in the matter. Do you feel a little more open to the idea yet?"

"I think I am; I know you wouldn't even suggest such a thing if you didn't think I was up to it."

"No of course I wouldn't, you just don't believe in yourself, so I'm telling you I have more than enough belief in you, because you are a unique talent and you deserve to be at the top of your game."

Jake gasped out, "Oh darling, hold me please." He shuddered, it was as if a lightning bolt had suddenly struck him and loosened the scales from his eyes, showing him a prognostic vision, a revelation. He knew instinctively what his future was going to be, it was all going to come to pass, his wildest dreams were coming true!

Jim moved from his own chair to sit on the arm of Jake's. He put his arms around him, holding him close, and kissed his forehead. He knew Jake had come to a sudden realisation, an epiphany.

"You believe now, don't you?" he said.

"Yes darling, I do!"

They stayed like this for what seemed ages, until they realised sleep was calling them.

Over breakfast, they calmly discussed some of the details and practicalities they would need to sort out, as well as the order things would have to be done in. One thing Jim was relieved about was the fact that Jake had applied for an Equity card a year ago; he was now a fully paid-up member, so he could work professionally anywhere. Jim pointed out three things. Firstly, they would have to hurriedly arrange an audition with the team at The Capital, which would include himself as theatre manager, the artistic and musical director, stage manager, choreographer, etc. Secondly, once they knew Jake had secured the job, they would have to speak with Monty Sharman and inform him that Jake would be leaving. It would mean they would be liable to pay the penalty clause in his contract, but that couldn't be avoided. They both hoped that Monty would be magnanimous enough so that they would all part amicably. Thirdly, Jake was going to need a full-time dresser, Ricci was the obvious favourite, they would have to ask him if he wanted the job, negotiate a fee and pay him of course. If he didn't, perhaps he might know someone else who would like the job. Jim said that he would arrange a date and time for an audition when he got to work, he said he had already spoken to a number of people about the prospect of Jake applying and they were all enthusiastic about it, especially knowing Jim had the Capital's best interest at heart.

"I suggest that you contact Adrian and ask him to let you borrow whatever sheet music you think you'll need. Don't tell him you're auditioning, or it might get back to Monty before we talk to him. You could tell him you're doing a charity do somewhere and their pianist wants you to take your music along. It's only a little white lie, I'm sure you'll be able to convince him, love."

"Oh, I think I'll be able to manage that."

"Yes you will love, I know he's always been sweet on you, you can twist him round your little finger!"

"If you like you could take a run over to Ricci's after I've gone to work, you can sound him out about being your dresser, but make sure you swear him to secrecy!"

"Good idea, I'm sure Ricci won't say anything."

Chapter 20

"You look absolutely stunning," Ricci said, admiring his own handiwork. "Pink really suits you, the sequins make it ultra-camp, they can't fail to hire you sweetie."

"I really hope so Ricci, but I'm so nervous, suppose I make a complete mess of it?"

"Look at me darling. Now listen to your Auntie Ricci, you are not going to mess up, you'll show them you're the consummate professional that you are, they will adore you, it's just pre-audition nerves."

"Yes, you're quite right, once I get on the stage I'll be fine, just like I always am."

"That's more like it sweetie, you're a winner, remember that."

"I'm so grateful to you, Ricci, for doing this for me at such short notice, you really are a pal."

"It's my pleasure darling. Just think, when you get the job, we'll be working together permanently, won't that be wonderful!"

"Yes it will, I wouldn't have wanted anyone else. I'm thrilled that you've agreed to do it, after all, it was you who started me off on this road."

"I saw your potential straightaway. OK, I think you're ready for the hair darling!"

The strawberry blonde wig was beautifully coiffured in a sweeping bouffant style, it was the biggest Jake had ever worn but it looked perfectly in proportion when Ricci placed a salmon-pink ostrich feather stole around his shoulders. Jake admired himself in the mirror,

"Ricci, you're a magician, the wig looks magnificent. It feels as if it's totally me, I think you've definitely found my style."

"I was sure it was right for you as soon as I saw it, clever me!"

"Clever you indeed. Now, am I going to manage to walk in those baby heels you've brought for me to wear?"

"You can slip them on and have a go, I think they're better than flatties, they'll give you extra poise and make you feel even more feminine."

Jake lifted each foot for Ricci to slip the pink satin shoes on. He stood up and took a few tentative steps and to his surprise he didn't fall down or turn his ankle; he felt as though he'd been wearing them for years.

"Just as you said, Ricci, they give me that extra feeling of completeness being this woman Rusty L'amour!"

Ricci gave Jake a complete once over, making sure that every detail was just perfect.

"Once they've seen you in the feathers, you can drape them over a chair or drop them to the floor if you think they're going to hinder you, it'll be a nice touch. Don't forget the deep butch voice the first time you speak, then you can do it the way you normally do. There, you're ready sweetie."

"Would you let them know I'm ready Ricci? The pianist has my music, I'm walking on to the tune 'A Lovely Dream Walks By'!"

"What a brilliant choice, I'll go and tell them, you'll be a sensation, sweetie."

Jake wished he could have seen Jim before going on. He

began to have a little last-minute wobble of panic, but then he thought, *you don't need Jim's approval, you already have it, he's waiting out there willing you to do well, so get out there and wow em!*

Ricci came back in. "You're on girl, come on follow me."

Jake followed Ricci down the corridor and up some steps to the backstage area near the wings. Ricci squeezed Jake's arm to encourage him. "I'll cue the pianist for you, then off you go." Ricci walked into the wings, caught the pianist's eye and nodded his head decisively. He began to play.

A Lovely Dream Walks By!

Jake walked serenely out onto the stage, half turned, waited for a few seconds then placed the feathers on top of the grand piano, looked at the pianist and in a deep manly voice said, "Alright mate!"

He heard a ripple of laughter from the auditorium, walked to the microphone and took it from its stand. Still in manly voice mode he adjusted his tits and said, "Cor blimey, you don't get many of these to the pound," which caused a ripple of laughter.

Then in a breathy feminine voice, "I nearly didn't make it here tonight you know, the conductor wouldn't let me off the bus until he'd put a new roll in and punched my ticket!"

The innuendo wasn't lost, loud laughter erupted from the stalls. He waited for it to subside before giving the pianist the nod to play the introduction to his song. Before he even started to sing, Jake felt he had them.

When he finished his song there was loud applause, the auditorium lights came up and a man who had watched his audition called out, "Thank you Mr Wiggins!"

Jake picked up the feathers, remembering to thank the pianist before walking off stage. He felt he had done his best, the rest was up to them. He could see Ricci standing in the wings looking positively gleeful.

As Jake got to him, Ricci trilled excitedly, "You were fantastic Jake, you surpassed yourself darling. C'mon, let's get you changed so that you can relax."

"Relax? I won't relax until I've had at least three whiskies, darling!"

When they reached the dressing room, they found Jim waiting there for them. He was sat in a chair with his legs stretched out grinning from to ear. He jumped up and strode to Jake, giving him a big hug,

"Darling, you were amazing, how do you feel?"

"I don't know what I feel at the moment Jim, I just hope they liked me."

"Like you? They loved you! They just need to put their heads together now to decide whether they will book you or not and under what terms. I think they like to do a bit of posturing to make it look as if they had to make a hard decision. They know my opinion and I've declared my bias, so we just have to wait to see what they say, it shouldn't be too long though."

"They'd be fools if they didn't make him sign on the dotted line here and now," Ricci remarked.

"Thank you, Ricci darling, my number one fan."

"I'd better get back to see what's happening, as soon as I hear anything, I'll let you know."

Ricci helped Jake by taking off his wig and helping him undress. He put the wig on its stand and hung the frock on the rail while Jake began to remove his make-up.

Ricci said, "I'll make you a nice cup of tea, you can't have anything stronger because if you have to see anyone it will give the wrong impression to be smelling of strong liquor. You can have your whisky later."

"A cup of tea will be lovely, thank you Ricci."

They talked about Jake's audition, Ricci saying he thought it was the best thing he'd seen Jake do.

"That line about hardly making it to the theatre because the bus conductor wanted to punch your ticket was inspired, absolutely hilarious. When did you come up with that?"

"Just before I went out onto the stage, it just came to me."

"Well it was genius, pure genius sweetie, and your voice was as clear as crystal!" *Jake secretly knew where the idea had come from of course!*

Jake washed and dried his face, moisturised to replenish his skin, then slipped on a pair of comfortable slacks and a polo shirt. He sat down and began to drink his cup of tea.

Shortly afterwards Jim came back in and said, "They're asking to see you upstairs love, come with me."

"Have they told you what their decision is, Jim? Have I got it?"

"No sorry love, I'm as much in the dark as you are, but we're about to find out!" Jim secretly winked at Ricci as they left the dressing room.

"See you in a while Ricci," Jake called back nervously.

Jim led Jake up to the artistic director's office, to Jake it seemed like the walk of a man who was about to have a sentence pronounced on him. He would have thought Jim would have been told.

Three people were seated in the room, the artistic director, musical director and choreographer. The artistic director, a tall slender man called Ian Laithwaite who looked to be in his sixties, with a pleasant face, smiled politely and asked Jake to take a seat. Jim remained standing by the door,

"Thank you for such a wonderful audition, Jake," he said. "We felt we should tell you of our decision personally, rather than inform you by letter. We would be delighted for you to perform here at The Capital. Congratulations! We will draw up a contract, would you be able to start next week?"

Jake stood up and shook the man's hand. "Thank you, I'm absolutely thrilled, I would be delighted to start next week subject to my manager agreeing the contract."

They all smiled and the musical director and choreographer came and shook his hand. They both said how much they were looking forward to working with him, they all felt that everything about Jake, his voice, his look, deportment and his humour, were exactly right for The Capital. Jake felt a million dollars as he thanked them and left. Jim came out with him.

"Well done darling, I told you they loved you. Would you like me to show you around the theatre?"

"Yes please love, I'd like that, and while you're showing me around you can explain why you didn't tell me I'd got the job when you came into the dressing room to get me!"

Jim looked surprised. "How did you know?"

"Because I can read you like a book, my love!"

"I didn't tell you because I thought professionally, it was better for you to hear it from them, they were the ones who were making the decision to take you on board."

"I know, I completely understand, Jim. Wow, it hasn't sunk in properly yet love. I'm going to be top of the bill at the famous Capital and you're the one who made it all possible!"

"No I didn't darling, you did, I only presented you with an opportunity, it was you who clinched it. I'm so proud of you."

Jim led Jake to front of house. They walked through the foyer into the auditorium where Jake saw for the first time the view that the paying customer would see. He took in the richness of the place, the red velvet curtains framing the stage, the carved plaster cherub sculptures painted in gold leaf, the boxes at the side of the stage.

"I've got goosebumps Jim, what a fantastic theatre, it's so grand and beautiful!"

"It is, isn't it? I can't think why I've never brought you here to see it before."

"Well I'm here now."

They walked down the centre aisle to the front of the stalls and turned to face the back of the theatre. Jim pointed out the gantry of spotlights and the control room underneath the upper circle that operated all the sound and lighting.

Jake asked, "What's the seating capacity, Jim?"

"Two thousand three hundred and fifty-nine, and they'll all be coming to see the greatest female impersonator ever!"

"Oh Jim, that's scary. Hey, we'd better go back to Ricci and tell him the good news, he'll be wanting to get home, then we had better think about contacting Monty to break the news to him. I wonder how he'll take it."

"You leave him to me love, I'll put it in such a way he'll be glad to let you go."

Jake was in a state of euphoria; he felt as if he would explode, his emotions were a mixture of joy, excitement, pride and trepidation. He couldn't wait to let everyone know what had happened this wonderful, amazing day.

Chapter 21

Monty had agreed to see them tomorrow evening at the club, so they booked a table at their favourite restaurant for dinner, where they enjoyed the delicious food and a good bottle of Nuits St George served by Michelle the gorgeous waiter. Jake wasn't looking forward to tomorrow evening at all, but there was no way of getting out of it. Jim, of course, was completely unfazed by the prospect and he politely reminded Jake that he had an obligation to thank Monty for giving him his first break and launching him into the spotlight, it had enabled him to get some valuable experience. Jake felt justifiably chastised by Jim reminding him of this fact. It was a wonderful evening which gave them the opportunity to celebrate Jake's achievement in securing a plum job where he would be able to see more of Jim.

"I don't know if it has occurred to you Jim, but you'll be managing me twice now, you're my personal manager as well as my manager at the theatre!"

Jim leaned over the table and whispered to Jake, "I can manage you as many times as you like, Miss L'amour!"

They both laughed so loudly all eyes in the restaurant turned on them, which they thought was even funnier.

Jim said, "You're going to have to get used to everyone looking at you when you're famous!"

They left the restaurant and climbed into the taxi, both of them high on the day's events and the prospect of a steamy night. Jake was on a promise.

The next day, Jake had arranged to go with Ricci to

meet his friend Michael at Burmans. They would need to hire a number of quality gowns and accessories for him, his appearances would require two gowns, one for the actual performance, another one for the finale with the whole cast on stage. They all needed to be jaw-dropping creations that would draw gasps of delight and admiration from the audience, prompting envy from the women and curiosity from the men; lots of feathers, sequins, headdresses, different coloured wigs, gloves, etc. Michael was delighted to meet Jake and couldn't have been more helpful. It was obvious that Ricci had told Michael all about him and his coup in landing a prestigious job at The Capital, also the fact that he was going to be his dresser.

Jake got the distinct impression that Michael fancied him; it wasn't arrogance on his part, he just knew, he could tell. Jake wouldn't have been interested in him though, even if he had been single and available, he wasn't his type, but there was no harm in using the man's attraction for him to his advantage so as to get the best frocks, the best deal possible, he would be sweetness personified. In one hour, they had managed to fill a ten-foot rail with the sort of dresses you would expect to see royalty wearing at grand society balls. Jake created an open account at Burmans which meant he could hire costumes and be billed for them each month. Ricci arranged for the gowns and accessories to be delivered to the theatre with instructions that they were to be covered, boxed and labelled 'Miss Rusty L'amour C/O Mr Jim Hartnell' This would ensure they would be safely taken care of once they arrived. They thanked Michael for all his help and left to go home.

When Jim came home that evening, Jake told him all about the costumes he'd chosen and had sent to the theatre for his attention. He mentioned that he'd opened an account with Burmans as it seemed the sensible thing to do; Jim agreed. Jake also told Jim that he had phoned his mum and told her the good news about his forthcoming debut in the West End and how thrilled she and Ted were.

He cooked them a cheese omelette each and accompanied them with a bowl of mixed salad as it was a quick and easy meal before they set off for their meeting with Monty Sharman.

"I've got a few things to show you. What do you think of this first of all?"

Jim showed Jake the press release The Capital publicity team had put together to take full advantage of the fact they had a new 'leading lady'.

FEMALE IMPERSONATOR JAKE HARTNELL-WIGGINS AKA 'RUSTY L'AMOUR'
to be the new leading *lady* at The Capital Theatre.

Rehearsals are underway for the debut performance of Rusty L'amour, the alter ego of Jake Hartnell-Wiggins, who will take over this month from singer Selena Dreyton who left unexpectedly earlier this week.

Mr Hartnell-Wiggins, an accomplished entertainer, will be delighting audiences with his spectacular lavish costumes, songs and unique brand of witty humour. This leading *lady* with a difference has that extra something that makes him unique! Get ready to be thrilled, the West End will not have seen his like before, and probably never will again! Tickets are available now from the box office for his debut performance on Saturday 22 November at 7.30pm. Book early as we expect there will be a high demand

to see this fabulous original artiste.

"Jim it's wonderful, I think they've hit exactly the right tone, and I love my new double-barrelled name, but we're on a tight timescale, aren't we?"

"I knew you'd like it, it will be in the papers on Wednesday, hopefully the *Evening News* and the *Evening Standard* will print it. Yes, it is a tight timescale, we've had to work quickly because of it, your first rehearsal is on Thursday, then dress rehearsal on Friday, Saturday is the big day, with your opening night performance at 7.30pm."

"Have you been able to get an idea of what I'm going to be paid ahead of them drawing up my contract?"

"I thought you would ask me that," Jim replied, handing him a slip of paper. "Will that be OK?"

"This can't be right, surely they've made a mistake?"

"No they haven't, you're well worth that amount, don't underestimate your worth love. This is only interim, you wait until you're drawing capacity crowds, they'll have to think again then!"

"Fantastic, totally unbelievable, I'd never have dreamed they would pay me that much!"

"We have put Ricci on the theatre payroll as your dresser too, so that's all taken care of. He will just need to sign his contract of employment, he can do that on Thursday when he comes in for rehearsal."

"Good, that's marvellous."

"Right, we ought to get going to see Monty then, we don't want to keep him waiting."

"OK, I'll get my coat."

Chapter 22

Monty Sharman smiled, shaking them warmly by the hand he ushered them into his office.

"It's always a pleasure to see you both but I hope nothing is wrong. What can I do for you?"

"Thank you, it's good to see you too. It's like this Monty, I won't beat about the bush, Jake has been given a once-in-a-lifetime opportunity to be the lead in a West End theatre production. We have come to respectfully ask you to release him from his contract with you with immediate effect, so that he can take up this new role. We will of course honour the clause that states he will be liable to pay £1,000."

Monty looked shocked.

"We know it's very sudden and we're sorry for that, but he can't possibly turn this down, this will mean his name going up in lights in the West End. Who knows what it might lead to?"

Monty leaned back in his chair rubbing his chin and looked at them both. "If I can get a word in Jim, I won't pretend I'm not shocked and disappointed, because I am. The Black Orchid won't be the same without you, but I'm also absolutely delighted for you too, Jake. Congratulations, what a fantastic break for you. Which theatre is it?"

"The Capital," Jake replied.

"Wow, the breaks don't come much bigger than that do they?" Smiling sincerely, he went on, "You won't need your cheque book today Jim, I won't have it said that Monty

Sharman ever stood in anyone's way." Standing up, he went to a metal filing cabinet and lifted out a file, he took some pages from it, saying, "This is your contract." And to Jake and Jim's surprise he tore it straight in half. "I know this sort of thing is only to be expected in the entertainment business, you couldn't have done better for the club, so consider yourself released with my blessing, with two provisos though!"

"What are they?" Jake asked curiously.

"You buy me a drink in the bar and you let me have complimentary tickets for your opening night performance!"

"That's wonderful, Monty, you're on, you are a real gentleman, sir."

They went out to the bar and Jim said, "I think champagne is called for, don't you Jake?"

"What else, what better to drink to Monty's health?"

They sat at Monty's table and Jim ordered the champagne. Several regulars came up and said hello to Jake like he was their best friend in the world, saying they couldn't wait to see him on Saturday night when they came in. Jake felt slightly sad and a little guilty that he would be disappointing them.

"I just want to make an announcement, people need to know about this," Monty said, leaving the table and walking onto the empty stage. "Ladies and gentlemen, if I could just have your attention for a few moments, I have an important announcement to make. Our much-loved female impersonator Jake, otherwise known as Rusty L'amour, is unfortunately leaving us. He is about to make his mark on the West End stage at The Capital Theatre this very weekend. I'm sure you would like to take this opportunity to wish him well for his future success!"

Jim popped the cork from the bottle of champagne. There

was a groan of astonishment from the regulars as Monty continued.

"I'd like to propose a toast. Please raise your glasses for Jake, and you must all buy tickets to go and see him."

Everyone stood up, raised their glasses and drank to him. "To JAKE!"

Someone in the club shouted out, "Give us a song then!"

Jim looked at Jake, shrugged and lifted both hands up and said, "There's no way you can get out of it. Jake, up you go!" He pointed to the stage.

Under his breath, Jake said, "But, I don't have anyone to play the piano for me!"

"They won't mind, sing something they know and ask them all to join in."

He stood up and climbed the steps as they all cheered and clapped him on.

"Thank you, you're very kind, but you're all going to have to help me out because I don't have a pianist."

A heckler shouted out, "That's not what we heard, you usually have it tucked between your legs!"

Jake laughed, responding with, "Oooh, cheeky! You all know this one, 'I only want to be with you'."

They all joined in, everyone thoroughly enjoying themselves. When the song ended, they started chanting "More, more!" He just curtsied very proficiently and blew them all kisses as he came offstage and sat down again. The place was a buzz of chatter, the atmosphere one of joyful bon homie.

Monty and Jim, looked delighted, Monty said, "They're all going to miss you so much."

This brought tears to Jake's eyes but he held his emotions in check so as not to appear foolish. With a lump in his throat he said, "Please tell the girls I said goodbye Monty, I'd hate them to think I had forgotten them."

Jim could see he was on the verge of a flood of tears so he squeezed his hand, smiled at him, and said, "Hold it together until we get home love, you'll be fine. I'll get him home now Monty, he's got a hectic schedule over the next few days, Thanks for everything."

"My pleasure, I am so looking forward to seeing you perform on Saturday Jake. Break a leg, goodnight."

Chapter 23

Jim had told Jake that Vera and Ted were coming up to see the show, so he was absolutely delighted about that. He said they were staying at The Cumberland Hotel. Jim had invited them to come to his dressing room after the show. Jake was on an adrenalin high, the pace of the last two days had been hectic, his first rehearsal had proved to be a revelation due to the fact he'd discovered there were some choreographic moves to master and remember for the finale. Steven, the choreographer, wanted two of the male dancers to link arms with him and lead him on stage, they then had to move centre stage, turn and do leg flicks in either direction, turning their heads in the same direction as they were kicking in, while the other members of the troupe danced around the stage. He had chosen an appropriate costume to show off his legs. It was showgirl style with Burgundy draped satin folds and bright fuchsia-pink ostrich feathers around the waist. He was wearing a body form with false boobs for only the second time which still felt quite strange, but there was no way you could tell his tits weren't real. He wore a matching headdress which was studded with diamanté stones and ostrich feathers, his sandals had baby heels that were also covered with glistening stones, he wore fish net tights, the effect was totally amazing. He had found the first rehearsal was nerve-racking and hard work, he had never sung with an orchestra before, but his number went well and he soon picked up the moves he had to do.

The dress rehearsal was completely awesome and went like

a dream, which built Jake's confidence no end, making him impatient and eager for the real performances on Saturday. Ricci had been so efficient, nothing was too much trouble for him; he was such a good friend and they had a good laugh together. He also had the knack of bringing Jake back down to earth if he got too carried away and above himself. Jim had watched the dress rehearsal; he had been totally enthralled with Jake's performance and spellbound with the spectacular finale. Jake looked so stunning, he was totally convincing as a woman, he knew for certain that Jake would be a resounding success.

Once Jake had changed, Jim took him out through the stage door and round to the front entrance so that he could see all the photographs advertising the show. They walked back inside the main entrance into the foyer and Jake was amazed to see a large life-size cardboard cut-out of himself. He could hardly believe it, it all seemed so unreal, but wonderful at the same time. They went back to Jake's dressing room to say cheerio to Ricci, they found him busy putting things away and making sure everything was alright for tomorrow's opening.

Jake thanked him for all his hard work and said he would see him tomorrow. Jim and Jake then left by the stage door, saying cheerio to Bert the stage door keeper. A lone photographer appeared out of the shadows and took a photograph; he looked very pleased with himself, and as he was backing away he said very pointedly, "Thanks very much Mr Wiggins, that will do nicely. You can see it on the front page of *The Sunday Globe and Star* very soon." Then he turned and left in a great hurry.

Slightly taken aback at this encounter with him, Jake and Jim wondered why a picture of them leaving the stage door would be worthy of the front page of any newspaper. But then they thought it was obviously in connection with the opening night.

The Sunday Globe and Star was a law unto itself. It was renowned as being one of the gutter tabloids whose penchant was for printing sensational, juicy exposés of prominent people; they had wrecked many people's lives in the past.

"He could have had a proper photograph, if he had stopped and asked, I'm sure that one won't be very flattering," Jake said.

"Never mind," Jim commented. "It's his loss."

They forgot all about it as they walked to their car. They were both quite hungry, so they stopped on the way home to get a Chinese takeaway as neither one of them wanted to be bothered with cooking or preparing food. They could have an easy night as tomorrow was going to be unbelievably exciting and hectic, so Jake needed to preserve his energy and stamina in order to be able to cope with its demands and be at his best. Jake poured Jim and himself a well-earned drink as Jim laid the table and put the plates and the food out. They sat and ate their meal, Jake talking animatedly between mouthfuls about all the events of the day, how he was thrilled to bits that his mum was going to see him perform on stage for the first time.

Jim explained to Jake how so many important people had been invited to the opening night performance – dignitaries, like the Lord Mayor of London, other people who were connected to the production in some way, but not directly involved in it, financial backers, contractors such as Burmans Costumiers, Hair Creations, newspaper arts reporters, all sorts of influential people who were somehow instrumental in making the show happen, or could further impact on publicity. Jim could see Jake was tired so he suggested that he have an early night.

"You look all in love, I'll run a nice hot bath for you so that you can have a nice relaxing soak before you go to bed."

"Thank you, Jim, that will be lovely. I don't think I've ever felt so tired. I'm not complaining, I'm loving every minute of it but I didn't realise this work would be so exhausting!"

"Oh yes, it's hard work darling, not just physically, but mentally too, not least because you have to think about and remember so many things, but you'll be fine after a good night's sleep."

Jake woke up the next morning feeling completely rested, ready for his preparations before the show. He had booked an appointment with Sharon at The Studio to have his legs waxed and his nails done as he wanted to look and feel perfect for his performance. He showered then he and Jim had breakfast together before Jim left for the theatre. He reminded him that a taxi was booked for five thirty to get him to the theatre in plenty of time for Ricci to make him up and get him ready. Ten minutes after Jim had left, Jake jumped in his car and drove for his appointment. Sharon and the other girls greeted him, they were delighted that he was now starring in a West End show. Sharon said she was so thrilled for him when she'd seen the article in the *Evening Standard*.

"You really deserve it. When I came and saw you at the Black Orchid, I thought to myself he's far too good to stay in this place for long. You see, I was right, wasn't I?"

"You certainly were Sharon, but I have to say, the club was a good training ground for me, it helped prepare me for a professional career. I'll always be grateful to Monty Sharman and the Black Orchid for that."

"Well you were wonderful when I saw you there, and you'll be even more wonderful at The Capital. We will definitely be coming to see you."

"Thank you, Sharon. When you do, be sure to come backstage to my dressing room and have a drink."

"How lovely, we certainly will. Now brace yourself, this wax is going to feel a bit warm and it'll sting like hell when I pull it off!"

"I can stand it love, it's got to be done, the things we girls do in the name of vanity, eh?"

"Ooh, you are a one," Sharon said, laughing as she eased sufficient wax from the top of a strip away from Jake's leg to give her something to catch hold of. She had enough leverage then to rip it clean off, hairs and all!

Jake grimaced. "That wasn't too bad, keep going sweetie, it'll soon be over, as the actress said to the bishop!"

Sharon gave a squeal of delight and chuckled, "Mr Hartnell-Wiggins really, you crease me up!"

Despite their jovial banter, Sharon was able to expertly wax and moisturise Jake's legs in no time at all, then she gave him a manicure and applied false nails. Jake paid, tipped her well and said a cheery goodbye to all the girls who were all wishing him well for his opening performance. Jake went home and listened to some relaxing music, remembering not to drink too many fluids as it was too much of a palaver to have to go to the loo with all the drag on.

He tried not to get anxious about what was going to happen later; he told himself that he knew his words and his moves perfectly, so there was absolutely nothing for him to worry about. Jake's taxi dropped him at the rear of the theatre, just off the dirty-looking side alley with its black metal fire escapes which led to the stage door. He paid the friendly driver and gave him a tip. Walking to the stage door, he entered and was greeted cheerfully by Bert who wished him all the very best.

Ricci was completely organised when Jake walked into the dressing room, all his make-up was laid out. He smiled at Jake and gave him a hug and a kiss and said, "Hi sweetie, how are you? We'll soon have you made up and ready for you to wow them."

"I'm fine thanks Ricci love, it's strange but I don't feel at all nervous!"

"That's because I'm nervous enough for the both of us darling. I'm only kidding, you're sure to get a few butterflies later on, it wouldn't be natural if you didn't."

Jake noticed there was a pile of envelopes on the table. "Are these for me, Ricci?"

"Of course sweetie, but just strip to the waist and put your body form on then I can get your brows covered up before you start opening them, then you can have a few minutes, OK?"

Ricci began applying paste over Jake's eyebrows.

"Yes fine, gosh there are flowers as well, aren't they gorgeous, who are they from?"

"Yes I'm glad you like them, they're from me sweetie to wish you all the best for the show."

"Thank you Ricci, you're such a darling, I wouldn't be here but for you."

"Hmm, well, I can happily say exactly the same sweetie, now let's get your face on darling."

The speaker on the wall of the dressing room came to life with the sound of the orchestra tuning up and the indistinct chatter of people coming into the auditorium to take their seats.

Ricci handed Jake the pile of cards, he opened them as they came, there were greetings from Lorenzo, Ricci and Toby, Jim, Monty, the guys and girls in the dance troupe, Sharon and the team at The Studio, Michael from Burmans, Vera and Ted, Ian the artistic director, Pauline and Ned. He left the others unopened as Ricci needed to get on. It was all he could do to stop himself getting emotional over them, but he drew on reserves of self will and remained calm.

Then the overture began, the dance troupe came on and did their introductory routine before the well-known cockney compère, Danny Denver, was heard enthusiastically thanking them and welcoming everyone to The Capital theatre, the famous home of international variety. He told a couple of jokes to get them warmed up and laughing before introducing Karl and Carlotta Zarinski, a husband and wife knife-throwing act from Russia.

"And now ladies and gentlemen, I'm very pleased to introduce our first act for you this evening, they've come all the way from Russia, so please give them a very warm welcome, the Fabulous Zarinskis!"

The music of composer Aram Khachaturian's 'Sabre dance' began, interspersed with bangs and gasps from the audience as knives thudded into balloons on the revolving board that Carlotta was strapped to, just missing her by inches.

The door to the dressing room opened just as Ricci was applying Jake's lipstick. It was Jim looking so handsome and debonaire in his evening dress suit.

"Hi girls, everything all right?" Looking at Jake in the mirror, he went on, "There's a packed house out there all eager to see you my darling, I know they are all going to love you, you're looking fabulous. Wonderful work as ever Ricci. Jake, I'll pop in to see you just before you go on. Must dash, see you later!"

"Now that was a match made in heaven darling, I'm so

pleased you listened to your wise Auntie Ricci when I told you he was a real catch and you shouldn't let him slip through your fingers!"

"Yes Ricci, you've always steered me along the right path."

Applause and Danny Denver's voice came out of the speaker. "Weren't they brilliant ladies and gentlemen? I'll bet *she* doesn't argue with her husband eh?"

The audience erupted into laughter and applause at the joke.

"We have something a little more gentle for you now, he's one of the funniest ventriloquists in the business. Please put your hands together for Buddy and his lovable pooch Pepito!"

"There's just this act; one more, then Marvello the magician before the intermission. You're the first act in the second half love, your make-up's finished but we need to get a move on. I'll put gloves on and help you put your tights on, we don't want you laddering them with those nails, then I'll dress you and put your wig on. You can relax for a few minutes before we put your shoes on you."

"I'm sure we'll be OK for time, Ricci, you're such a marvel."

"Yes I know, like marvel the bloody magician, if I go any faster I'll disappear in a puff of smoke up my own arsehole!"

They both roared with laughter; it cut through the tension they were both feeling.

"What was so funny?" Jim said, as he walked in. "I could hear you outside!"

"Oh just something Ricci said, I'll tell you later love."

"I just came to tell you how Danny is going to introduce you." Jim read from a piece of paper. "He'll say, *and now the star of our show, the girl with hidden assets, Miss Rusty L'amour, give* him, erm, her a warm welcome, *I'm confused,* I'm sure you'll think of something witty to say as you go on love!"

"It doesn't need any thinking about darling, I'll reply in a deep butch voice, *you're confused mate? How do you think I feel, and my assets are definitely staying hidden OK.*"

"Absolutely brilliant, you'll have them on your side right away, you're going to knock em dead love. I'll be here waiting for you when you come off. I love you very much, break a leg."

"I love you too darling, I know you'll be cheering for me."

Jim blew a kiss and left. Ricci stood there holding Jake's wig.

"Wig," he said assertively as a prompt for Jake to lean forward to assist Ricci to put it on his head. Once on, he titivated and sprayed it with lacquer. Kneeling down, he said, "Right, shoes and we're done gal."

When Ricci had put them on him, Jake stood up and viewed himself in the mirror.

"Not bad for a farm lad, eh Ricci? You've done wonders again love!"

"Thanks Jake, I'll be watching from the wings, give em everything you've got sweetie, like you always do, they'll love you."

When Marvello had finished his act, the first curtain call for Miss Rusty L'amour to make her way backstage came over the loudspeaker. From the wings, Jake and Ricci could hear the audience returning to their seats in anticipation of the second half and seeing the star of the show. They stood talking to Danny Denver before it was time for him to stroll briskly in front of the audience and introduce Jake.

"And now, the act you've all been waiting for …"

The introductory banter between Danny and *Jake* worked

like a dream, even before he spoke to the audience to say good evening and introduce his song, he was getting loud applause and wolf whistles. His superlative performance brought them out of their seats shouting for more.

Chapter 24

On his way back to the dressing room so many of the dancers and the backstage crew were congratulating him it was unbelievable. When he entered his dressing room, Jim and Ricci were waiting, both with beaming smiles and congratulations, they hugged and kissed him saying how well he had done. Jake sat down and Ricci removed his wig for him until he needed to don it again for the finale; he scratched his head with relief to be free of it. He looked at himself in the mirror, he was glowing with elation.

"Thanks Ricci, it feels good to get that off for a bit." He felt dazed and other worldly as if it was all a fabulous dream. "Now I'd better have a pee otherwise the finale could have a gushing water feature." He dashed into the loo and when he came out he said, "What a relief."

There were three acts in the second half, a comedian called Sammy Williams, an up-and-coming pop group called The Meteorites and a trio of puppeteers who wore black clothing and stood behind a black screen so they could not be seen by the audience as they expertly worked their marionettes. Jake, Ricci and Jim talked excitedly about the after-show party at The Dorchester, Park Lane, Jake saying he had never been in such a swanky hotel before and was really looking forward to it. The time seemed to pass very quickly and in no time at all Jake was making his way to the wings to walk back on stage to join the whole company for the grand finale.

Everything went without a hitch, the audience loving

every moment. They stood up clapping and cheering wildly as Jake entered stage right wearing his showgirl costume, was escorted by two handsome bare-chested male dancers wearing scanty tight sequinned shorts that left nothing at all to the imagination; they were certainly big boys. It was an outrageously camp spectacle, totally ground-breaking, the West End theatre hadn't seen anything so suggestive and flagrantly 'gay' ever before, but judging by their reaction they loved it and they wanted more. A beautiful bouquet of flowers was brought onto the stage and placed in his arms. His world had changed; he wasn't fully aware of it yet but stardom had arrived with sequins, glitter and adulation. There was no turning back now. It seemed as if they didn't want to let him go. Jake thought he was never going to get off the stage, but finally the wave of applause, whistles and cheers subsided sufficiently for him to make an exit. Making his way back to his dressing room he looked at the card attached to the bouquet and saw that they were from Jim with the message,

To my darling Jake, the toast of London Town. I love you so very much. XXX

Jim and Ricci were waiting for him with even more praise and congratulations than earlier. Jake gave Jim a kiss to thank him for his bouquet. Ricci had poured Jake a celebratory scotch and ginger ale, he sat him down, gave him his whisky then knelt down to unfasten his shoes and pull them off. Jake sighed as Ricci lightly massaged his feet.

"Ooooh you are a darling, thank you Ricci!"

"You were a triumph, darling," Jim said. He looked so excited and proud. "Don't start to take your make-up off or anything as there will be a few people calling to see you. Just enjoy your drink and relax love, you've earned it."

Almost on cue, there was a knock on the door which Ricci answered. Jake heard Bert the stage door keeper's voice say, "There's a Mr and Mrs Beavis asking to see Mr Hartnell-Wiggins."

Jake rose out of his seat and turned to welcome a very excited Vera and Ted. "Mum, Ted, how lovely of you to come," Jake said kissing his mum and shaking Ted's hand. "Did you enjoy the show?"

"Oh Jake it was wonderful, very entertaining but you were incredible, I couldn't believe it was you up there. I'm so proud of you!"

"Yes you were marvellous Jake," Ted added. "The whole experience was grand, I'll bet you're proud of him too, Jim?"

"I certainly am Ted, he's worked so hard and so has Ricci here."

Ted shook hands with Ricci and Vera did the same. She said, "It's lovely to meet you Ricci, Jake's told me how it's all thanks to you he started doing drag. I'm so pleased you're looking after him, you have a real talent to make him look absolutely gorgeous the way you do!"

"Thank you, Mrs Beavis, it's lovely to meet you too."

There was another knock at the door. Ricci said, "Excuse me," and opened the door, it was Bert again. He introduced the well-known impresario Lou Darnell, saying he wished to see Mr Hartnell-Wiggins.

"Show him in Ricci, hello Mr Darnell I'm Jim Hartnell, Jake's manager. Please let me introduce you to Jake. Jake, this is Mr Lou Darnell, the famous producer of so many hit West End shows."

Ricci looked at the tall dark handsome man dressed smartly in a light-grey suit, he smiled and shook him by the hand and said hello.

"I just had to come and meet you and say what a wonderful performance you gave this evening. I think you are definitely the new West End star and I would like you to appear in my televised Saturday Extravaganza."

"Oh thank you Mr Darnell, that sounds absolutely wonderful, I'm honoured. I'm sure Jim my manager will be able to come to an arrangement with you."

"Yes I'm sure we will. I'm delighted to meet you Jake, please take my card Jim, I'd like you to call me at ten o'clock on Monday morning so that we can discuss the arrangements, will you do that?"

"Of course, Mr Darnell, thank you so much for taking the time to come backstage."

"My pleasure, I have to say I was curious, I thought I might be disappointed when I met you in person close up Jake, but I am even more amazed, you are totally convincing as a woman, young man, I'd have you on my arm anytime!"

Jake smiled broadly at him. "Well thank you for such a compliment, sir," Jake replied coyly.

They shook hands again and Mr Darnell turned to Jim and said, "Ten o'clock Monday morning Jim," then he left.

All of them gaped at one another in astonishment.

Jim said, "Jake, you've only gone and got the great Lou Darnell chasing after you to sign you up for his TV show!" He ran to Jake to hug and kiss him, Ricci gave him a kiss too. Jake looked as if he was in shock.

"You deserve it sweetie," he cooed. "You've worked really hard!"

"So have you love, and I won't forget it, whoo hoo, fancy that, it's incredible!"

Vera and Ted, having watched the whole scene, were incredulous and full of excitement. They both rushed to Jake to say how excited they were for him that he might be appearing on television, they couldn't wait to tell Pauline and Ned and all their friends.

"It's been a wonderful experience seeing you on stage and to be able to come to your dressing room love," Vera said to Jake, "but we'll be off now and leave you to celebrate."

"Oh you're not coming to the after-show party with us then Mum? You'd be very welcome."

"No, it's very kind of you," Ted said, "but you should be able to enjoy yourselves with all your friends and colleagues, without having us tagging along. We'll feel a little out of place anyway, but thanks all the same, we are both so pleased the evening has been such a success for you."

"Well, as long as you're sure, but I promise you, I'll be sending you tickets to see my future shows. I'll send Pauline and Ned tickets too. Bye Mum," Jake said, giving her a big hug and kiss, then shaking Ted warmly by the hand, "I'll let you know how we get on with Mr Darnell."

"Yes you must, but from what I saw, it looked as though he's determined to get you on his show. I think he was smitten with you Jake."

"Smitten, I thought he was going to propose to me there and then!" They all laughed.

"I'm so pleased you were able to come this evening," Jim said. "As soon as we can we'll come down to Brighton again to see you, we'll spend some quality time together, go out for a nice meal somewhere."

"That would be so nice Jim, now promise you'll look after Jake, see that he doesn't work too hard, *all work and no play makes Jake a dull boy,* you know!"

"Don't worry Vera, I'll make sure he gets plenty of rest and relaxation. Would you like me to call you a taxi to take you back to your hotel?"

"No, that won't be necessary," Ted replied. "Thanks all the same, we want to have a little walk before we head back."

"OK but be careful out there, the West End can be a bit tricky at night. I'll see you both to the door."

"Bye Jake, bye Ricci," Vera and Ted said, waving goodbye.

"Cheerio, it was lovely to meet you Mr and Mrs Beavis," Ricci said smiling.

"Bye Mum, I'll call you soon darling."

Jim took them through a part of the theatre that they hadn't seen, giving them bits of information about different things. He led them backstage through the wings, down the steps by the side of the orchestra pit, into the auditorium and on through the theatre to the front entrance. He said goodbye to them again but not before Vera had kindly remarked, "I hope you don't think I'm being rude Jim, but look after little Ricci, he's a real treasure and he obviously thinks the world of our Jake."

"Bless you Vera, we know we could never find another Ricci. He's a dear friend, goodbye both, take care."

He waved them off as they set off down Shaftesbury Avenue, towards Piccadilly Circus. He went back to the dressing room to find Jake out of his costume, with his make-up and nails removed. Before he went to wash his face, get changed, they both thanked Ricci, saying goodbye to him and going on to the party.

Half an hour later their taxi pulled up in front of The Dorchester and the concierge came forward to open the door for them.

"Good evening gentlemen, welcome to The Dorchester."

"Would you direct us to the Simmington suite please?" Jim asked.

"If you'll kindly follow me sir, I'll take you there."

They both followed the man into the sumptuous lobby, into the lift which took them up to the fourth floor. The concierge led the way to a set of double doors opposite, he pulled them open and the whole room of people erupted into loud cheers and whistles.

The concierge, surprised, looked at them saying, "Have a pleasant evening, gentlemen," and retired, closing the doors behind him.

The crowd of people, many of whom Jake didn't know, suddenly burst into the song – 'For he's a jolly good fellow' – and champagne corks began to pop as Ian Laithwaite the artistic director came up to them, took Jake by the arm, congratulating him on his tremendous success and said, "I'll introduce you to a few people, Jake. Come with me, I think this is going to be some party!"

The next morning, although he was slightly hungover from an excess of champagne, Jim had been out to the local newsagent and got hold of the ones that had the reviews in them. He quickly had a glance at them before he began making breakfast and taking it up to Jake.

He had anticipated they would be good but they were fantastic. One piece read:

Mr Jake Hartnell-Wiggins was an amazing Tour de Force as 'Miss Rusty L'amour'!

Another stated:

Sensational, He Is A Must-See Spectacular Female

Impersonator!

One more proclaimed:

The Man's A Triumph As 'Miss Rusty L'amour'!

The Sunday Globe and Star ran a very different headline:

Farm Labourer to Shooting Star!

Jim had left that particular newspaper in the office, he didn't want Jake to see it. He carried the breakfast tray upstairs and gently woke Jake.

"Wake up sleepy head, breakfast."

Jake murmured then groaned and complained, "Oh my head, I think I had too much to drink last night!"

"I think everyone did, me included. You'll feel better when you've had a cup coffee and something to eat love, sit yourself up."

"Oooooh never again," Jake groaned as he eased himself up in bed, propping the pillow up behind him and holding his head. "Thank you for getting breakfast darling but I think I'll just have black coffee."

"I've been out and bought the newspapers, would you like to see the reviews?"

"Yes please, what are they like?"

"They're glowing, absolutely glowing."

"Oh darling, I know you're my greatest fan." He patted Jim's hand and said, "Would you read them to me please?"

Jim poured Jake his first cup of strong coffee and started to read out the superlative reviews as Jake took a sip of the hot drink.

When Jim had read the first one, Jake's eyes were wide and he was expectantly waiting to hear more.

"Go on, next one!"

Jim smiled, saying, "OK the *Gazette* said, 'Sensational, he is a must-see spectacular female impersonator', the *Sphere* said, 'The man's a triumph as miss Rusty L'amour'!"

He finished reading them all out except the *Sunday Globe and Star* muck, he decided he would suppress that one until some other time, he didn't want to spoil Jake's happiness. Jim knew that Jake would be really angry and upset at them for dragging his distant past back up to hurt him and potentially damage his career. He was angry about it himself; the headline alone was a not-so-subtle reference to him accidentally shooting his father in self-defence all those years ago. Jim had read the whole piece, and it was basically casting doubt as to it being an accidental shooting, the paper made it sound like Jake must have wanted to kill him. It was definitely libellous as far as Jim was concerned, and he knew that Jake would think so too. They would have to put the matter in the hands of their solicitor and let him deal with it. But for now, Jim wasn't about to spoil the morning for Jake, he would tell him some other time. He could see Jake was ecstatic about the reviews and had started eagerly buttering and eating a piece of toast.

Speaking with his mouth full, he exclaimed as a joke, "My god Jim, do you think they liked me?"

"Silly, they adored you."

"When I was talking to Ian last night he said that he was astounded by the response in the theatre, he said he felt that people had been longing and waiting for a different kind of act, and they had found it in my unique and glamorous characterisation of Rusty!"

"Well Ian certainly knows what he's talking about, he said the same to me, adding Jake has got the balance of comedy, intrigue and glamour just right. These reviews are going to help enormously when I negotiate with Lou Darnell!"

"What I don't understand is how I am going to be able to do a live televised Saturday Spectacular for him when I'm contracted to The Capital and work every weekend!"

Jim gave a little chuckle. "Ha ha, well that's easy, it's a 'Saturday Spectacular' in that it's televised on a Saturday night, but it isn't recorded on a Saturday, it's done on another night, and I think it's a Sunday, in which case you will be free to do it because we're closed on Sundays, but it will mean you won't have a day off that week, sorry love!"

Jake lifted the back of his hand to his forehead and said in a mock self-sacrificing way, "I'll do anything for my art darling."

Jim swiftly put his hand under the bedclothes, taking hold of Jake's cock. "Oh will you now, well we'll have to see about that then won't we!"

"Seriously Jim, stop it for a minute, you mentioning a day off, you very rarely get one, if ever. I think it's about time that you received a proper wage on the books for managing me. What do you say?"

"I say that's your minute up, I want to manage you right now!"

"Oh you managers are all the same, you must have your pound of flesh. Give me a kiss then!"

"I want more than a pound's worth, c'mere."

Chapter 25

Jake's solicitor, Edward Southerby, a senior partner in the firm of Woolston, Southerby and Snape, had interviewed Jake and Jim at their office in Gray's Inn and been shown the article in *The Globe and Star*, along with historical local newspaper accounts that Jake had obtained pertaining to the events leading up to the shooting at the farm. He was explicit in declaring that the article was defamatory in nature and that Jake could, if he so wished, sue the newspaper for defamation of character. He explained all the legal details, the positives and negatives of taking legal action and pursuing damages. After listening and asking a few questions, Jake and Jim decided that going to law was their only course of action and they instructed Edward to proceed. They were not prepared to stand by and let the gutter press try to destroy Jake's character by their divisive and scurrilous accusations. If it meant that Jake had to go to court, then he most certainly would, but what they hoped would happen was for the newspaper to realise that nothing was to be gained from that and agree to settle out of court.

Either way, it would mean that there would be considerable publicity and speculation over all the personal details of Jake's private life, it would be like washing his dirty linen in public. He knew it could turn people against him and lose him fans. But for Jake it was a matter of principle, he was not going to just stand by and have his hard-earned reputation ruined, he was determined to fight this all the way.

Fortunately he didn't have to wait too long for a development.

After a couple of months he received a telephone call from Edward Southerby, who told him that the newspaper had said that they were prepared to settle out of court and would print a retraction apologising for causing any distress to Mr Hartnell-Wiggins. All he had to do was go to their office and sign the papers agreeing to this, as well as the substantial amount of compensation they had negotiated for him. Jake and Jim were over the moon that it had all been settled so quickly. They had stood up to a giant of the newspaper industry, who thought they could just print whatever lies suited them in order to sell more copies of their scurrilous rag, and they had won. However, in terms of stress, the whole sorry business had taken its toll on both Jim and Jake. Thank god litigation didn't go on and on, it was over. Well over in one sense, but it meant that Jake would now be able to answer questions from the media and during television interviews without being gagged by sub judice.

He was able to tell his side of the story when he was interviewed by *City Voice*, a magazine that specialised in articles that featured prominent celebrities and focused on current affairs. After that, he refused to talk about that aspect of his private life at all. Thankfully, since the article had been printed, it didn't appear to have done Jake's career, or his popularity, any harm at all, in fact just the opposite. He was receiving more fan letters than ever, and offers of work were pouring in. But he still wouldn't want to go through an experience like that again, not even for the thirty thousand pounds compensation he had received.

Chapter 26

So many things had happened in the whirlwind three years that followed Jake's astoundingly successful debut performance at The Capital and his subsequent television appearance for Lou Darnell. Most were good, but the blow of losing his mother had hit Jake very hard and he had struggled to continue his career for a while, but Jim was his solid rock and stalwart, helping him to hold it together and not go on a dramatic self-destruct. Friends had also been tremendously kind and understanding, as had his employers and fellow artistes. Vera and Ted had played down Vera's ill health as neither of them wanted to be a trouble or a burden to anyone. When she first went to see her doctor because she had been feeling unwell and had a lack of appetite, he sent her for scans and tests. They diagnosed that she had liver cancer and she was given the prognosis that she had three months left to live at the most. It came as a devastating shock to both of them, not least because it was such an incredible short span of time in which to come to terms with it, put her house in order so to speak, and prepare for the inevitable. It was typical of Vera that she remained strong, focusing her mind on alleviating as much distress as possible from her beloved Ted, her family and friends. She had private medical insurance so after talking it all over with Ted, she arranged that as soon as her disease began to get difficult and unmanageable at home, she would go into a hospice where she would be cared for and looked after by medical professionals, taking the burden of caring away from Ted, even though he had said he would look after her at home. She made sure her will was up to date, arranged for a private cremation, stating that she would like everyone who so wished to attend a memorial service at a later date, wearing the brightest colours they could possibly find.

She made a point of seeing Jake, Jim and all her dear friends before her illness progressed too far. With its inevitable dramatic skeletal looking weight loss, she did not want them seeing her like that, she wanted them to remember her how she was before this horrendous thing took hold of her and she made sure that everyone had a keepsake to remember her by. It was a brave, unselfish decision, one she hoped they would understand and accept.

Jake was just grateful that her last days would be as comfortable as possible with optimum pain management. On a lighter note, he was pleased that Vera had been able to watch him on television in the starring role on Lou Darnell's Saturday Spectacular, as well as numerous chat show appearances with hosts and actors who were household names.

In the letter she had written and left for him, she stated how much she loved him and how proud she was of him for his momentous achievements, despite the traumatic setbacks he had overcome in his early childhood and his teens. Above all she was content in the knowledge that he was successful and happy and he had found the enduring love of a good and trustworthy man in dear Jim.

After the funeral, which had been attended only by Ted and Vera's hospice carers, Ted arranged a memorial service for her at their local church in Saltdean. Jake and Jim thought it was the most colourful, uplifting and joyous occasion you could have possibly imagined; everyone had honoured Vera's memory by attending in glorious technicolour clothing. It gave him the opportunity to see Pauline and Ned who had come down to pay their respects. They both looked in good health, and apparently the farm was doing really well. Pauline said if it hadn't been for Vera's generosity she felt for sure that they would have gone under and had to sell up. They were thrilled that Jake had made such a great success of his move to London and they had really enjoyed watching him on television.

Jake introduced Jim to them and they went to have lunch together at the local pub Vera and Ted used to go to. The landlord had put on a delicious carvery which everyone enjoyed along with sharing anecdotes and stories about Vera. Jake had a long talk with Ted, asking him if he had any future plans. Surprisingly, Ted revealed that he was thinking of selling the house and moving abroad to France, he and Vera had discussed the possibility of doing it together before she became ill as they both loved the area of Provence. When she was told that her life expectancy was practically zilch, Vera told him that he should go ahead and do it anyway, she would be with him in spirit. He felt that he no longer wanted to continue living in the house they shared as it held far too many raw memories of Vera's last days with him before she had to go into the hospice.

Jake said, "If that's what you want to do Ted and it will make you happy, you go ahead and do it. You know Mum would have approved, but you must keep in touch. We could always come over and visit for a holiday once you've settled in."

"I would love to have you both, you'd be most welcome."

"You could always come and stay with us too. We're shortly moving to a much bigger house we've bought in High

Wycombe, Buckinghamshire, as we've kind of outgrown the Hampstead house now. It's a grade II listed manor house with lots of character, it will be much better for entertaining guests and holding parties, it will be a lot more private for us too. You must come up and see it; stay with us before you move abroad."

"That sounds great, I'll definitely take you up on that Jake. Jim was telling me earlier that there's a movie opportunity in the pipeline for you, it could be a great opportunity."

"Yes Ted, we're really excited about it, I've read the script, it's hilariously funny. I think it would be a fantastic experience and it would put me out there in front of a whole new audience. Jim's negotiating a contract for me which involves me getting a percentage of box office sales, so fingers crossed!"

"What's it about?"

"Basically it's about a man who tries to join the navy and he's turned down because he has flat feet. He decides to apply as a woman and somehow manages to get accepted by sweet-talking the male doctor doing the medical examination and agreeing to go on a date with him. He does the same with the man doing the entrance examination and passes with flying colours. It's all very tongue in cheek, totally unbelievable in real life of course, but it works wonderfully as a piece of farcical comedy."

As they were talking, Jim came to them and said, "I think we ought to be going now Jake, we both have a busy day tomorrow. It's been good to see you again Ted, you know where we are if you need us, or you want to talk."

"I'll get your coats," Ted gestured, just as a woman came up to him obviously wanting to engage him in conversation.

"That's OK Ted, we can get them, you can talk to this lady."

They went to the gents, then fetched their coats, waved to

Ted who was still talking to the woman and left.

Jake had been at pains to keep as low a profile as possible, so as to avoid fans and the press turning it into a circus but inevitably it had somehow leaked out and when they left the pub there were flashing cameras and fans asking for autographs. He didn't ever mind signing autographs, after all it was his fans who had helped put him where he was, but he disliked the press intruding into personal aspects of his life.

I guess it must have reminded him of how the press hounded him when he was a young boy after he was found by the police, and also after the incident at the farm. One good thing though, they had shown some respect and not bothered him at the church, so he waved and smiled to the cameras and treated it as an impromptu photo opportunity.

He thought of his mum. Jake felt that he owed a lot to Ted for the way he had loved and cared for his mum all those years ago, after the brutal way his dad had treated her. He had restored her faith in human nature, loved her the way she had always wanted and deserved to be loved, he had brought her true happiness, for that he was very thankful. She hadn't had an easy life until he came along, unfortunately she hadn't had an easy departing either, but she had died in the knowledge that she had found her true love.

Chapter 27

On the way back to Hampstead, the two of them talked about lots of things, how they thought Ted was holding up without Vera, Jake remarking that he thought Ted was looking a bit gaunt and had lost weight, wondering if he was looking after himself properly. They discussed their move down to the new house in Buckinghamshire, which Jake had humorously christened 'Buck House' because it was a camp queen's residence. Jim saying that he hoped the decorators would be finished soon as he wanted to put the Hampstead house on the market. Two months later they had moved and were settling into their new home. Jake was very happy with his choice of interior decor and furnishings which Jim had left entirely in his capable hands, advising the interior designer that he'd hired to deliver his concept for the house until it was perfectly accomplished. The Hampstead property was sold, it went in the first week that it was put on the market. They got an excellent price for it as it was in a very quiet desirable area, so they were both delighted about that.

It wasn't long before Jake broached the subject of a housewarming party. Jim had been expecting this and wasn't at all surprised, in fact he had been having thoughts along the same lines himself, but hadn't said anything as he knew Jake liked to instigate these things. So they began to plan it together, which caterers they would get in, they would invite all their show business friends, as well as making sure to invite those special people who had been influential in Jake's career, not forgetting those who had potential to be in the future.

They set a date for a Sunday the following month as Jim had pointed out it wasn't wise to hold it any later due to not knowing when shooting would start on the film. Jake agreed. They chose a date and started writing a list of names which soon grew to such an enormous number it had to be whittled down to a hundred guests. This would make the number more manageable in terms of fitting people in the house; the marquee on the lawn enabling Jake and Jim to socialise properly. The society caterer they chose was Delauney Caterers who specialised in providing everything required. The food was served by flunkies dressed in eighteenth-century livery, with frock coats and knee breeches; Jake felt that these would provide a suitably ostentatious flavour to the party. The canapés would consist of delicacies such as beluga caviar, smoked salmon blinis, pâté de foie gras, cocktail sausages as well as a large buffet of assorted sandwiches, salad accompaniments and delicious desserts available in the marquee, not forgetting oodles of quality champagne. There were ample tables and chairs set out for people in the marquee as well. Jake intended it would be the most talked about party of the year, anybody who's anybody would be there.

Jim received a letter from the studios that week. He turned out to be right about the film schedule, as he usually was when it came to business affairs. The commencement of filming *Dames On The Briny* would be just two weeks away.

It looked as though 1973 was going to be a momentous year for the two of them and it was great that it was being shot at Borham Wood, it was only a stone's throw from where they were living.

Their housewarming party was a tremendous success. Jake

and Jim decided that they would greet their guests in the hall as they arrived, this was in case for some reason they were not able to mingle sufficiently to talk to everyone during the party itself, at least then no one would be able to say *we never even got a chance to talk to them!*

The food was superb, and the liveried footmen provided excellent service. One footman/waiter offered Jake a canapé, he was so gorgeous, Jake thought to himself, *I could eat **you** let alone the canapé, shame you're not offering anything else love!* He took a smoked salmon blini and undressed him with his eyes, fantasising to himself, *if I wasn't a happily married woman, I'd soon have you upstairs and out of those fancy breeches young man!* Thankfully, these days Jake's sexual misdemeanour's merely consisted of these little excursions into flights of fancy, the days of him actioning any of them were over, it was too dangerous now because of who he was. There were too many people willing to take advantage of someone who was a famous celebrity, a household name, he wasn't about to lay himself open to being blackmailed or robbed, or perhaps worse. Jim kept him on the straight and narrow, giving him everything he wanted and satisfying all his sexual needs. He had so much to be grateful for he wasn't about to ruin everything for a quick bit of extracurricular sex. Homosexuality had only been legalised six years ago and there was still ignorance and hostility out there, it was never wise to be too explicit in what your predilections were and he was always careful to make sure his act was very tongue in cheek, containing harmless innuendo; he couldn't afford to offend or displease his public.

However, among his closest friends he was totally accepted for who he was, and he was thoroughly enjoying being in their company tonight. The champagne was flowing like water and he was relishing being lady of the manor in their new home. Lots of his friends commented on their beautiful house, the classy interior design and decor, and said what a wonderful party it was. The other main talking points were how he appeared to be riding on the crest of a wave, his career lurching forward from one success to another. It seemed you couldn't open a newspaper, turn on the radio or television without seeing, hearing or reading about him.

One of his friends remarked, "And soon we'll see you on the silver screen too. I wouldn't be surprised if America and Hollywood won't be clamouring to sign you up next!"

"I don't know about that, I'm just enjoying it all while it's here. I'm not naive enough to think that it always will be, I'm having a ball and making the most of it while I can darling!"

The whole evening more or less went along these lines, with friends and show-business people commenting and congratulating him on his success and wishing him well for the future. Everyone was enjoying themselves; Jake's attention was drawn to a noisy group of about six people on the other side of the room who for some reason were clustered around and bending over a tall glass-topped sideboard.

He worked his way through the guests to a secluded spot a short way away from where they were, he was curious to see what they were doing. He saw a young man from the film company cutting lines in a white powder on the glass with a bankers card, then others were leaning over a line and snorting it up their nostrils through a small tube. Jake was absolutely horrified, he had never seen this before, but he had heard about it from someone somewhere so he knew exactly what was going on. He was furious. His immediate thought was to charge over and confront them, He was about to shout at them, *how dare you bring that shit in here, get out of my house and take your filthy drugs with you,* but a small sensible voice inside his head made him hold back. *I mustn't cause a scene. If someone was to call the police to report a disturbance and they did a raid and found cocaine here, they would haul us down to the police station, it would be in all the papers, and on top of the salacious* Sunday Globe and Star *article three years ago, it could ruin my reputation, some people have long memories.*

They hadn't seen Jake, they seemed oblivious to him or anybody else, they were intent only on getting their share of cocaine. Jake looked around the room to see where Jim was. He could see him talking to some friends so he quickly made his way over to them, smiling and looking as natural as he could.

Catching hold of Jim's arm, he said, "I'm so sorry to interrupt, Jim, could I have a private word with you for a moment? Sorry to drag him away, please excuse us won't you."

"Is there something wrong Jake?"

"Yes there is Jim, we've got a problem. There are people over there taking cocaine, I want them out of our house as quickly and quietly as possible without the whole house knowing what's going on."

"The cheeky bastards. OK, leave it to me love, I'll deal with them. You just smile for the guests and carry on as if nothing has happened."

Jim went over to the group, smiling. He said quietly, "If all you guys would like to finish this up and follow me, I've got something much more interesting lined up for you in the next room!"

The guy who had been doing the cutting looked at Jim curiously, so Jim winked at him. The little runt smiled knowingly.

The glass had been cleared so he said, "Sounds interesting. Lead the way my good man."

Jim turned and walked towards his private study. He had kept it locked so that none of the guests would go in there and disturb the papers that were on the desk. He reached the door, took the keys out of his pocket and unlocked it. Holding the door open and ushering them all in, he stepped inside behind them and locked the door, putting the keys back in his pocket.

He walked over to the man he had spoken to before and punched him hard in the stomach. He keeled forward clutching his guts. As he did so, Jim put his arm up his back in a half nelson as he groaned in agony. He stood behind him and watched to see what the other two weedy looking guys might do. He didn't think either of them were the type to want to have a fist fight which he was relieved about.

"What the hell's going on?" one of them asked as one of the women started snivelling in fear.

"I'll tell you what the hell's going on, you drug-taking morons are going to leave my house right now. T police have been called, but providing you don't cause any trouble you can leave by the side door before they arrive but you'd better be quick, they'll be here before you know it."

"Let go of my arm, you stupid prick, we're going."

Jim pointed to the way out. The others began to file past him giving him filthy looks. He let go of his captive who followed them quickly out of the door, but not before he'd shouted an empty threat to Jim to *watch your fucking back*. They got into their cars and there was a screeching of tyres on the tarmac of the drive as they hurriedly left to avoid what they thought was the imminent arrival of the police.

Jim locked the back door, secured his office and went to find Jake. He found him talking to Rodney Griffiths, the manager of a video production company who had done a promotional video for them. He walked up to them, said hello to Rod, as he liked to be called and said, "I've seen to that Jake, everything's fine now."

"Thank you darling, I appreciate that. Rod was just telling me that he's interested in possibly doing some filming in the grounds here. I said that he would need to speak to you about it. I understand he's willing to pay very handsomely for the privilege!!

He gave a little chuckle. "I'll leave you boys to talk business, enjoy the party Rod."

"Thanks for that Jake, best wishes for the film."

"Thank you," Jake replied as he manoeuvred over towards the bar, he needed another glass of bubbly. He wondered how Jim had managed to get rid of the unwanted guests, but he would have to wait until later to find out. In future all their party guests would have to be vetted a little more closely.

The rest of the evening went extremely well. Jake had received several invitations from close friends to attend dinner parties, he and Jim always enjoyed dining with friends, but he made a point of saying his acceptance would be dependent on not having any work commitments. People seemed to understand and accept this. The caterers left at midnight along with the majority of guests, but the party continued well into the early hours with the last few guests, twenty or so, leaving around 3am. Among them were the actors and socialites Margo Langford and her husband Alan Drake, Arty Minkel the film producer, Ronnie Marquis, the chat show host who had earlier spoken to Jake about getting him back on his show with a line-up of other guests that would interact together wonderfully to make unforgettable television. Jake thanked him, saying that he would look forward to the invitation. Their dear friends and neighbours the Harpers and other show-business friends made up the remainder.

Jake and Jim retired to bed, their main topic of conversation being the group of drug takers. Jake asked Jim what had happened when he took them into his study. When Jim had told him how he dealt with it, Jake said, "My god Jim, that was so brave of you, weren't you scared?"

"Scared? I was fucking terrified. Luckily none of them were ready to have a go, otherwise I don't know what might have happened!"

"Oh my brave darling, thank you," Jake said, giving him a kiss. "Thank god they didn't, I'd never have forgiven myself if you'd been hurt."

"Well I'm not, so we can forget about it now, they didn't spoil the party, we didn't let them. We can pride ourselves on hosting a magnificently successful party."

"Yes, we did do rather well, didn't we? Sleep well darling, goodnight."

"You too sweetheart, I love you, goodnight."

Chapter 28

The Tuesday of the week after the party, Jake walked into his dressing room and found Ricci sitting at the dressing table with his head buried in his hands crying. He went over to him, put his hand on his shoulder and asked, "Ricci love, whatever's the matter, why are you crying?"

Ricci lifted his head up a little and, in a muffled voice between sobs, blurted out, "Toby has left me!"

"What? I don't believe it sweetie, when did this happen?"

"Last night, he told me he had met someone else. They had been seeing each other for some time and he had fallen in love with him and they wanted to live together. Oh Jake, I don't know what I'm going to do without him!" Ricci put his arms around Jake and sobbed uncontrollably into his shoulder.

"Oh you poor love," Jake sympathised, patting Ricci's back. "There now, you have a good cry."

Ricci gradually stopped crying after what seemed like an eternity to Jake. He felt awkward and didn't really know what to say for the best, he didn't want to make the situation any worse, but he felt really sorry for his friend. Ricci seemed to suddenly pull himself together, he looked at Jake in embarrassment.

"What must you think of me, Jake? I'll be alright now I've had a good cry. We must get you ready." He began to busy himself preparing the make-up.

"As long as you're sure you're alright, darling." Jake took off his coat, then went to wash his hands and face before returning to moisturise before being made up. He looked at Ricci who looked so fragile and vulnerable and his heart went out to him.

"You must come home with us tonight after the show. I won't let you go back to your flat alone."

"Oh no Jake, I couldn't possibly impose on you."

"I won't take no for an answer, sweetie, and if you're worrying what Jim will think, he'd say exactly the same. After we leave here, we can stop off at your place so you can put a few things in a bag."

"It really is good of you to do that for me."

"What are friends for, sweetie?"

Jake didn't show it in his face so as not to let on just how concerned he was for Ricci. He and Toby had been together for a long time and you heard such dreadful things that could happen when long-term relationships end. He wasn't about to leave Ricci to go home to an empty flat to brood on his own, he needed to know that he had friends who loved and cared about him. Meanwhile, he did his best to jolly him along to try to take his mind off things a bit. Thankfully, Ricci managed to hold himself in check and do his job getting Jake ready for a performance that went very well despite Jake being somewhat preoccupied with worrying about him.

After the show, when Jim found out what had happened, he wholeheartedly agreed that Ricci should come back home and stay with them. They called at Buckley Road and waited outside in the car while Ricci went in to get his personal effects. Jim and Jake talked about the situation.

"I really can't believe that Toby would do this to him," Jim said.

"I know, what a bastard he turned out to be, after everything

Ricci has done to keep him on the straight and narrow. Do you think it could have happened because Ricci has been out at night working, which left Toby to his own devices?"

"I don't know, possibly, but maybe it would have happened in any case."

"I guess we'll never know, but we'll help him as much as we can to get through this. It's certainly not going to be easy for him though, it's such a damn shame."

"Yes, it is, ssssh, he's coming out. Oh gosh look Toby's with him, and Ricci doesn't have a bag, be careful what you say, we don't want any unpleasantness."

Toby walked around the car to the driver's side and tapped on the window. Jim wound the window down. Toby looked as though he had been crying.

"Hello you guys, I'm really sorry about all this. Would you mind coming in for a few minutes? I don't want to say what I need to say to you on the street."

"Hello Toby," he and Jake said in unison. "Yes OK Toby, no problem."

Toby and Ricci turned and began to walk back inside as Jake and Jim got out of the car. Jim locked the doors and they followed them inside. Jim exchanged glances with Jake as they were walking upstairs as if to say, *I wonder what's happening?*

As they entered the flat, Toby looked downcast, and said, "I've got some humble pie to eat guys. I need to apologise for any inconvenience I may have caused you, due to my bloody stupidity. I've already apologised to Ricci and asked him if he'll have me back. Graciously he said he will, but I wouldn't have blamed him if he'd told me to sling my hook. I behaved like an immature schoolboy. Basically as it turned out, the guy I got involved with was after what he could get out of me financially, when he found out there wasn't anything, that was it, finito. I've been a complete fool and I can't begin to tell you all how sorry I am. I hope you'll forgive me."

Jim did no more than shake him by the hand and give him a great big hug.

"If Ricci has forgiven you Toby and you're going to make a fresh start, then I for one couldn't be happier. What do you say, Jake?"

Jake gave Toby a very serious look. "I agree with you Jim, but I'll tell you this Toby Anderson, if you ever hurt my friend like this again, I'll cut your bloody balls off. You could never find anyone who loves you the way he does. Now come here and give me a hug, you silly bugger!"

"I know that now Jake, I always knew it really, I must have been off me rocker!"

Ricci embraced Jake and Jim, and with tears in his eyes said, "Thank you for being true friends and being there for me. I can't tell you how grateful I am."

"You would have done the same for us I'm sure, Ricci."

"Would you stay and have a drink with us?" Toby asked.

"Some other time, it would be a pleasure, but I have to drive home and Jake's a little tired, but we'll definitely get together soon I promise."

"Yes we will," Jake agreed, "but you two have got some making up to do, so we'll leave you in peace. I'll see you tomorrow, Ricci love."

"Yes of course, darling, bless you, goodnight."

"Thank you both, I can't tell you how relieved I am that you're still my friends, goodnight!"

Jake and Jim left the house, neither of them said anything until they were in the car.

As Jim drove away he said, "That was a surprise, I never expected that, did you?"

"No I didn't, I just hope they can put it all behind them and be strong together now. Ricci and I will have a good talk tomorrow evening."

"I think Toby is suitably remorseful and regrets what he did. I'm sure they'll work through it."

"I do hope so, they were always so good together. I think it was a case of Toby being completely beguiled by a younger guy, he must have been blinded by infatuation and allowed himself to be completely taken in by him. I'm just glad the heel showed his true colours as it brought Toby to his senses."

"Well, we've done our bit love, it's up to them now."

"Yes." Jake gave an involuntary gaping yawn.

"We'll soon have you home love, you look worn out."

"I am, I'm ready for my bed, it's been a long day."

Chapter 29

Shooting of the film was going well and Jake found the whole experience quite exhilarating. He was working with actors who he very much admired and who were kindly helping him with their encouragement and helpful suggestions. The director, Arnold Wiseman, was a man who had many well-known successful films under his belt, a consummate professional who teased the best performance he could from his actors. He was firm but fair, making it clear to everyone exactly what he wanted. Jake found the whole process incredibly tiring though, he had to be on set early in the morning and into make-up and costume, often there was a lot of hanging around until you were required for a scene and sometimes filming stretched into the early evening. Because of the storyline of the film, it was necessary to shoot some scenes at sea, on board ship, this was a totally new experience for Jake and one he hadn't particularly enjoyed. He had been advised to take a sea sickness pill, however, despite that, because the sea had been quite choppy, Jake had still felt rather queasy. Luckily he hadn't got sea sick and was able to carry on shooting his scenes. The August weather was typically hot so by the time he got home he was absolutely exhausted, he was also stressed with the fact that he had only been released from his commitment to the theatre for two weeks, so his scenes would have to be shot and in the can to allow him to resume his main line of work within that period.

He needn't have worried on that score though. Arnold

Wiseman saw to it that he met Jake's deadline as there was a penalty clause involved in the contract that meant if he went over schedule it would cost him money, and seeing how it was a low-budget film, he intended keeping it that way! Jake had completed all his scenes and been released from the studio, but there was still some work going on before it would be finished. Several weeks later, Arnie Wiseman called him and asked him if he would like to come and see some of the rushes, prior to the film being released later in the year. Jake and Jim went along to the studio for a private viewing along with other members of the cast. Jake felt quite jittery about it, he didn't particularly like watching himself as he was extremely self-critical and would see flaws in his performance, things he would have done differently, but overall he was happy with the film, he knew he wouldn't be getting an Oscar for it, but such is life!

Jim was over the moon with Jake's performance and thoroughly enjoyed the film, congratulating him at every opportunity. Looking back at the two weeks, Jake was particularly pleased that he had been able to invite Ricci and Toby into the studio and onto the set as his guests to watch some scenes being filmed. It was good to see them enjoying the experience together and it was obvious that they had overcome Toby's indiscretion and moved on.

Over lunch in the studio canteen, they listened intently as Jake described some of his scenes, Ricci asking questions about Jean Scholson, an actress in the cast whom he had long admired. Before the day was over he had been able to pluck up the courage to go over to her and ask her for her autograph. He came back to Jake and Toby literally glowing with excitement and admiration that he had spoken to her.

"Ooooh she was absolutely lovely and didn't mind signing my autograph book one bit. She's even more gorgeous in real life than on the screen, I can't believe it, I've actually met Jean Scholson."

"Calm down Ric, don't go burstin a flippin blood vessel, you'll bring on one of yer migraines."

"You're a philistine Toby, you wouldn't understand. I've seen all her films, she's wonderful, you must be so proud working along such a star, Jake!"

"I am Ricci, it's a real privilege, she's one of the greats," Jake said with emphasis as he looked at Toby.

"Pardon me, I stand corrected you two, what do I know!"

Before *Dames On The Briny* was put on general release in November there was a gala preview at the Odeon Leicester Square which was a red carpet affair attended by the glitterati of the show-business world, held in the presence of Her Majesty The Queen. Jake was excited as after the showing he would stand in line with the director, producer, other cast members et al to be presented to Her Royal Highness and touch the gloved hand of the royal personage.

When the picture was put on general release, Jake's fan club secretary contacted him to let him know that the number of members had shot up, he was getting cards and letters from adoring fans from all over the world, telling him how much they loved him, asking for signed photographs. More importantly, the film seemed to have hit the right spot for the public at that particular time, it was breaking box office records and the money was rolling in. Consequently, Jim's office was receiving requests for personal appearances, being sent numerous film and theatre scripts, many of which were completely unsuitable or inappropriate and were discarded straightaway. Saturday morning's post however, produced one that absolutely shone out as being the perfect foil for Jake. Amazingly, it was going to take him trans-Atlantic to appear in the title role of a major musical production on Broadway called *Goodbye Mrs McGiver*. Jim was so excited, he couldn't wait to tell Jake about it after his performance that evening.

Jake went wild with excitement when Jim told him, giving him the script to take home to read, stating that it was a fantastic opportunity to break into the American market and make a real impact stateside in a role that appeared to be tailormade for him.

Later that evening after dinner, Jake started to read *Goodbye Mrs McGiver*, a story about an Irish chorus girl. Set in nineteenth-century New York, it tells how she gets a break in a leading role and rises to stardom in show business and marries a rich prominent businessman. Her career changes as she matures and she gets acting roles, she is politically active and finally leaves the theatre world to become a Democratic politician, who supports the downtrodden poorer workers in America. She is hugely popular and becomes a candidate for the Presidency. Jake couldn't put the script down. Jim bought him a whisky and placed it on the table beside him.

"What do you think, is it good, do you think it's right for you?"

"Good? It's amazing! It's as if it were actually written for me, it has humour, pathos, and it's a superb story." Jake took a swig of his drink and continued. "Now please let me finish reading it, love!"

"Yes, of course, carry on darling, I haven't seen you this excited since your first night at The Capital!"

Jim wasn't sure whether Jake had heard all of what he'd

said or not as his head was buried back in the script, he was completely engrossed already. When he'd finished reading it, he knew it was right for him.

"I want to do this, Jim. First thing on Monday morning, please ring the producer and let him know."

Chapter 30

After Jim had spoken on the telephone with Jerry Felmeyer, his contact in America, to tell him that Jake wanted to do the show, things began to move very quickly indeed. It was only a matter of a couple of months in which so much happened, Jim had secured a fantastic deal with the American theatre company for an incredible amount of money, they had both ended their employment at The Capital, having given sufficient notice for them to find a replacement for Jake and hire a new manager. They parted the company amicably and began preparing for their move to the States for a period of at least six months. Their notice had spanned the Christmas season, which their bosses had much appreciated.

So in mid-January they flew from Heathrow, flying into La Guardia airport. From the moment Jake and Jim arrived in New York, they loved it, it was so fascinating, bloody cold, but fascinating. They were met at the airport by a theatre representative, a Mr Harstock. He drove them to the apartment they had been privileged to be given to stay in while they were in Manhattan; the director of the theatre, Theo Sneldeim, had leased it for them at their expense, apparently it was a tax-deductible perk for visiting stars such as Jake. Avery Harstock was a very personable, pleasant young man in his late thirties and he was absolutely charming; he was thrilled to meet Jake.

He showed them around the high-rise apartment at 421 West 42nd Street which commanded a magnificent view of Manhattan taking in the Hudson River and Long Island. It was a spectacle that both of them would never forget; it was going to be a pleasure to stay here.

There was the biggest bowl of fruit on the coffee table and there was a lovely bouquet from the theatre management. They thanked Mr Harstock, who said they were to call him Avery. He said he was looking forward to dining with them that evening.

After he'd left, Jake's first comment as he stood looking at the view from the window was, "Wow Jim, it's like we're on top of the world!"

"We are Jake, we're on the 31st floor. It's fantastic, isn't it? It's like being in a dream that I never want to wake up from!"

"Imagine what it would be like to live here all the time, I'd love it!"

"I'm not so sure you would darling, but it will be great for us while we're here. Let's have a look at the bedroom."

They walked through the gorgeous apartment marvelling at the luxury of it, the ensuite bedroom was the height of opulence. Jake was impressed.

"Look at the size of that bathtub, you could get both of us in that!"

"We could certainly test that theory out sometime soon."

"Maybe once I get over my jet lag darling, I need to take a nap before we go to meet Mr Harstock at the theatre. They're picking us up with a chauffeured limousine at six thirty this evening, for a tour of the theatre, and supper afterwards with Mr Sneldheim, Mr Harstock and their wives."

"Good thinking darling, I'll need a nap myself, I suspect it might be a long evening."

When they woke up from their well-needed rest, they showered and dressed, deciding to leave the promising pleasure of sharing the bathtub until another time.

Jim poured them both a drink, and handed Jake a whisky, and remarked, "They've certainly supplied a well-stocked bar, there's something to satisfy most people's taste. We can clean our teeth just before we go, and suck a mint so that it isn't obvious that we've had a drink, we don't want to come across as two lushes."

"Good idea, I think they have been incredibly generous. This is the life, eh Jim?"

"I'll say, cheers darling, here's to a great evening and a successful run on Broadway."

"Who would have thought we'd ever be raising our glasses to that! Cheers my darling."

They kissed and stood looking out of the window at the view across the Hudson River as lights were beginning to illuminate all the buildings, the effect was magical and so romantic.

"We must get ready darling, they've requested us to wear dinner suits and bow ties, so they're obviously taking us somewhere swish and want to show us off."

Jim felt that there was a hint of nervousness in the way Jake spoke, so to put him at his ease he reminded him in a subtle way that he had nothing to be nervous about.

"That's OK darling, I want to show you off too. I love you so much, and I know we will have a superb evening. These people want to make us feel welcome and enjoy the company of a celebrated star from jolly old England, they'll just adore you sweetheart."

"Oh you smoothie you, I love you too darling. I hope the food's good, I'm feeling ravenous."

Their limousine pulled up in front of the famous and

historic Minchams theatre, a stone's throw from Pelegrino's restaurant where they would be eating later. As they stepped out of the car, Avery was there to meet them, He greeted them warmly and led them towards the entrance. Once inside the foyer, he introduced them to Theo Sneldheim and his wife, Nina, who enthusiastically shook hands with them.

Avery then introduced them to his own wife Berenice, who Jake thought looked absolutely gorgeous. She was wearing a long formal evening dress in a flattering dark peach colour.

Jake made the comment, "What a gorgeous gown you're wearing, I'm so jealous, it's better than some of mine!"

They all laughed hilariously at his remark; any awkwardness between them was immediately dissipated.

The theatre had looked small from the outside but its outward appearance belied it's interior. Inside it was a rococo dream, with deep red plush everywhere, plasterwork garlands and cherubs adorning the walls, it was like stepping back in time.

Theo explained that Minchams had been completely restored from a near derelict building some ten years ago, and whereas the decor had a period look, everything else was thoroughly up to date with all the latest technology, lighting, sound system, etc.

Jake and Jim were impressed. It was a truly beautiful theatre and Jake said that he would be privileged to perform on its stage.

Theo kindly remarked that he would be following in the footsteps of some of America's greatest actors and actresses, such as Paul Lombard, Carol Manning, Evie Ronson, to name but a few, so he was in excellent company. They spent a good three quarters of an hour looking around, before leaving to walk the short distance to Pelegrino's.

The restaurant was high end, very posh, the tables covered in bright-white table linen, the waiters in white shirts, black trousers and bow ties, with neatly folded white cloths over their arms. They were perfectly attentive, efficient, but not overly intrusive.

The ambience was relaxed and pleasant. They were escorted to a table in an alcove by the maître d', who had greeted Theo with such exuberance that it was clear he was a regular here, which bode well for the cuisine. Once they were all seated, the maître d' signalled to the wine waiter to come and take their order for drinks, and when he had gone their main waiter brought menus for them. Theo, having asked Jake and Jim what wine they would like, ordered it and a bottle of champagne as well. When the champagne had been poured, Theo stood and officially welcomed Jake and Jim and proposed a toast for a successful production and a long run for *Goodbye Mrs McGiver*. With glasses raised and smiles all round, they drank wholeheartedly to that.

The evening was delightfully pleasant and the food out of this world, everyone talked animatedly saying how excited they were to have Jake as the 'leading lady' for the production; they all felt that it couldn't fail to be a sensational hit. When the evening was over, they all said their goodbyes and Jake and Jim were waved off in their limousine which took them back to the apartment.

Rehearsals started two weeks later, after Jake had lived morning, noon and night with the script to make sure that he knew his lines perfectly, Jim had helped him by prompting and encouraging. Jake was introduced to all the cast who were absolute sweeties and made him feel so at home. The next few days were a whirlwind of trying on costumes that had been made especially for Jake from the measurements that had been sent over as soon as the contract had been signed. Jake was used to extravagant costumes, but the ones made for him for this production were in another league. Lavish wasn't the word for them, they were outrageously opulent, and he couldn't wait to wear them onstage.

Rehearsals went smoothly, apart from one incident when Moira, one of the dancers, had to be replaced after falling while on stage and breaking her arm. She was in absolute agony, but so livid, she berated herself loudly – and with the choicest of language – for being clumsy and taking herself out of the show. Everyone felt so sorry for her, poor love! Her replacement, Zena, soon allayed everyone's fears by quickly getting to grips with the well-choreographed routines and slotting in very well. When it came to the Press Night, to which members of the press, critics and dignitaries were invited, things could not have gone better, everything was flawless, a fitting testimony to everyone's hard work from the stagehands, the orchestra, the chorus, dancers to the main characters, not least Mrs McGiver played in his own inimitable way by Jake.

Chapter 31

In a run-down apartment of a tenement block in Morrisiana, the Bronx, Diego and Rosita Alvarez were having their umpteenth argument that week. Their arguments had become a way of life and would often flare up spontaneously over seemingly nothing at all. They had been married for twenty-two years, their two children Santiago and Marianna had both left home, no longer bothering to contact their parents. This evening they were shouting and raving at one another above the sound of their blaring television which was tuned to a station broadcasting a spotlight on Broadway shows. Rosita was in the kitchen preparing their meagre supper, Diego was lying on the settee half watching the programme and trying to think of some way to get up his wife's nose in retaliation for her constant nagging at him to go out and get some work to bring more money in. She managed to eke out the housekeeping to make it last until the next benefit cheque came in. She always made a point of taking a little out of it and putting it to one side for emergencies. She kept it in a Matzo tin at the back of the cupboard, along with the loaded gun that was there for their protection. This was not a good neighbourhood. Rosita wasn't exactly sure how much was in the tin, she didn't get many opportunities to count it, but there was a tidy sum, should they ever be in trouble. They had no health insurance, so it was a necessity in case either one of them needed medical treatment.

She no longer loved her husband. If you'd asked her she wouldn't have been able to explain why, she just didn't. She didn't think he loved her either, if he ever had at all. She couldn't say she hated him exactly, but she resented the way he treated her, when she did her best to feed and clothe him and pay the bills. It was all on her shoulders, he did nothing. She walked from the kitchen into the living room holding a plate with his sandwich in one hand, and a cup of tea in the other.

"Supper Diego, please sit up and eat it, you can't eat lying down."

"I can eat lying down if I want to, woman, but I will sit up."

That was one of the things she resented most, his habit of calling her woman, as though she was nothing to him, just an object of scorn.

"Phwoor, why can't you look like she does?" he said, pointing to the television screen. Now that's what I call a woman!"

Just then the presenter on the programme announced that you could see Mr Jake Hartnell-Wiggins, the famous female impersonator, in *Goodbye Mrs McGiver* at Minchams Theatre on Broadway, and to contact the box office as tickets were still available.

Diego suddenly roared with laughter. He said mockingly, "Oops, my mistake, it's a man, but even he looks better than you, ha ha, mmm, lovely sandwich."

He continued to chuckle as Rosita walked back into the kitchen to get her supper, but instead she found herself stooping down, opening the cupboard and reaching in to take out the Matzo tin. Opening the lid, she calmly lifted out the gun, walked back into the living room, put the gun against the back of Diego's head and pulled the trigger. She felt the warm splatter of his blood hit her face, and the television screen now had a blob of brain cartilage running down it. She felt numb as she went back to the kitchen. Grabbing the money from the tin, she proceeded to count the notes. Surprisingly there was nearly three hundred dollars.

She went to the bathroom to wash her face and brush her hair, then went to the bedroom to change her bloodstained dress. She returned to the kitchen to pick up the money. She put it in her purse, walked past the dreadful scene in the living room not even noticing it, and took her coat from the hall stand. Putting it on, she opened the apartment door into the dimly lit corridor, stepped out, closed it behind her without locking it. She felt liberated. If she hurried, she would just be able to catch the last performance.

When Rosita arrived at the theatre and walked in to buy her ticket, the box office clerk noticed she had a strange look on her face as though she was in a trance. Her whole demeanour was odd, all she said was, "One in the stalls." The clerk was also surprised at her general appearance, it was unusual to see such a scruffy, dishevelled-looking woman coming into the theatre. She thought that by the way she was dressed she wouldn't have been able to afford to buy a ticket because they certainly weren't cheap, but then she thought, *you can never tell with people though can you? Perhaps the poor woman had been saving up, or a friend had bought it for her.*

Chapter 32

Goodbye Mrs McGiver had taken Broadway by storm, with rave reviews for the opening night's performance that were beyond what anyone could have hoped for. Jake was a smash hit, the critics, the public, and it seemed most of America loved him. The only adverse reaction came from a few religious fanatics, who said he was a perverse travesty, but no one it seemed was taking any notice of them. The show was a triumph and it was set to run indefinitely.

Jake was scheduled to stay with the show for six months, with his understudy, an American female impersonator called Rod Farrell aka Minti Julep, stepping in from time to time in order to give him a well-earned rest. This gave him and Jim a chance to do some sightseeing in New York, which included going to the top of the Empire State building.

When they were atop of the skyscraper on the viewing platform, Jake said, "Isn't it wonderful Jim, this reminds me of that film which Deborah Kerr and Cary Grant starred in. I can't remember the name of it."

"No, I can't remember the title either, but you're not Deborah Kerr and I'm certainly no Cary Grant!"

"Oh you are to me love, you're Cary Grant, Tyrone Power and Errol Flynn all rolled into one, but especially Errol Flynn!"

"Thank you darling, I'll try to remember that tonight when we're in bed!"

"Oh good, that should be fun then, I can't wait!"

During their time in America, they also enjoyed an

unforgettable trip to Niagara Falls and a weekend in Las Vegas which they both found amazing.

Midway in his fifth month at the theatre, Jake returned to the show playing his role with renewed vigour after a well-earned break. During a Saturday night performance while Jake was on stage doing the spectacular 'Parade In Central Park' number, a loud gunshot rang out and all pandemonium broke loose. The woman who had fired the shot had the gun knocked out of her hand by a man sitting directly behind her, she was then overpowered and wrestled to the floor by the people next to her in the same row and held there until the police arrived. The incident put most of the audience into a blind panic as they rushed to escape from the theatre.

The scene on stage was a similar one. Most of the cast who were onstage at the time had fled, the curtains had been closed to hide and protect the small group that were clustered, knelt down on the floor, attending to poor Jake who had been shot.

When the bullet hit him, the searing pain in his right arm had caused him to pass out, he had sunk to the boards as if he was dead. His fellow actors all thought he had been fatally shot, until Jake came round then they discovered that he had just been wounded in the arm. There was blood everywhere; he was as white as a sheet and weakly asking for Jim. The paramedics arrived and took him to the Santa Royale hospital where he was treated for his gunshot wound. Luckily the bullet had passed straight through his arm and hadn't done any really serious damage. The police later found the slug embedded in a piece of scenery.

Amazingly, no one else had been harmed. Jim was informed of what had happened, he immediately left the apartment, grabbed a cab and went directly to the hospital. In a private room, at Jake's bedside, he found him looking very pale and obviously suffering from shock, but Jake smiled up at him and said, "Oh Jim darling, I'm so pleased to see you, I thought I was a gonner!"

Jim sat on the chair next to Jake's bed. He took hold of his hand and said with consternation, "My poor darling, how are you feeling? What a dreadful thing to have happened, what have the doctors said?"

"They tell me that the bullet went straight through my upper arm, miraculously only causing a flesh wound. They say they will keep me in here for observation for a couple of days, then I can go home and continue to rest. I don't know why anyone would want to shoot me, I didn't think my performance was that bad!" He smiled weakly.

Jim replied, "This is no time for jokes, Jake, I could have lost you. Whatever possessed the person to do such a thing?"

"It was a woman apparently, I overheard one of the cast telling someone. She was probably jealous of the gorgeous frock."

Jim gently tutted at him and said, "Tssk, Jake you are funny, I love you so much, but I know you're putting a brave face on things. When you leave hospital, I'll discuss with the theatre about you finishing with the show and returning home."

"I'd love that Jim, I'm tired now, I need to sleep."

"You sleep my love, I'll be here when you wake up." Jim leaned forward, kissed Jake on the forehead, then sat back and let him rest.

While Jake slept, Jim had a word with the doctor, who was a young, good-looking Puerto Rican guy. He just wanted to check out what the real situation was. Jim asked him how he felt Jake would recover, he told him that his thoughts were for Jake to pull out of the show and go back to England. The doctor was in agreement with that, adding that physically Jake would mend quickly, but he felt it wise to be aware there could be some psychological trauma involved. The mind would take longer to heal than the body and a shooting was not an everyday occurrence to be easily overcome.

Later, the nurse told Jim that Avery Harstock had rang to find out how Jake was and asked if he would be able to receive visitors tomorrow. She had told him that it would be fine for him to have visitors tomorrow. Jim thanked her and sat by Jake's bed and waited for him to wake.

The next morning, when Jim walked into Jake's room it was absolutely filled with flowers and fruit. Avery and Berenice had sent a bouquet as well as an enormous basket of fruit, so had Theo and Nina, members of the chorus and orchestra had sent flowers and cards too, as well as Rod Farrell who would be stepping in for Jake until he was well again. Jake looked a lot brighter due to a good night's sleep. He beamed when Jim appeared. They kissed, and Jim told him that everyone had sent their love and wished him well, he had telephoned Ricci, Toby and Lorenzo, Ted, Mary and Howard, Pauline and Ned, he had been on the telephone most of the evening.

Before leaving to visit Jake, Jim had watched the different network coverage on TV that morning, it was the big headlining lead story of the day. One newspaper headline read:

Female Impersonator Shot On Stage By Crazed Gun Woman.

Jim bought a copy on his way in, but he wasn't going to let Jake see it, at least not until he was completely well.

The later editions of the newspaper had printed a lot of

background information on the woman who had shot Jake. The police had released information that earlier that evening they were called to a tenement block in Morrisania in the Bronx after someone had called 911 to report the noise of a gunshot in one of the apartments. On attending, they were appalled at the gruesome scene and the discovery of the body of a Hispanic male aged around fifty-five, who had been shot at point blank range in the back of the head. On investigating further, they ascertained from a search of the apartment that the man's name was Diego Alvarez and his wife's name was Rosita. His wife was missing and none of her relatives knew her whereabouts, she had not been in touch with any of them. The neighbour who had contacted them said she had heard them having an argument, and later she had heard a gunshot. The police then assumed that this was a domestic, that Rosita Alvarez had shot her husband after an argument and fled the murder scene. They had put out bulletins for her to be cautiously apprehended, were she to be sighted.

When police arrived at the theatre they arrested the woman. When they asked her name, she told them it was Rosita Alvarez. This meant they were able to link her to the earlier shooting of her husband, and this shooting of a Broadway star on stage, but they couldn't understand why she had shot Jake. It was only during a police interview later, that she explained.

"I shot him because my husband had said he fancied her, why couldn't I look like she did? When he found out it was a man dressed up as a woman, he laughed at me and said, even a man looked better than me." Rosita lowered her head into her arms on the desk in front of her and gently sobbed. The lieutenant, who had interviewed her, felt strangely sorry for her, as she was from an underprivileged background and obviously had mental health issues. She had also been the victim of marital abuse; she had been examined by a female doctor and she was covered in bruises.

He obviously didn't condone what she had done, but he felt she was more to be pitied and helped than sent to prison or the electric chair. He hoped that a decent defence lawyer would be able to save her from the electric chair and get her a secure hospital sentence on the grounds of diminished responsibility. If that did happen, at least she would be fairly well looked after rather than go to prison. Strange to say, she would probably have a better life …

At La Guardia Airport in the VIP lounge they sadly said their goodbyes to Avery and Berenice who had become such good friends, but they had promised they would visit Jake and Jim in England and stay with them later in the year. Berenice hugged and kissed both of them and wasn't able to hold back her tears; she was going to miss them dreadfully. Avery gave them both a handshake and hug, wishing them a safe journey home.

"Promise you'll ring and let us know that you've arrived home safe and sound?"

"We will," Jake and Jim said in unison.

They walked through the departure gate, turned and waved to them both, and boarded the plane.

Midway into their flight as they were sipping their in-flight champagne, Jim suddenly turned to Jake and said, "What do you think of this idea darling? When we get home, we could start looking for a suitable place to buy in the city centre that we can turn into your own cabaret/supper club. We could make it a really swish place where everyone would want to come to see you, a place that anyone who's anybody would want to be seen in. We'll look for a place in the city that's up for leasing, we can fit it out with a cabaret stage, I can hire the staff and run it, as well as continuing to manage your career. That way it'll be our very own venture, we cut out all the middlemen, it will also free you up to be more available for other opportunities. You'll be working for yourself, be able to pick and choose what you want to do, when you aren't being showcased in your own exclusive club!"

"Oh Jim darling, what a wonderful idea! What would we call it?"

"Why, Rusty's Place of course!"

"Did you just think of that name?"

"Yes, good isn't it?"

"Good, the whole idea is inspired darling, yes, we'll do it. Let's drink to that, cheers!"

"Cheers my love, here's to Rusty's Place."

Chapter 33

The flight from La Guardia airport, New York, was an uneventful one, apart from a little turbulence midway that had unusually disquieted Jake. Normally he wouldn't have batted an eyelid, but his recent experience had rattled him.

Jim warned Jake on the plane that the recent events were big news at home, because he was famous, with almost pop-star status, the incident would have been reported worldwide, therefore attracting strong media attention. There would undoubtedly be a large press contingent waiting for them when they got off the plane, he wanted to mentally prepare him for it. So before disembarking, Jake donned a pair of sunglasses to alleviate the glare of the camera flashes. They both decided that the best way to deal with the press was to smile and make one quick statement that hopefully would appease them, giving them time to make a hasty retreat.

Their American trip had been both successful and traumatic.

When their plane touched down at Heathrow airport, they were met by a bombardment of press reporters, photographers and TV cameras, all wanting to get a good shot of Jake with his arm in a sling, due to his shoulder being strapped up. Some of them wanting to know how he was feeling after being shot on stage by a deranged woman who had tried to kill him. When pressed by a BBC correspondent for a statement, and asked "How are you, and what would you like to say to your fans, Mr Hartnell-Wiggins?" Jake smiled at the camera, waved at the crowd of fans who had come to see him, and replied ironically, "I'm fine, she was a lousy shot. Tell them I'm so happy to be back home in England and I'll be having a well-earned period of rest and recuperation."

They forcefully jostled with the media crews to make their way through the mêlée on the tarmac and get to their waiting closed-in buggy that would take them to the VIP lounge to undergo customs security checks. Once that formality was over with, they were escorted through a private walkway to their waiting limousine at the entrance.

This would take them to the peaceful sanctuary of their Buckinghamshire home. Once in the car, Jim told Jake to sit back and relax, they would be home soon, the journey only takes about an hour from here. Jake breathed a sigh of relief, took off his glasses, leaned back into the comfort of the soft padded leather seat, and closed his eyes. The car journey gave Jim time to gather his thoughts and run some ideas through his head. Jake had fallen asleep beside him which Jim was thankful for, he didn't see the small crowd of reporters milling around outside the gates to their drive that led through the few acres that surrounded their secluded home 'Buck House', the name Jake had called it in deference to the Queen's residence, Buckingham Palace, because he said there was a queen living here too.

Jim looked at Jake, reaching out and gently squeezing his hand. He was concerned about him, as he knew the shooting had affected him badly, which was hardly surprising.

Outwardly, most of the time he seemed OK but he wasn't sleeping well and had been prescribed some tablets for anxiety by the doctor, on discharge from the hospital. Hopefully when he reached home, and settled into a period of normality, he would begin to feel a lot better.

When the press saw the car arrive and slow down to wait for the automatic gates to open, they ran towards the limousine and frantically took photographs through the windows, until their driver was able to proceed through the gates and up the drive to their house. Jim thought the house was such a welcome sight in the sunshine of the June day, he was glad to be back.

"We're home darling," Jim said, touching him on the shoulder to wake him up.

"Oh are we? That was quick, I must have dozed off."

"You've been sound asleep since we left the airport love, it must be a combination of jet lag and your medication."

They got out of the car and went towards the house. Pru Cossins, their housekeeper, stood in the open doorway to greet them. She was a young attractive woman in her early forties, slim and vivacious with long curly ginger hair. She had answered the advertisement that the boys had placed in the situations vacant section of the magazine, *The Lady*, before they set off on their American trip.

Live-in Housekeeper required. A theatrical couple located in Buckinghamshire require a housekeeper/cook for large manor house. Accommodation consisting of a one-bedroom flat provided. Must have previous experience, references required.

Out of the seven applicants that had applied, she shone out as the obvious candidate for the job. She had come with impeccable references; her dynamic personality, skills and confidence were exactly what Jim and Jake required.

"It's so lovely to see you both, how was your flight?" Pru asked.

Jake smiled at her, and replied, "Not bad at all, we hit some turbulence halfway across, but we survived it."

"You survived a lot more than that I'm very glad to say. I couldn't believe it when I heard about the shooting on the news. Anyway, we won't talk about that, I've made you both a lovely lunch." Looking at Jim she said 'hello', he kissed her on the cheek and they all went into the house, leaving Dennis the chauffeur to bring in the luggage. Pru told them they had a mountain of post and there were a lot of telephone messages too, she had put them all in the office.

Jim and Jake thanked Pru and said that they would have a rest, freshen up and change before they came down to eat in about an hour. When they came down, Pru had just finished laying the table. She brought out the lunch of a salmon salad with new potatoes and French beans, with fresh sourdough bread, and a chilled elderflower pressé to drink.

When she had finished she said, "I hope you enjoy your lunch."

They said thank you and she left them to eat. They didn't realise how hungry they were. The food was absolutely delicious. The house looked immaculate, thanks to Pru's supervision of the cleaners employed from the local village. They had certainly made the right decision in hiring her, she was a treasure.

They finished their lunch and Jake said, "I suppose we should make a start on the post and see what messages we've had."

"Yeah, I'll start opening the letters, if you'll read the messages."

"Fine, I'll take the message book into the lounge, it's more comfortable in there. You could bring the post through as well, rather than stay in the office on your own."

"Yes I will love, because if there's anything really important I can share it with you straight away."

They both made their way to the office. When they saw the amount of post, Jake said, "I think it's going to take us some time to go through all this love. Ooh, guess who the flowers are from? Dear Monty Sharman, what a darling."

"You're telling me, there are a couple of telegrams here that we should look at first, you grab the message book, I'll bring the mail sack."

Walking back to the lounge, they sat next to one another on the large settee and Jim read out the telegrams. One was from Arnold Wiseman, the film director expressing regret over the shooting incident and wishing him well for the future. The other was from Ian Laithwaite, the artistic director at the theatre where Jim and Jake had worked just prior to their American trip. He said more or less the same but added that there was always an opening for Jake at The Capital.

"That's so kind of them, how sweet of Ian to say that."

Jake opened the message book and saw that Ricci had rung and spoken to Pru to say how sorry he was that his spectacular run on Broadway had been marred by such a dreadful incident. "We're just so grateful that you are OK Must meet up soon, if you need anything you know where we are. All our love Ricci and Toby." He read it out to Jim and he said, "You should ring him Jake, I expect they've been really worried about you love."

"Of course darling. Yes, I'll ring them later when we've sorted this lot out, it looks as though the rest of these are all get well messages, people really are so kind."

"Yes, they are love," Jim replied with a distasteful look on his face, as he screwed up a letter and threw it in the wastepaper bin. "But there are some really unsavoury characters around too."

"What was that then?"

"Some sad obnoxious moron choosing to write vile homophobic obscenities to us. You don't need to see it darling."

"No I don't, I've had hate mail before, as long as it isn't threatening. If it is, we should show it to the police."

"No, that isn't necessary, it's just a load of disgusting filth, not worth bothering about. Shall we have a nice cup of coffee? I'll go and make us one."

"Oh what a lovely idea, yes please, I'll give Ricci a ring."

As Jake dialled the number of the telephone at Buckley Road, he pictured the house. He would need to let it ring for a while to give Ricci time to get down the stairs. It seemed an interminable time before a voice Jake didn't recognise answered the phone.

"Hello."

"Hello, could I speak to Ricci please?"

"Hold on I'll give her a shout. R I c c yyyyy! I think she's in, yes, she's coming down, it's the phone for you love."

"Thanks, Tony, hello?"

"Hello Ricci, it's …"

"Jake, oh my sweetie, how are you? We've been worried sick, but we didn't like to keep ringing in case you were resting."

"I'm fine, honestly, still recovering from the awful shock you know, but I'm getting better. Look, why don't you and Toby come down and spend the weekend with us? It would be lovely to see you both, your company will do me good."

"Well we'd absolutely love to of course, but only if you're up to receiving visitors."

"Of course, I'm not a complete invalid darling. I'm just

having to manage with my arm in a sling, which is an irritating inconvenience really. Other than that I'm alright."

"And how's Jim, is he OK?"

"Jim, yes he's fine, he's just bringing our coffee in if you'd like to say hello."

"Yes I would please sweetie."

"I'll just pass you over, here you are … it's Ricci love."

"Hi Ricci, how are you?"

"I'm good thanks Jim, it's wonderful to talk to you both, we've been so worried. It was a dreadful thing to have happened. Jake has just kindly invited us down for the weekend, but I'm concerned it might be a bit too much for him, what do you think Jim?"

"Oh has he, yes, well, it will be lovely to see you both, we've got a bit of catching up to do. If you're aiming to get here for lunch on Saturday, I can send Dennis to pick you up, you don't want to be messing about with trains and taxis. Shall we say ten thirty? We'll have lunch about twelve thirty."

"Thank you, that will be wonderful Jim. My god, I'll feel like royalty, that'll get the neighbours' curtains twitching, seeing a chauffeured limousine in the street!"

"Good, just don't wear your diamond tiara. We'll see you both on Saturday then."

"Looking forward to it, see you soon, sweetie, bye."

"Bye Ricci."

"That was nice of you to invite Ricci and Toby for the weekend, love."

"Well, I thought it would be good relaxing company for us both, most of our other friends would probably have made other arrangements or be entertaining themselves. I'd better let Pru know we have guests coming for the weekend so that she can cater accordingly."

"Yes, we can tell Pru later, let's have coffee."

While they were relaxing over coffee, Jim broached the subject of Rusty's Place again, to see if Jake was still as enthusiastic about the idea of opening their own club as he was when Jim first mentioned it on the plane journey home. He didn't want to push him too hard, but he didn't want to procrastinate about it either because it would be a fairly long-term project.

"Of course I want us to go ahead with it, darling. If you're worried about my health, please don't, it's a bit like falling off a horse, the best way to get over it is to get straight back in the saddle again. In my case, that means putting a frock on and getting out there in front of an audience. I'll be fine."

"My brave darling, I love you so much."

"I really want to talk to Ricki about it this weekend/ I'm hoping she will be my dresser again. I've no idea what she's doing at the moment. The last I heard, she was doing her own drag act at the Majik Mushroom in Putney."

"That would be good for you if she could. Let's just hope when we're all set up and ready to roll, she'll be available, but I would think we're talking about a year down the road before then. I will contact some commercial estate agents to see if they have anything suitable to lease on their books. Once we find somewhere we can then set about designing the layout and fitting it out to our requirements. I can't wait."

"It will be fantastic. I've got so many ideas in my head. The wine waiters could be bare-chested hunks with false white collars, black bow ties and skimpy black shorts, leaving nothing to the imagination, a take on the bunny girls at the Playboy Club."

"That's a brilliant idea love, it would certainly bring the ladies in."

"Yes and our gay brothers and sisters, which I welcome, but at the same time, I don't want people to think it's a gay club, we want to appeal to a broad social spectrum, especially the rich and famous. We've certainly got plenty of show-business friends that will gladly support us."

Jim continued opening the post. Opening a large heavy envelope, he began to read the accompanying letter, then laughing out loud, he said to Jake, "Hey, there's a script here from a film director who wants to make a gay spoof version of *Some Like It Hot* with you in the lead, what do you think?"

"Oh great, I'll do it, that should be the end of a beautiful career," Jake replied chuckling.

"Well you never know darling, perhaps he's a visionary ahead of his time."

"With visions like that Jim, I'm surprised he makes a living. What would you like me to tell Pru to do for lunch on Saturday, Jim?"

"Mmm, I don't know, how about macaroni cheese, a mixed salad and crusty bread?"

"Sounds good to me, I'll go and let her know."

Chapter 34

Jake and Jim saw the limousine pull up outside so they went to the front door and opened it as Ricci and Toby got out of the car.

"Darling, how wonderful to see you, it's been much too long. You're looking well considering what you've been through, you poor love."

Jake embraced and kissed Ricci on both cheeks, agreeing with Ricci's comment.

"It's lovely to see you too Ricci, you're right, it has been too long, but we'll catch up on everything this weekend."

"Hello Jake, great to see ya cobber. That's certainly the way to travel, what a motor. You look well considering your arms in a sling, hope it's not the wanking arm!"

Ricci cut Toby a withering look, and exclaimed, "Toby, behave yourself, you uncouth lout!"

"It's alright Ricci," Jake said smiling, "I'm well used to Toby's graphic vernacular. Hello Toby, you enjoyed the journey then?"

Toby leaned forward and kissed Jake's cheeks, being especially careful not to hurt his arm.

Jake stage whispered so that everyone could hear, "I'm ambidextrous by the way."

Chuckling, Toby replied, "I always knew you had special qualities. Yeah it was so smooth and comfortable. Wow, some place you've got here, you two, a bit different from our place, eh!"

Ricci frowned and commented, "Yes it is, but we'll make the most of it while we can."

Jake didn't really understand the remark. He thought perhaps Ricci was having a dig at Toby, but he was to find out later what he meant.

"Come on in, we'll show you around before we have lunch."

Jim led the way in, Toby followed him and Jake put his good arm around Ricci's shoulders as they walked in and said, "It's so good to see you Ricci, I've really missed you darling. You must tell me all your news and bring me up to date. You're looking really well."

The tour of the house brought out mixed feelings for Jake, he wanted to show them the place but he didn't want them to feel that he was showing off or in any way trying to diminish his two friends or make them envious. They were shown their room, which was the largest and prettiest of the guest rooms on the front of the house; it looked out over the landscaped garden, along the drive to the trees beyond.

"Oh Jake darling, this is such a lovely room, just look at that view. Thank you both so much for inviting us."

They had both seemed genuinely interested in seeing everything around the house, and their comments were full of admiration. The feeling Jake got was that they were pleased he and Jim had achieved so much for all their hard work.

"We'll leave you both to settle in and unpack. Lunch should be in about half an hour."

"Thank you," Toby and Ricci both said.

Toby continued with, "We'll see you later."

When Jake and Jim went back downstairs, Pru was finishing laying the table for lunch. There was a delicious smell of melted cheese wafting from the kitchen.

Ricci and Toby joined them about fifteen minutes later. Ricci, immaculate as ever, looked lovely in a pair of oatmeal-coloured slacks with an open-necked silk shirt, patterned in brown shades with hints of orange and yellow, which he wore over his belt.

"You look lovely Ricci, what gorgeous colours. Come and sit down darling, we've a lot of catching up to do. Lunch won't be long. You boys can sit together on the other settee."

"Thanks Jake, we certainly have, haven't we? I want to hear all about the good parts of your tour, you can show me all your photographs and press cuttings later. It is so lovely to see you."

They chatted together and in no time at all Pru came in with the salad and bread and said that lunch was ready to be served. So Jim got up and said that they should take their places at the dining table. Pru came back into the room carrying the largest dish of macaroni cheese that Ricci had ever seen.

"Oohh that looks beautiful, and it smells divine."

"I hope you're both hungry, there's plenty of it."

"I could eat a scabby horse and come back for its tail," Toby said in his broad Aussie brogue.

"Oh I'm so pleased," Jake replied, "because it's scabby horse and salad," which made them all laugh.

Jake saw Pru look a little dismayed, so he said, "Thank you Pru, it's absolutely lovely, ignore our schoolboy humour, we don't mean any offence."

Pru didn't say anything as she went back to the kitchen, and it was obvious that she didn't find the remarks funny in the slightest.

"Oh dear, I think I've upset Pru. Jim, you wouldn't like

to have a quick word with her after lunch and smooth things over, would you darling? I'd hate to lose her, she's a treasure."

"Yes of course love, no problem."

Ricci glowered at Toby and commented, "Of course if a certain Australian gentleman would think about what he was going to say before opening his big antipodean mouth, it wouldn't have happened!"

"Oh pardon me I'm sure, It's just my turn of phrase."

Jake jumped in quickly as he didn't want anyone making a big deal over it and spoiling lunch. Passing the bowl of salad to Ricci, he said, "Well let's just eat shall we, enjoy our food, and we'll say no more about it. C'mon help yourselves."

Thankfully, Ricci and Toby settled down and tucked into the food; everyone thoroughly enjoyed the meal, Jim kept the conversation light-hearted and there was some jovial banter between him and Toby. Despite this, Jake had noticed that Ricci didn't seem his usual self, and felt that under the surface, there was something amiss. He made a mental note to get him on his own at some point and find out what was troubling him.

Chapter 35

Jim had done a brilliant job of smoothing things over with Pru. He reported back to Jake that she was fine about the whole silly incident. She had said it was the shock of hearing Jake say, *it's scabby horse and salad,* as she hadn't heard the remark Toby had said at all, which put the whole thing out of context. Jake was relieved and would make it up to her with a little gift. He knew she liked nice perfume, so he would get her some.

Jake took the opportunity of suggesting that they all go for a walk to help them digest lunch. Everyone thought it was a super idea.

"I'd love to see the garden and grounds darling," Ricci enthused.

As they walked through the house and out into the back garden, Jake said proudly, "I'll take you through the rose garden first, they are spectacular at this time of year, not just for their colour, but their beautiful, sweet fragrance too."

Jim said, "The garden has been such an important part of Jake's recovery since we came back from America, he has found it so peaceful and therapeutic, he has spent hours out here enjoying it."

"It's a real credit to you Jake, you must have green fingers," Ricci said admiringly. "They're so gorgeous."

Jake thought this would be an ideal opportunity to get Ricci to himself and find out if his suspicions were correct, if there was something troubling him or not, so he said, "Jim, why don't you take Toby to see your shed and greenhouse, while I give Ricci a tour of the flower beds?"

Jim immediately cottoned on to what Jake was trying to do. He had seen that Ricci seemed quite subdued and not his usual self, he hoped that there was nothing wrong between him and Toby.

"Yes, love, that's a splendid idea. C'mon Toby, let me show you my handiwork, Jake and Ricci can be alone to catch up."

"OK cobber, lead on, have ya got a secret watering hole in ya shed then?"

Jim thought it was funny that Toby had guessed his little secret; he did keep a nice bottle of his favourite single malt whisky and two glass tumblers hidden behind a shelf. It was handy for when he wanted time on his own to think and relax and fancied a drink. He loved Jake to death, but there were times when he needed to be on his own. The shed wasn't anything out of the ordinary, but with his basic knowledge of carpentry, Jim had fitted it out really well with shelves and cupboards to store his bloke paraphernalia, it suited his own needs. There were a couple of small comfortable chairs and a table and even a transistor radio; sometimes it was nice to get out of the house and into the fresh air for a change of scene.

When Toby saw it he said, "Nice little place you've got here mate." He sat himself down in the chair and enquired cheekily, "Any liquid refreshment going?"

"I don't have any beer I'm afraid, but I do have a rather special single malt whisky, will that do?"

"Sure will mate," Toby replied enthusiastically, rubbing his hands together.

Jim reached behind the shelf and pulled out his bottle of Laphroaig. It was his favourite tipple with its beautiful silky smoky taste. He poured two fingers of the liquid in each glass and said as an instruction, "This is really special stuff, Toby, it deserves to be treated with respect, and savoured, not just knocked back in one gulp." He held out the glass for Toby, "Here you are, try that my friend."

"OK, I'll treat it gently, it certainly smells good," Toby said, sniffing the lovely amber liquid. "Cheers mate."

While Jim and Toby were savouring the delights of the connoisseur whisky, Jake had steered Ricci to a bench near the rose bed to have a sit down.

"OK, Ricci love, c'mon tell me what's bothering you, I know something's the matter."

"Is it that obvious darling? I've been trying to put on a brave face as I didn't want to burden you with my troubles, you've had enough of your own lately."

"You won't be burdening me, a problem shared is a problem halved, as they say, now tell me."

"We've got to get out of the flat and find somewhere else to live, Lorenzo's selling the place and moving back to Sicily, I don't know where we're going to go."

"I'm so sorry to hear that darling, I know you love it there. How long have you known about this?"

"He told us just last week, when I went to pay our rent."

"Do you know if he's put it on the market yet?"

"I'm not sure, but he definitely said he was going to."

"I think I just might have the very solution to your problem, Ricci, but I will have to speak to Jim about it before I can tell you what it is. Let's go and find them, shall we?"

As they walked off to find the boys, Ricci was quite bewildered and asked him, "What is it Jake, how can you possibly have an answer, just like that?"

"Aagh, you just wait and see, this can be sorted out very simply indeed."

Chapter 36

"Oh so that's what you get up to as soon as our backs are turned? Secret imbibing, eh!"

Jim and Toby hadn't seen Jake and Ricci coming and were slightly startled by Jake's loud challenge.

"Good god Jake, creeping up like that I nearly spilled my liquid gold."

"You might need another one of those when I tell you what I've got on my mind." Looking at Ricci, Jake said, "You and Toby stay here for a few moments if you don't mind, I need to have a word with Jim."

Jim quietly protested, as he thought Jake was going to tell him off. "We were only having a quiet little tipple, Jake."

"That's OK, I don't care about that silly, I just need to talk to you about something important, in private."

Jim was wondering what on earth was so important that it warranted Jake dragging him away from their friends. "Oh, OK, please excuse us for a while guys."

When they had gone out of earshot of Ricci and Toby, Jim asked, "What is it Jake?"

"I've found out what it is that's been troubling Ricci. They're having to get out of the house at Buckley Road, because Lorenzo's selling the property and going back to Sicily. I thought it would be nice to go and see Lorenzo and ask him not to put it on the market, but to let us buy it. That way Ricci and Toby and the other tenants would still have a roof over their heads, and we would acquire a good house that would bring us in a little income, what do you think?"

Jim looked really taken aback. "I know you mean well, darling, and like you, I'd do anything for Ricci and Toby, but it needs to be thought through properly Jake. We don't know how much Lorenzo would want for the place, and besides, we are about to embark on looking for premises to start our new club."

"I agree, we do need to go into this sensibly, but I take it you're not completely against the idea then?"

"No I'm not, I do love you, you've got a heart of gold." He pulled Jake to him and planted a great big kiss on his lips, then he let him go and pulled back. "Have you told Ricci about your idea yet?"

"No, all I said was that I thought I had the solution to their problem."

"Well, we can't leave them in suspense now, I'll bet the poor buggers are wondering what the hell we have in mind. We'll have to tell them what we want to do so as not to get their hopes up, in case it doesn't happen. Then we'll have to go and see Lorenzo and speak with him as soon as possible."

"Let's go back now Jim, you can tell them what it is we'd like to do. I think they'll be over the moon."

Jim and Jake walked the short distance back to the shed where Ricci and Toby were waiting. They both looked questioningly at them, curious to know what they might have been discussing, as Ricci had told Toby he had confided in Jake.

Jim smiled and said, "Here we are guys, sorry about that, let's go back to the house, have a nice cup of tea and we'll tell you what's on our minds."

"The suspense is killing us, mate, what's going on?" Toby

asked.

"Yes, thanks Jim, a cup of tea will be lovely," Ricci said, trying to calm Toby's impatience. "We'll do whatever you say, it's not long to wait."

When they reached the house, Jake went to make a pot of tea and left the three of them talking in the lounge. Jim started to explain that Jake had thought of a great idea which he had told him about.

"Jake and I are thinking of asking Lorenzo to sell us the house in Buckley Road, so that you guys and the other tenants in the house can continue living there. It all depends whether the price is right, he might want too much for it. What do you guys think?"

Jake walked into the lounge with a tray of tea and biscuits and was a bit unsure of the situation as there was a deathly silence and Ricci and Toby's faces looked as though they were in a state of shock.

"I see Jim's told you about my idea, now all you have to do is tell us if you like it or not."

Ricci was the first to speak. "Darling, we're absolutely gobsmacked that you'd both consider making such a wonderful gesture in order to help us out, but we couldn't possibly let you do that, it would be asking far too much."

Jim explained, "But you haven't asked us Ricci, we're offering. Anyway, it's not entirely altruistic on our part, we would think of it as an investment, not just in the property, but also in you, our friends. You're not aware of our future plans, because we haven't told you about them yet, but we're looking into opening our own club in the West End and Jake was hoping that you would be his dresser there. So you see we're not just wanting to do this for you two, it's for us as well."

Ricci started to cry and Toby put his arm around him as he said, "You two are amazing, I don't know what to say, other than thank you. You guys are the best friends ever, not everyone would do something as kind as that. Don't cry love, everything's going to be alright now."

"Good, there's no time like the present," Jim said. "I'll give Lorenzo a ring right away, and say that we would like to call round and see him. I won't tell him what it's about, we can surprise him when we see him."

Jake felt he should impress upon Jim, the need for urgency. "Make it as soon as possible Jim, we don't want to miss the opportunity to make our bid before he puts the place on the market."

"Yes of course, Jake." He had already dialled the number, and it was answered very quickly.

"Ello."

"Hello Lorenzo, this is Jim Hartnell, Jake and I were wondering if we might call round and see you this evening, if you're not doing anything?"

"Oh, whata da surprise, that woulda be very nice, yes, whata tima you like?"

"Would, say, around eight o'clock suit you?"

"Yes thata willa be fine, I seea you then."

Jake looked at Jim and said admiringly, "My word, you don't let the grass grow under your feet do you love!"

"There's no point hanging about and losing an opportunity. Have you guys got your head around the fact that we might be your next landlords yet?"

Ricci got up from where he was sitting, ran over to Jake and kissed him on both cheeks, moved over to Jim and did the same to him, as he said, "Thank you both of you, it will be wonderful."

"Well we haven't clinched a deal yet, but I have a good feeling about it. Let's have a drink, eh?"

"I'll ask Pru to do supper for six thirty, if that's alright," Jake said, looking at Ricci and Toby. "We can have it together, then Jim and I can shoot over to Kilburn to see Lorenzo. I'm sure you'll be able to amuse yourselves while we're gone."

"That's great, yes I'm sure there will be something good on TV," Toby said, tongue in cheek and giving Jake a wink.

Chapter 37

Jake found the drive to Buckley Road had been very pleasant, it had stirred all kinds of memories of the area where he used to live. He had driven because Jim had had a drink at suppertime. He parked in the only space available, which was a few doors away. As he was locking the car, a man came past and, recognising him, asked for his autograph. He went on to say, "I have been a fan of yours for a long time. Could you sign it to Derek, please? You are looking very well, I was so sorry about what happened to you in America."

Jake finished writing in the autograph book, and said, "Thank you, you're very kind."

The man shook him by the hand, looking very pleased with himself for being in the right place at the right time. He and Jim walked towards Lorenzo's house, as the man continued in the opposite direction.

"Good god Jim," Jake said chuckling, "I don't believe it, he had a real autograph book, it's so much better than trying to write on some of the things I've been asked – a handkerchief, a shirt cuff, envelopes, cigarette packs and much worse. I turned over a page and saw the previous autograph he had acquired was Larry Grayson's, so I couldn't be in better company could I!"

They both laughed as Jim pressed the doorbell to Lorenzo's flat. They had previously agreed to let Jim broach the subject of buying the house. The door opened and Lorenzo very excitedly invited them in.

"Hello my friends, pleasa to come in, it isa so gooda to see you."

Once inside the door, Lorenzo embraced Jake and hugged him and did the same to Jim.

"Go ona through, you know da way Jake, it isa wonderful to av sucha famous guests, I ama onoured."

Lorenzo stepped aside and beckoned them to enter the open door to his flat. Lorenzo began fussing over them like an old mother hen.

"Sita ere ona da couch, you wanta I maka soma tea?"

Jake replied, as he was looking around, "That would be nice, it's so good to be in this house again, I have such lovely memories of my stay here, but first tell us how have you been keeping Lorenzo? You're looking very well."

"I ama fine thank you, I musta ask you the sama thinga Jake. Ava you recovered froma thata terrible incident?"

"Yes, completely thanks, I'm raring to get back to work again. I have a television spot coming up soon, a guest appearance on the Justin Feldman show, and Jim's negotiating with producers for me to do Mrs Macgiver in the West End."

"That isa wonderful, Jake, you ara biga success, anda you deserve it, I willa make the tea now, eh, then I canna tella you mya news."

"Oh, yes, thank you Lorenzo."

He went into his kitchen and while the door was closed, Jim whispered to Jake, "When he mentions selling up and moving back to Sicily, you look surprised, and I'll take it from there, OK?"

"Yes Jim," Jake replied, smiling. "I think I can manage that, I am an actress, remember."

Jim smiled and pursed his lips, blowing Jake a kiss, then

gave a chuckle. "This could be your best part yet."

Jake laughed and said, "Cheeky devil."

The door opened and Lorenzo appeared carrying a tray.

"I opa you lika cannoli, it is a da delicacy froma my country, I buy it froma da Sicilian bakery ina West Hampstead, it isa delicious."

"I've never eaten it before, but it looks gorgeous."

Lorenzo put a little table in between them and poured the tea, asking them both if they wanted milk and sugar. He put the cannoli on fancy little china plates, handed them their tea and put the plates on the table, accompanied by little dessert forks. "Thera you are, enjoy." Then he put his own tea and cannoli on a side table next to his armchair and sat down with a sigh.

"What beautiful china Lorenzo, what is it?"

"It isa da Crown Derby, a pattern called 'Olda English Roses', a little indulgence, I coulda nota resist, please eat, tella me whata you think of a da cannoli?"

Jim was the first to take a bite, and talking with his mouth full said, "Mmmm, so delicious, thank you Lorenzo."

Jake, a little more delicately, with less cake in his mouth, said, "Scrumptious, I shall have to visit the bakery and get some of this. Whereabouts is it?"

"It'sa in a da parade of shops, justa down froma da tube station."

There was a lull in the conversation as they all ate their cannoli and sipped tea, smiling at one another, then Lorenzo started to speak. "I musta tella you both somathing, I ama going back ome to my beautiful Sicily."

Jim seized his opportunity. "That will be a nice holiday for you Lorenzo."

"No, sorry, nota da oliday Jim, I ama going ome to stay, I ama selling da ouse."

They both acted surprised, Jake saying, "Selling up? Is that a recent decision, Lorenzo?"

"No, Jake, I ava been thinking about it fora longa time, my hearta isa there."

Jake asked him, "Do you have family at home?"

"Yes, I ava da brother anda uncles, aunts, anda many cousins, my father and mother ara dead now, they died a longa time ago."

Jim said, "Well I'm really surprised, I thought you had settled down to life in England."

"I ava enjoyed my tima ere, I ava meta nice people lika you anda Jake, but I stilla av a ouse ina my ome village, Cammarata."

Jim looked surprised. "Oh I didn't know you had property over in Sicily as well, have you put this one on the market yet?"

"No, nota yet, but I willa soon, I ama being very sentimental, I don'ta wanta to sell to a developer, anda av them spoila da place. I wanta someone to buy it who loves it asa it is, that away it elpsa people to ava da accommodation who can't afford to buy a ouse."

"That is very good Lorenzo, you never know what they might do to it. If you don't mind me asking, I'm just being nosy, but how much will you be putting it on the market for ?"

"I thinka ita willa be twenty-five thousand pounds."

"Lorenzo, please don't be shocked, but you mentioned being sentimental about this house. Well I can't stand the thought of developers getting their hands on it either, because I am very sentimental about it too, it's where I met the love of my life, Jake. So what would you say if I were to make you an offer of twenty thousand pounds cash, here and now. That way you get your wish to keep the house as multiple occupation and the tenants who are here will be able to remain and we get to own a house that is filled with beautiful memories for us?"

"Oh Jim," Jake said, and began to cry, but it was no act, he was so moved by what Jim had said.

Lorenzo's jaw had dropped open with shock and for several moments he didn't know what to say, you could see he was deep in thought. Then he suddenly stood up, went over to Jim, grabbed his hand and shook it.

"Thata isa fair price, you ava da deal." He then threw his arms around Jim and said, "I coulda nota wish fora anything better, than my friends to ava this ouse." Then holding out his arms to Jake, he grasped his shoulders and kissed him on both cheeks.

Jake said, "I can't believe it," as he wiped a tear from his eye, "how marvellous."

"Thisa calls for a drink," Lorenzo beamed, as he walked over to a pretty lacquered cabinet in the corner. He turned the small key in its lock and dropped the front down to reveal a selection of bottles and glasses. "I ava beena keeping this champagne fora da special occasion."

While Lorenzo busied himself opening the champagne, Jim looked over at Jake, caught his eye, and winked victoriously at him. Jake gave a broad grin back, just before Lorenzo popped the cork and poured them each a glass of celebratory bubbly.

"Eera you are," he said giving them both a glass and returning for his own, "Letsa drinka to us anda youra new ouse."

"To us, new horizons," Jim said.

Jake joined in with, "To Buckley Road and Cammarata."

They each took a sip and all smiled with satisfaction.

"I will go and see my solicitor first thing on Monday morning, Lorenzo."

"I willa do the same."

"Have you said anything to any of the tenants yet?"

"I tolda Ricci anda Toby, buta no one else."

Jim said, "If I were you, I would let Ricci and Toby know they don't have to leave, but I wouldn't tell the others about our plans yet, in case they get worried. Now we have shook on it and have a gentleman's agreement between us that we will buy your house, and we will not renege from that."

Lorenzo replied in agreement, "That isa very good, I cannota believe it, I can now maka plans anda prepare to return home to Sicily."

Jake was ecstatic and pronounced poetically, "It's like buying a parcel of happiness with all your beautiful memories tied up in it."

Chapter 38

When Jake and Jim arrived back home, they walked into the lounge with long faces. Ricci looked excitedly at them and asked, "Well, how did you get on?"

Jim, who could manage to keep a straight face without laughing when trying to fool someone, whereas Jake found it impossible, said, "He's already sold it."

Ricci and Toby shrugged with resignation. Toby said, "I guess that means we're on the move then old girl!"

"Yes, never mind guys you tried, and less of the old please Toby."

Jim, bursting into a smile, exclaimed, "Yes we did, and we succeeded, he's agreed sell to us!"

Totally surprised, Ricci said, "Oooh you were kidding, how wonderful. Isn't it great Toby?"

"Sure is Ric," he said smiling. "Did you have much trouble convincing him to sell, Jim?"

"Not a bit of it, he told us that he was going to sell up and move back home, we both looked surprised. I asked him if he'd put the house on the market yet, and how much he wanted for it. He mentioned that he didn't want it to fall into the hands of developers, as he wanted the place to stay as it was with separate flats. He admitted to being sentimental about the place. That gave me an opening to say that we also felt sentimental about it as well, it was the house where Jake and I met and fell in love. When he told me the price, I made him an offer for cash and he took it, we shook hands on it and we are both seeing our solicitors tomorrow, it was as simple as that."

"Brilliant," Toby said with admiration.

"We didn't mention that you were staying with us this weekend, and that you'd told us about his intentions, so make sure you guys keep that to yourselves, OK?"

"Yes of course," Ricci agreed. "We wouldn't want to say anything to jeopardise the deal, would we Toby?"

"Oh absolutely not love."

"We should have a drink to celebrate our success," Jake suggested. "What would you like, Ricci?"

"I'd love a gin and tonic please, sweetie."

"How about you Toby?" Jake said as he was pouring Ricci's gin.

"I'll join you in a whisky and dry ginger ale, please Jake."

Jake continued pouring drinks for all of them. He handed Ricci and Toby theirs, then he gave Jim a whisky, held up his glass and said, "Here's to Buckley Road, may it always be a haven for those living there."

"Buckley Road," was said in chorus as they all chinked glasses.

"Well done both of you," Toby said. "I don't know where we would have ended up if we had been forced to move out."

Jim replied, "I'm sure you'd have found somewhere, Toby."

"Maybe, but not as nice as the home we have there."

The rest of the evening was spent in easy pleasant conversation; Jim and Jake talked about their plans to look for a West End property to lease, that they could turn into a club. They told them they would call it Rusty's Place.

"That's the best possible name you could have thought of," Ricci said. "And if you'd really like me to dress for you again Jake, I'd be only too delighted to, I was so happy doing that when you were at The Capital."

"Oh darling, that will be marvellous, we make a great team you and I."

The drinking and chat went on late into the evening, they finally retired to bed around midnight. They slept in late the next morning, and spent a leisurely pleasant Sunday, until Dennis the chauffeur brought the car to the door at seven thirty to take Ricci and Toby back home.

Jake had suggested to Ricci and Toby that it might be better if Dennis dropped them off in the next street just in case Lorenzo should happen to see the limousine outside. They agreed that would be best.

The next morning, Jim spoke with his solicitor, putting the arrangements for purchasing the Buckley Road property in his hands. Within the time frame of two months, everything had been finalised, the contract had been signed, Lorenzo, bless him, had said his goodbyes and moved out. He had been very generous in leaving every stick of furniture in situ, stating, "I ava no needa ofa any of it."

Jim and Jake were now the proud owners – and new joint landlords – of their romantically memorable house, and didn't make any changes, apart from changing the name on the tenants' agreements, giving the outside a new coat of paint, new stair carpet throughout, and the house a new name to mark its new beginning. The sign hanging in the arched doorway read The Haven. They pointed out to Ricci and Toby that they would have no objection to them moving downstairs to Lorenzo's garden flat if they felt it was better than their current bedsit, the only proviso being that they would be responsible for the general upkeep of the small garden. Ricci was thrilled at the thought of having the open-air space of a garden to sit in during the summer and Toby said, "Jeez Ric, that's great, we wouldn't have to climb up all those ruddy stairs."

"No, but you would have to mow the lawn and do the weeding, love."

"I don't mind that, I'd enjoy it."

They asked if they could have a look at it, to help them decide. Jake and Jim opened it up to show them. It took no time at all for them to give it the once over, weigh up the pros and cons and come to the conclusion that it was too good an offer to turn down.

"We'd love it guys, but it depends what rent you'll be asking for it."

"It's the same as what you're paying now, we don't want to charge you any more. Obviously there may be annual incremental increases in the rent in the future to offset inflation, but that's it."

"In that case we'll take it, you beaut Jim," and he shook his hand.

Toby and Ricci lost no time in beginning to pack up their belongings so that items could be carried to their new flat, when the time came to move it all downstairs. Jake had said that the sooner they moved, the sooner they could advertise and let it to a new tenant/s. They had given Lorenzo's place a good spring clean and earmarked where they wanted to place the furniture. They had enlisted the help of Tony who had taken over Jake's bedsit, his boyfriend Doug and Amir, as many hands make light work, giving them the next Saturday morning as moving day; they were all only too pleased to help.

Three weeks later, Ricci and Toby were ensconced in their new flat and loving it, pleased that they had made the decision to move from upstairs. Jim had advertised the top-floor flat and had been inundated with applicants for it. He had made a conscious discriminating choice to let it to a man in his thirties called Tristram, who was obviously a gay guy. He was a hairdresser and worked in a unisex salon in Neasden, called Scruples. Jim felt that he would more naturally enhance the harmony and well-being of the house, rather than taking a chance on a straight guy, or a female. He was a professional person, his references were top drawer and he confided to Jim that he had a long-term relationship with a married friend, who would be the only person that he would have visiting as he was the only man he wanted to entertain. Jim thanked him for his honesty and said he hoped he would be very happy in the house. Rightly or wrongly, Jim somehow suspected the friend might be his sugar daddy, but, hey ho, whatever works, it really wasn't any of his business anyway!

Chapter 39

The lone shadowy figure climbed over the perimeter wall and walked through the shrubbery towards the large house. He had parked his car away from the main road, hidden by some bushes. His eyes now accustomed to the dark, he was able to see the size of the house. *What a place*, he thought, *there should be some good stuff to be had here*, he just hoped there would be no guard dogs or burglar alarms in the place, he didn't fancy being attacked by a Rottweiler or being collared by the police and carted away to prison. He had been lucky so far though, on the previous occasions he had robbed places, he had managed to gain entry easily and get away with a good haul of stuff because the places had been empty. It looked as though it might be the same here, he hadn't heard any dogs barking, a good guard dog could usually sense when there was a prowler about, and as well as alerting its owners, would also let the intruder know it was time to make his getaway. He was avoiding using his torch until he was inside the house as he didn't want anyone to know he was in the grounds.

He edged his way around to the rear of the property, avoiding stepping onto the course gravel path by keeping to the lawn or edge of the garden. He was hoping that he might be lucky and find an open window somewhere, so he wouldn't have to risk making a noise using his jemmy. Unfortunately, he didn't find one, but there was a small window that he knew he'd be able to get through, if he could jemmy it open. His adrenalin pumping, he was on edge, alert to any possible telltale signs of animal or human activity that would curtail his enterprise. He moved onto the border under the window, removing the crowbar from his sack. He lifted it to the metal frame and began to try to lever it open as quietly as he could. After a couple of prises, he felt it begin to give, it had opened sufficiently for him to reach his hand in and lift the latch. He pulled it open a little too enthusiastically and the hinge made a metallic creaking noise. He waited for a minute, poised, listening, hoping if there was anyone in the house that they hadn't heard the noise. He shone his torch in and saw that the room was a downstairs bathroom. The toilet was located under the window which was handy, it would be very useful to stand on. He picked up his bag and hoisted himself up onto the ledge, he lithely twisted his body so that his legs were through the window, placed his feet onto the toilet cover and nimbly stepped down to the floor below.

He opened the door and moved silently into a thickly carpeted hallway. Shining his torch beam around, he saw a staircase ahead of him. His usual method was to do upstairs first as there was often money and jewellery up there; he preferred cash and jewellery to anything else, it was easier, although he wasn't averse to acquiring the odd small antique item, like a clock. He liked this area, it was very affluent, so there was always the possibility of rich pickings to be had. He chose isolated places with no immediate neighbours, that afforded him the concealment of trees and shrubs. This house fitted the bill exactly.

Chapter 40

What was that! Jake woke up startled from a deep sleep and sat bolt upright in bed. His first instinct was to nudge Jim, but of course he wasn't there. He had stayed up in London in a hotel, as he had several important meetings to go to in connection with the club, so it was easier to be in town, rather than have to commute. Jake had heard a strange grating noise from somewhere downstairs, it sounded as though someone was trying to break in. Jumping out of bed, he reached for his dressing gown, and putting it on he moved quickly over to the door. Quietly opening it, without switching the light on, he peered out. He could see a torch light sweeping animatedly around the walls and floor. Someone was in the house and whoever it was, was coming up the stairs. Jake quickly went back into his bedroom, closing the door carefully so as not to make a sound. He fumbled to find one of the wooden barley twist candlesticks on top of the chest of drawers, very nearly knocking one over. He grasped it firmly and stood nervously waiting for the intruder to come through the door. He had no time to call the police, and anyway, he would be heard making the call. Jake's heart was pounding in his chest as the door began to slowly open. *Damn,* Jake thought, *if the intruder shone his torch on the bed, he would see that whoever had been asleep had got out of bed, he would have to be quick.* As the figure entered the room, Jake lifted up the candlestick and brought it down with a thwack on the back of his head. The man – he knew it was a man now because of the deep groan that had escaped from him – sank down, landing in a crumpled heap on the bedroom carpet.

Jake immediately turned on the light and looked down at the prone figure unconscious on the floor. He then went over to the bedside table and picked up the telephone intending to call the police. But he looked back over towards the burglar and from where he stood he now had a better view of his face. He paused from dialling 999. It was odd, but something in the back of his mind was telling him that the face was familiar. It suddenly occurred to him who he thought it was, just as the person began to groan and come to, holding his head.

"Terry, is it you?"

The man, still clutching his head, looked up at Jake alarmed.

"Eh, yeah, who the devil are you, n how do ya know my name, n was it you as it me?"

Jake looked down at him and said sternly, "Don't you get on your high horse with me Terry, of course I hit you, I had no idea who you were, or what you were going to do. What do you mean by breaking into my home? Give me one good reason why I shouldn't call the police, and don't get any ideas, I'll hit you again if you try anything."

"I don't know any toffs who live in houses like this, so ow do ya know who I am, who are ya?" He tried to get up, but the effort only succeeded in making his head throb more painfully. "Ouch, ooo you must have given me one heck of a bloody clout, you could've bloody done me in."

"I would have thought getting hit over the head is an occupational hazard in your line of work, you obviously don't remember who I am, but I never forget a face, or name, even though it has been a long time."

Two of the main reasons why Terry probably hadn't been able to recognise Jake was the fact that he had lost his broad Midlands accent and was no longer living in a bedsit in Kilburn. But, when Jake really thought about it, why would he remember him anyway, it wasn't as though they had made mad passionate love or anything, they had simply flirted on a bus and never seen each other again, and it was over twenty years ago.

"Well are ya goin ta tell me who you are or not?"

"It's Jake, Terry, don't you remember? In the sixties, you chatted me up on the top deck of your number sixteen bus when you came to take my fare. You told to write my number down and give it to you as I got off the bus. I didn't have any paper so I wrote on a discarded cigarette packet. You called me once, but I mentioned that the police were at the house, and you suddenly hung up, I can understand why now."

"Oohh, yes, I remember now, I warned you to be on the lookout for pickpockets in Oxford Street. Blimey, you've changed, and ow da ya come to be livin in a swanky place like this?"

"Let's talk about you first Terry, when did you get involved in doing burglaries and why?"

"What da ya wanna know mi bleeding life story for, you're gonna call the rozzers on me, ain't ya?"

"Not necessarily. Now, how is that head of yours, do you feel sick or dizzy, or have blurred vision? I should get you to hospital if you do."

"Oh, a right little Florence Nightingale we are now, aren't we, after nearly cracking mi ead open. No, I'm OK, just a splittin eadache that's all, I'll survive."

"Yes and you're a right hypocrite, Terry. Beware of

pickpockets indeed, more like beware of burglars in the middle of the night." Jake then softened a little and said, "Why don't you try to get up off the floor? You can take your shoes off and lie on my bed, if you like, then you can tell me what made you start robbing people."

"That sounds cosy," Terry said as he started taking his shoes off.

"Here let me help," Jake replied, "and don't get any silly ideas like that, I'm not interested."

Jake finished taking Terry's shoes off and helped him up. Terry put his arm around Jake's shoulder so that he could help him over to the bed.

"Thank you, that's much better."

"It all started after I'd met my missus and she became pregnant. Ya don't earn much as a bus conductor ya know, I needed to find extra cash. I got talking to a geezer in a pub one night, I was moanin about the cost of livin and tryin to make ends meet, an ee told me he did some blagging on the side. He let me go on a job with him and gave me some pointers. After that I was hooked."

"Didn't you have any thought for the poor people you were robbing?"

"The people who lived in the houses I chose to rob weren't poor by any means."

"Yes I know, maybe they weren't, but it's not just about the things you steal, it's the psychological effect that the robbery causes, the feelings it stirs up, fear, violation, the emotional effects it has on the victim, the experience could ruin their lives."

"Well, I ain't about to ruin your life am I, you're about to ruin mine by turning me over to the police."

"Have you stolen anything from in the house?"

"No I ain't, I didn't get the chance."

"No and you're not going to either. Did you break anything or do any damage getting in?"

"No I didn't."

"I think we can safely say that the crack on the head I gave you is punishment enough. I won't be calling the police, and I hope this experience will make you think again about doing burglaries. What would your wife and child do if you went to prison?"

"I wouldn't know, she left me last year, went off with another bloke."

"I'm sorry to hear that Terry, how's your head feeling now?"

"My headache isn't as bad as it was, but there's a bloody great lump come up."

"Can you see alright, you don't feel sick or dizzy or anything?"

"No, I feel OK, but I could murder a cup of tea."

"I'll go and make one, if you promise to lie quietly and rest."

"Yeah OK, this bed's lovely and comfy."

"I won't be long then," Jake said, still concerned that he might have given him a serious head injury. "Don't go to sleep will you, it's not wise after a knock on the head."

He walked out of the bedroom and went quickly downstairs and into the kitchen to make some tea. He put the kettle on, laid out a tray with teapot, cups, milk jug, sugar, a plate of biscuits and two plates. Once the kettle had boiled, he made the tea, picked up the tray and went straight back upstairs. Walking into the bedroom, he saw straightaway that Terry wasn't in bed.

"Terry, are you in the bathroom?" he called. There was no answer. "Where are you, are you alright?" Jake placed the tray of tea on the bedside cabinet and walked towards the bathroom door, he pushed the door open gingerly, half expecting to see him lying prone on the floor, but once inside there was no sign of him. He walked in and out of the different bedrooms but he wasn't in any of them. He went back downstairs and went into the lounge thinking he may have followed him downstairs and come in here, but he hadn't.

Then the thought occurred to him that Terry had fled to avoid being turned over to the police; perhaps he thought Jake might have called them while he was downstairs making the tea.

Jake turned around, walked out of the lounge wondering where next to look, when Terry suddenly leapt up behind him, wrapping his arm around his neck and nearly throttling him. He felt something sharp digging into his side.

"I've got a knife, don't try anything stupid, or you'll get it. Where do you keep your money? Take me to it."

Jake was rendered useless by the fear of being held at knifepoint, his mind was in a turmoil, then he was suddenly jolted from inertia by the sharp menacing rasp of Terry's angry voice.

"Carm on, fucking move it, not so mouthy now are you, you didn't think I was going to leave here empty handed after being nearly killed by you knocking me on the head did you? I know yer've got money in the house and I want it."

Jake finally managed to blurt out, "I only keep a small amount of cash in the house, I think there's about two hundred pounds in the bureau in the study."

"Is that all? Show me." Jake began to walk in the direction of the study, where he and Jim kept a petty cash tin. Just as he was doing so he could have sworn he caught a glimpse of a fleeting figure disappearing around the corner, towards the hallway leading to the front door. He thought for one awful moment, *Oh no, there's two of them, Terry's got an accomplice searching around the house for valuables,* then almost immediately another scary thought occurred to him. *I know Terry's identity, maybe he won't leave me alive to tell the police who he is!*

Jake led Terry to the small office and he pointed to the drawer in the bureau where the cash tin was kept, along with the key in its lock. There was the unmistakeable sound of a police siren in the distance.

Terry snarled at Jake, "You called the fucking police, thanks very much wanker."

Jake felt a heavy smack on the back of his head and he crashed onto the floor unconscious.

Chapter 41

Pru had been lying in bed reading when she'd heard the strange noise from somewhere downstairs. She had got out of bed and went to her main door. Opening it a crack, she peered out onto the landing. It confirmed her worst fears, she could see a torch light beam dancing around, there was an intruder in the house. She closed her door and locked it, went to her phone in the lounge and immediately telephoned the police. She wondered if Jake had heard anything, if so, she hoped he wouldn't do anything silly like trying to confront whoever it was, but she didn't like the thought of leaving the safety of her flat to check on him and put herself in danger. Then she realised, unfortunately that it was exactly what she had to do, otherwise how would the police get into the house. She couldn't think how the intruder had managed to get inside, but it certainly wouldn't have been through the heavy front door.

She put on her dressing gown and slippers. Trembling and frightened she quietly left her flat, and going quickly along the landing she made her way to the backstairs as she thought they would be more likely to use the main staircase. Descending steadily in the dark, she listened for any sound, or any hint of torchlight, being careful to feel her way, holding onto the banister rail until she reached the bottom. She had no idea of how many intruders there were, or their whereabouts in the house, or worse still, whether they were armed or not. Her brain was racing and she was beginning to regret leaving her flat.

Nevertheless, stealing herself to go on despite her fears, she quietly opened the door to the small sitting room that she would have to go through to get into the main hallway, leaving it wide open as a means of escape should she encounter anyone. There was no one about. Trying to remember exactly where the furniture was placed, she carefully felt her way like a blind woman across the room. Once she had successfully traversed it, she fumbled for the handle of the door, wondering what on earth was going to be on the other side.

She needn't have worried, it was clear. She was in the main hallway as quickly as she was able she made her way along it, then suddenly, hearing an aggressive unfamiliar voice, she ran and darted around the corner. She heard Jake's voice saying something about going to the study, so he was obviously being held captive by someone. The good news was, it would take them away from where she was and she would be able to open the door. When she had opened it, she felt the cold night air wrap itself around her. Shortly afterwards with relief, she heard the pleasant sound of a police siren. She thought to herself, *thank god they came quickly*. She threw on the switches on the wall by the side of the door which illuminated the immediate outside area as well as the indoor lights in the hallway. She waited for them to arrive. The police car came to a fast gravel-scrunching stop on the drive and two uniformed officers ran from the car towards her.

"We had a call about intruders miss?"

"Yes, quickly, follow me. I think someone has my boss hostage."

As they turned the corner to go towards the study, they almost bumped into a man fleeing down the hallway. He turned and started to run to try and escape, but one of the young policemen darted after him and brought him down with a flying tackle that any rugby player would have been proud of.

"Aaurrgh, ger off me!" the man yelled. "You're hurting me!"

"Consider yourself nicked," the police officer said as he placed the handcuffs on him.

"Well done Chris," the other officer congratulated him. "I didn't know you could move that fast."

Turning to Pru he asked, "Where's your boss, miss?"

Pru quickly led him to the study where they found Jake sat on the floor with his back resting against the desk, clutching his head.

"Jake!" she exclaimed, "You're hurt, what happened?"

"I'm OK, I've just had a knock on the head that's all. He heard the police coming so he smacked me one."

"We'll be off now," one of the policemen said. "We'll take him to the station, he'll be charged with breaking and entering and grievous bodily harm. It appears he hasn't stolen anything, which is good news, but I'm sorry about your knock on the head, sir. Perhaps you should let a doctor look you over. By the way, the wife's a real fan of yours."

"Oh is she? Pru, please give the officer one of my signed photographs, there are some in the desk drawer here."

Pru opened the drawer and took a photo from the top of the pile that was in there.

She gave it to the policeman who thanked her, and said, "Thank you very much sir, she will be really thrilled with this. Goodbye then, we will be in touch."

Pru walked the policeman to the door. He spoke to her

quietly. "If I were you miss, I'd advise him to see his doctor. Goodbye miss."

"Yes, I will, thank you, goodbye officer." She watched the man get into the patrol car, and it took off up the drive. She closed the door and walked back into the lounge. Standing in front of Jake's chair, she said, "Perhaps I should call Doctor Pierce to take a look at you."

"No, don't do that Pru, I'll be fine. I'm sure a couple aspirin will do the trick. Where there's no sense, there's no feeling. I should have rung for the police when I had the chance to."

"What do you mean?"

"I'll explain later. Can you help me to get up please?"

Pru put her arm through Jake's and helped him to his feet.

"Help me get to the lounge, will you?"

"Yes, OK, put your arm around my shoulder, I'll support you."

Pru managed to get him into the lounge and sat him in his armchair, then, very concerned for him, she asked, "How are you feeling now, can I get you anything?"

"A couple of aspirin and a glass water please, Pru."

Pru went to the kitchen for a glass of water, calling in the downstairs bathroom to get a bottle of aspirin from the medical cabinet. She brought them in, handed him the glass of water, and shook two tablets from the bottle into his outstretched hand. Jake threw them into his mouth, took a gulp of water and tossed his head back to swallow them.

"Thanks Pru, you're an angel."

"Do you want me to call Jim and let him know what's happened?"

"No, it's OK, I'll ring him myself later. If you ring him, it will make him think I'm seriously hurt."

"Well, I think it is fairly serious Jake, you never know what a blow on the head can do, and you're suffering from shock too."

Jake realised she was absolutely right, but he made light of it, saying, "It might have knocked some sense into me. I can't believe I could have been so stupid. I recognised him you see, I'd met him once in the sixties. Why that fact should have caused me to take pity on him, heaven knows, I can't think what possessed me, I think I felt guilty for hitting him over the head."

"You hit *him* over the head?"

"Yes, he came into the bedroom, so I picked up a candlestick and whacked him over the head with it. I was going to call the police but when I recognised him, I couldn't believe it, I called him by his name and he responded to it, but he didn't recognise me. I still don't think he realises who I am, but he'll soon find out when his case goes to court."

"How do you know him then?"

"I met him on a bus years ago, he was the conductor, we just got talking, he flirted with me and cheekily asked me for my telephone number, so I gave it to him, but we'd never actually met again until now, and I now wish we hadn't done."

"Oh I see," she said, looking slightly intrigued.

"I'm not sure you do darling, but it doesn't matter, we were just ships that passed in the night."

"Would you like me to get you anything else before I go back to bed?"

"No thank you Pru, you get some rest."

"Are you staying down here or going back to bed?"

"I think I'll stay here thanks."

"In that case, I'll get a blanket for you." She went to the

cupboard and grabbed a fleecy blanket, came back and tucked it around him. "Get some rest now. If you need me, just ring."

"Thanks Pru. OK, I will."

Pru left. As she was going back to her flat, she thought to herself, *I really should have called the doctor out, what if anything should happen to him?* She went to her bed with a very uneasy feeling.

When Pru had gone, Jake suddenly had a wave of emotion descend over him, a mixture of shock at what had happened, mingled with a certain amount of self-pity and relief. He gently sobbed and thought, *how could I have been such a stupid fool?* He had the sudden need to hear Jim's voice, but he looked at the clock and it was only five twenty in the morning, so he resisted the idea and decided to try to get some sleep

Chapter 42

Jim hadn't had a very good night's sleep at all. He didn't know why, but he had felt strangely worried about Jake. He had woken up around three in the morning with a notion that something was wrong, and several times after that. He put it down to the fact that he and Jake were not apart from each other very often. He took a sip of water from the glass beside the bed and contented himself with the thought that he would find time to ring him before he left the hotel to go to his first meeting, to tell him how much he was missing him. He snuggled back down, and after what seemed like an interminable time, fell asleep again. His alarm buzzed loudly and woke him up at seven, he got up, went to the toilet, shaved and showered. *What a lousy night*, he thought, *the worst night's sleep I've had for a long time, it's being away from Jake and sleeping in a strange bed. I'll ring him after breakfast, he might be up by then.* He began to dress himself; he had chosen to wear his dark-charcoal-grey suit as he felt it looked very business-like and gave the right impression. He put on a white shirt and coupled it with his favourite dark blue Ermenegildo Zegna patterned tie. He looked at the final result in the mirror, pushed a stray piece of his fringe across his forehead and dabbed another drop of Aramis on his face. He thought to himself, *You'll do, as Jake would say, go knock em dead sweetheart.* Jim opened his briefcase and took out a folder. He would come up to his room after breakfast, pack his small bag and grab his briefcase, before checking out.

The Mirador hotel was a very good four-star hotel situated

in Queensway, just off the Bayswater Road. Jim had stayed here once, a long time ago, before he'd met Jake. He liked it because it wasn't pretentious or snobby, it had just the right luxurious touch, without being over the top. The rooms were pleasant, the beds were comfortable, and he hoped the breakfast was still as good as he remembered; he was feeling particularly hungry. The place had been completely refurbished since the last time he was here. The interior design was now finished in modern coordinating pastel tones, very relaxing, with a soothing preponderance of pale green. He took the keys out of the door, opened it, and left his room. He walked along the plushly carpeted corridor, down the curved staircase and into the dining room. There were several other guests already having breakfast. He sat at a table by a window so he could look out at the people going to and fro on their way to work.

The waiter came to the table, with a pleasant, "Good morning sir, may I take your order?"

Jim smiled and replied, "Yes please, I'd like some fresh orange juice, bacon, scrambled egg and a grilled tomato, with some brown toast and marmalade, oh, and a pot of coffee, thank you."

"Thank you sir."

As he waited for his breakfast to arrive, he opened the folder of papers containing details of the commercial property the estate agent was going to take him to see. He and Jake had especially liked this one, because of its location and its potential to be transformed into the type of club they wanted. Jim just wanted to familiarise himself with some of the details. He took his biro from the inside pocket of his jacket and jotted down a few questions that he wanted to ask.

The waiter returned with a jug of orange juice. He poured

a glass, placed a jug of coffee, milk and sugar on the table and went away. Jim took a gulp of the orange juice's cold sharp freshness, finishing it off in one go. He poured himself a cup of coffee and continued looking at the description of the property. It was situated in Tavistock Place between Oxford Street and Regent Street in the heart of the West End and quite close to the London Palladium and London's theatreland. An ideal position for a nightclub to be in that it could provide an intimate after-theatre dining experience. Jim was hoping that the property would be suitable for conversion, as it had a ninety-nine-year lease on it.

He quickly gathered his papers and replaced them in the folder as the waiter had reappeared with his breakfast. Jim thought how nice it looked, he thanked the waiter and began to tuck in. When he had finished breakfast, he left a tip on the table and went back to his room so that he could telephone Jake and have a private conversation, rather than using one of the booths in the reception area.

The ringing tone went on for quite a while before Jake answered, he sounded very sleepy.

"Hello darling, I didn't wake you, did I?"

"Yes love, but it doesn't matter, I'm so pleased to hear your voice."

Jim could tell just by the sound of Jake's voice that something was wrong.

"What's the matter love, are you unwell?"

"Not unwell exactly, but I've got a sore head. We had an intruder last night and I'm afraid he hit me over the head, but don't worry, I'm OK."

"What? Bloody hell, I can't believe it, have you been seen by a doctor?"

"No, I didn't think it was necessary, I'm alright really."

"You can't be alright love, you could have concussion or be suffering from shock. You just take it easy, I'm coming home right away."

"But what about your appointments, love?"

"Oh bugger the appointments Jake, I can easily re-schedule those, I'm meeting the estate agent at my hotel at nine fifteen. I'll wait to see him to explain the situation, and I'll be on my way home. Is Pru in the house? If she is, ask her to look after you until I get back."

"Pru is here, please be careful, don't drive too fast, I love you."

"I love you too sweetheart, I'll be home as soon as I can, bye."

Jim hurriedly began to pack his bag. Thoughts were whizzing through his head, he wasn't usually prone to panic but this had put him into a bit of a flap. *What if Jake was making light of the situation, and he was seriously hurt, what if the place had been ransacked!*

He finished packing and zipped up his bag, he stuffed the folder into his briefcase, and grabbing hold of both of them, he picked up his key and left the room. He wasn't going to wait for the agent to arrive, he would leave a message at the reception desk, as the guy would be sure to enquire after him when he didn't show up in the lobby. He explained the situation to the female receptionist, asked her for a piece of hotel paper, and scrawled a short note apologising for not being able to keep the appointment, due to an emergency at home. He stated that he still wanted view the property and would be in touch soon. He wrote on the envelope, *F.A.O. Mr Grainger, Spellzer and Sons, Estate Agents*, then gave it to the receptionist. He paid his bill using the company cheque book, so that his expenses would be tax deductible, gave the woman a tip and said, "Thank you, please make sure that Mr Grainger gets the note," then he left the foyer and made his way to the hotel carpark. He threw his bags into the boot, got in the driving seat and started the worrying journey home.

Chapter 43

Jim found Jake lying propped up on the settee. He quickly went to his side, gave him gentle kiss on his forehead and said, "My poor darling, you look really pale, and I think you might have a temperature. I'm going to call Doctor Pierce and get him to give you a check-up."

"But I'm …"

Jim cut him off. "I won't have any buts darling, you're seeing the doctor."

He dialled the number and told the receptionist that he wanted the doctor to do a home visit, giving her brief details and saying it was a head injury.

"I'll put you through to the doctor," she said.

As soon as Jim had told the doctor what had happened, he said, "I'll come straight away."

"Thank you, doctor." Jim replaced the receiver. "He's on his way, love."

"I'd better have a quick shower and freshen up before he comes."

"Just take it easy then, don't rush around. Would you like some breakfast?"

"I would enjoy a cup of tea and some toast."

"I'll have it ready when you come down from your shower."

"Thank you darling," Jake replied as he went to go upstairs. "I won't be long."

Jim had deliberately not asked Jake any questions about the burglary in case he was still in shock. He appeared to be alright, but he would be happier once the doctor had seen him. He didn't even know if anything had been stolen. He felt dreadful that he hadn't been here to protect Jake when it happened. He began to prepare some breakfast for them both. There was a tapping at the door and he heard Pru's voice saying, "It's only Pru, how are you feeling Ja … oh hello Jim, I thought you were in London on business?"

"Hello Pru, yes I was, but I rang Jake this morning and he told me there had been an intruder and he'd been hit over the head. Jake's taking a shower at the moment, I've called Doctor Pierce, he's on his way to see him."

"Oh good, I tried to get Jake to let me call him just after it happened, but he wouldn't hear of it. It was me that called the police, the man was arrested trying to escape and we found Jake lying on the study floor."

"I don't know any details, I haven't asked Jake about it in case he's in shock. Can you tell me what happened?"

"I heard a noise and opened my flat door to look out, I could see a torch beam flitting around, so I knew someone had broken in. I was scared, so I immediately phoned the police, then I suddenly thought, how are they going to get in? I crept out of my flat under cover of darkness, felt my way down the backstairs, through the lounge and opened the front door so the police could get in. We nearly bumped straight into the burglar. He tried to run away but one of the policemen wrestled him to the ground and arrested him."

"You brave girl, I can't believe you went down the backstairs in the pitch black, thank you. God knows what might have happened if the police hadn't been able to gain entry!"

"Oh that's alright, Jim. The funny thing is though, when Jake was telling me what had happened, he said that he knew the person, he called him Terry. I wasn't sure if he was concussed from his blow on the head."

"We'll wait and see what the doctor says, but it's been a nasty shock for both you. You're feeling alright, aren't you?"

"Yes thanks, I'm fine, I'm just worried about Jake."

"That makes two of us Pru, as if he hasn't had enough to contend with recently, but I'll look after him, he's going to be fine too."

"Yes I'm sure he will be. Tell him I popped down to see if he was OK. I'll go now before the doctor arrives."

"Yes, I'll tell him, thanks for what you did Pru. I'll let you know what the doctor says."

Shortly after Pru had gone back up to her flat, Jake came back downstairs, so Jim put the toast on and made the tea.

"You look refreshed, are you feeling any better love?"

"Yes I am, but I'm amazed at the size of this bump on my head. You look." He leaned forward to let Jim see the back of his head.

"Bloody hell, it's enormous, he must have given you one heck of a whack!"

Jim poured them both a cup of tea and buttered Jake's toast. They sat at the table and Jake had just started eating when the doorbell rang.

"That'll be the doctor, you go into the lounge and I'll bring him through."

Jake took a gulp of his tea, left it on the table and went into the lounge, he re-arranged the cushions on the settee, and sat down to wait for the doctor. Jim opened the front door and was surprised to see a policeman standing there.

"Hello sir, would it be possible to see Mr Hartnell-Wiggins?"

"Yes, come in constable, I was expecting Dr Pierce, I thought you were him. Come on through, he's in the lounge."

"Who are you sir, if I may ask?"

"I'm Mr Hartnell, Jim Hartnell, Jake's partner. I hope your visit isn't going to put any pressure on him constable, he's had a nasty experience."

"Oh yes, I see, no I completely understand sir, I won't keep him long."

Jim led the way, and showed him in to see Jake.

"A policeman to see you Jake."

Jake looked surprised. "Hello constable, how can I help you?"

"I just wanted to let you know that the intruder Mr Terence Craven has been charged with aggravated burglary and the theft of monies totalling one hundred and seventy-five pounds. He will be remanded in custody until his court hearing on July 19. He has pleaded guilty so you will only need to provide us with a statement, you won't have to appear in court."

"That's a relief, at least I'm spared that indignity."

"Yes, I'm sure. Well, I won't linger as you're waiting for the doctor to arrive. If you could come to Buckminstead police station within the next week to make your statement it'll be over and done with. Oh by the way, he mentioned that he's acquainted with you, is that correct?"

"If having a brief conversation on the top of a London bus years ago could be termed as being acquainted, then yes, it's correct. We had never met since, until he broke into my house. A horrible coincidence, don't you think?"

"I see, yes, it must have been awful for you, but he's safely in custody now, so you don't have to worry on that score. I'll leave you in peace then. Goodbye Mr Hartnell-Wiggins."

"Goodbye constable."

"I'll see you out constable," Jim said, walking towards the hallway, the constable following him. He opened the front door for the policeman.

"Thank you, sir. I hope the doctor gives you reassurance that he'll be alright. Goodbye."

"Thank you constable, I hope so too. Goodbye."

Jim closed the door and went to re-join Jake in the lounge. He tried to jolly him along by saying, "He was the bearer of good news, at least you're not going to court."

"Yes Jim, I expect you're wondering about this business of him saying he knew me. It's exactly as I told the constable, except, well not quite exactly. We had a flirtatious conversation on his bus when he came to collect my fare, it was actually on the same day as Ricci's party. We never met again. But the fact that I had met him before clouded my judgement and I behaved like a stupid fool, because I thought it would make a difference when he realised I knew who he was. Silly of me. Oh Jim I could have been killed, and I would never have seen you again.." He ran to Jim's arms and began to cry.

"I'm here my love," Jim whispered, hugging and comforting him. "Try not to think about it. The fact that you knew of him isn't important, the lowlife is safely locked up now. You sit down and rest on the sofa, I'll go and get your tea, c'mon." Jim physically sat Jake down and went to get his tea; he found it had gone cold, so he made a fresh cup and took it to him.

"Here you are darling, drink this." He handed the teacup and saucer to Jake and looked at the clock. "I should think the doctor will be here soon."

It was actually another twenty minutes before the doorbell rang and Jim brought Doctor Pierce in to see Jake, after he had briefly explained that Jake had been assaulted by an intruder.

"Oh my word, poor man," he said, concerned. When he reached Jake he smiled and said, "Hello Mr Hartnell-Wiggins, I hear you've had a blow on the head. Let's take a look shall we?"

Jake turned his head so that the doctor could see the injury.

"Dear me, that is quite a nasty lump. Have you had any double vision or problems seeing?"

"No," Jake replied as the doctor asked him to turn back around and began to shine an instrument into his eyes.

"Do you have a headache or dizziness at the moment?"

"Yes, I have a mild headache, but it isn't too bad, my head just feels sore."

As the doctor put a thermometer into Jake's mouth to take his temperature, he said, "I'm not surprised about that at all. Have you vomited at all or feel nauseous?"

"No nothing like that I'm glad to say, I just feel very emotional and shaky."

He removed the thermometer, read it and put it away, then he took hold of his wrist to check his pulse, and looking sympathetically at his patient he remarked, "Well, I think your emotional state is only to be expected under the circumstances, Mr Hartnell-Wiggins, you've sustained a substantial head injury, and you're experiencing the consequences of that which is shock, the body's natural reaction. As long as you take it easy and get plenty of rest over the next couple of days, you'll be as right as rain. The bump on your head will subside fairly quickly, I'm sure. I prescribe lots of loving care, and, should you need them, paracetamol for your headache. If the headaches worsen, or you experience any of the things I mentioned earlier , double vision, dizziness, nausea then call me immediately, OK, but there is nothing to worry about, you're going to be fine."

Jake looked at him and said, "Thank you, doctor."

Looking on, Jim said, "Yes, thank you for coming doctor, you've put my mind at rest. I'll show you out."

The doctor said goodbye to Jake as Jim showed him out.

When he returned, Jim sat beside Jake, put his arm around him and said, "There you are, you heard what the doctor said, there's nothing to worry about, you just take things easy and let me look after you. I love you very much."

"I know you do, darling, I love you too. I'm sorry if I gave you a scare."

"It's scared me into realising that we need to have a burglar alarm fitted, as soon as possible. I'll see to it. I can't think why I didn't have the sense to do it when we bought the place."

Chapter 44

They signed the lease to the building in Tavistock Square a month after they had first been to view the property; they had both fallen instantly in love with it. Eighteen months later, after what had been a whirlwind of frantic activity, liaising with the architect, the landlord, builders, solicitors, suppliers and lord knows who else, they were finally beginning to see their dream of opening their very own club come to fruition. They were hoping that within a couple of short months they would be having a grand opening with their invited guests, friends who were the glitterati of the showbiz world attending their opening night. Jake wanted everything to be perfect, he would ensure that every attention was given to each little detail to ensure that it would be so. The club had to be a success, failure was not an option, they had thrown most of the money they had into buying the best of everything; no expense had been spared in order to make it the most lavish, the most tasteful, attractive venue in the West End. It had been designed to allow discerning celebrities, actors, singers, impresarios, rich businessmen and bankers to enjoy a pleasant evening out, a very pleasant, expensive evening out.

Jim and Jake's friends were aware of their latest enterprise, and there was a buzz of anticipation among them that was fuelling the jungle telegraph. Tongues were wagging in the right circles, providing free advertising. Jake had even been asked to do an interview by a trendy glossy magazine, and the subject of the club came up in conversation, Jake had made sure it would by mentioning it on a TV chat show appearance the week before.

Jim, as well as taking on the role of manager for Rusty's, was project managing the site, with considerable artistic input from Jake, who seemed to know exactly what he wanted, and usually if a difference of opinion occurred, managed to get his own way. Jim was just loving being at the helm again; it reminded him of his Capital days, he was in his element.

Jake and Ricci had been exceptionally busy, choosing new costumes for Jake's act. Custom-made, these complete outfits cost around three thousand pounds each, they were a bargain because they had used their usual costumiers and received a generous discount, otherwise they would have been considerably more. They had bought a selection of black satin shorts in various sizes for the waiters to wear. Ricci, who was an absolute wizard on a sewing machine, bless her, had cleverly bought a job lot of white shirts and some black bow ties, cut the collars and cuffs off the shirts and sewn them together with fasteners on the backs of each. These were to be the hunky waiters' outfits that Jake had envisaged when they first had the idea to open a club. They'd had leaflets printed and circulated around the city asking for young men with good physiques to apply for waiters' jobs in a new concept theatre supper club, which was due to be opened in September.

They had been inundated with applicants for just ten positions, with many being kept on the books in reserve. A well-known, well loved, veteran personality, Bobby Scott, who was a particularly good friend of Jake and Jim, had volunteered his services as resident compère/comedian for an incredibly low wage. He had made it clear that money wasn't his motivation, he dearly wanted to be a part of his friends' success in launching their new venture. Jake and Jim had been only too happy to take him on board, he was a gift from the gods, it meant they now had two big names to pull in the crowds; fate seemed to be smiling on them.

The 25 of September 1976 was designated as the club's official opening night, after it had been agreed for the different contractors to have it ready, completely fitted out, done and operational, a month before. This would leave them ample time to sort out any unexpected teething troubles with equipment. The chef and kitchen staff had their trial run prior to opening, their customers would be Jake, Jim, Ricci and Toby, Bobby Scott and his wife Trisha, and other invited guests who had all been instrumental in making the whole thing possible; this included some of the contractors and suppliers. There were about forty people in all, the evening went very well, with lots of the guests commenting on how good the food was. They needn't have worried about any catastrophes; there were a few minor glitches leading up to the opening night, but these were soon put right and the day finally came to launch the club.

Jim had never seen Jake so nervous. He put it down to the fact that there was so much riding on the success of the venture that Jake had got himself in a state. However, he knew that come the time for him to go on stage, he would be fine. Jim was so proud of what they had both achieved, Rusty's Place was ready to impress everyone who entered the doors.

Ricci was well organised for dressing Jake for the evening's performance, he was just doing a few final preparations. He had arranged all the bouquets and cards on top of a long side table, with the larger floral baskets on the floor underneath. He had been so impressed with the design of the two dressing rooms when Jake and Jim showed him what they were planning to do, now they were finished and he was actually using them, his admiration knew no bounds, they had thought of everything. They were spacious, air conditioned, the lighting was amazing, there was a massive wardrobe room for all Jake's costumes and accessories, the shower room and toilet facilities were great; he was sure that the artistes who used the other dressing room would find it luxurious, most of the top theatres couldn't boast such amenities.

He couldn't help but fondly think of Jake and Jim. What dear friends they were, and had always been, to him and Toby, so thoughtful, caring and generous.

Casting his mind back to how he had first introduced them at the party at Buckley Road, how they had been so supportive when he and Toby nearly split up, how they had bought the house in Buckley Road when Lorenzo was selling it and moving back to Sicily. Jake and Jim knew how much they loved living there, now they couldn't be happier living in the garden flat that used to be Lorenzo's.

Remembering these things made him feel so lucky to have such good friends, and how privileged he felt to be able to work so closely with Jake, doing a job he loved. He also recalled how he first convinced the new lodger who had arrived from the Midlands and was a bit green around the gills that he should consider doing drag. He was proud of that fact, he began to well up at the thought. Jake would soon be arriving to start getting ready. He put the present he and Toby had bought on his dressing table, he knew it would please him.

Jake arrived. On opening the dressing room door he exclaimed, "What gorgeous flowers, I didn't expect a bouquet from all of my lovers."

Ricci quipped, "There's over twenty of them there, love,

that's wishful thinking!"

"Yes, it might have been once upon a time, but I'm glad to say I'm now a happily married lady. Jim's the only man I want."

Ricci smiled at him and replied, "Yes I know darling, I should jolly well hope so too, you're not getting any younger."

Jake feigned a shocked expression with his mouth wide open, and said, "Well really, such abuse," but they were both chuckling, this was the usual sort of banter that went on between them.

They both loved it, if any strangers could have heard them, they would have thought there might be a fight ensuing, it sounded quite vitriolic sometimes, but to them it was just harmless fun.

Jake took off his coat, hung it on the clothes hook and walked over to his dressing table.

"Oh darling, is this from you?"

Ricci nodded.

"You shouldn't have," Jake said, as he undid the expertly wrapped package. "Mitsouko, it's so gorgeous, I'll wear it tonight." He gave Ricci a kiss. Ricci knew that Jake always liked to receive a gift of perfume and Guerlain fragrances were his particular favourites.

"I'm so glad you like it, I couldn't let this momentous occasion go by without getting you something. I've bought a present for Jim too, I'll give it to him later."

"Bless you Ricci, you're a sweetie," Jake said smiling. Then delving into his vanity bag he brought out an envelope and handed it to Ricci. "I've got you a little something too."

"What could it be?" Ricci enquired as he began opening the envelope. Jake looked on, waiting to see Ricci's reaction.

Ricci squealed with delight when he saw what was inside. "Two front row seats to see Jean Scholson in Scandal in Park Lane at the Drury Lane Theatre! How wonderful, thank you so much love." Ricci hugged Jake and gave him a kiss. "You couldn't have given me anything better."

What Jake hadn't told him was that he had arranged with Jean for Ricci to meet his favourite actress in her dressing room backstage, where she would have champagne waiting. Once Ricci had calmed down, he began to help Jake get ready. Jake was able to do most of his make-up himself, the only thing he often needed help with was his eyeliner, he didn't always have a steady enough hand, and tonight was one of those times, but Ricci never minded doing it for him.

"I think I'd better have a little drink darling, just to help my nerves," Jake said.

Ricci went over to the cupboard and poured Jake a whisky. Handing it to him he said, "You'll be fine love, you're only nervous because tonight means so much to you, but you'll knock em dead as always. You were brilliant at rehearsal, so don't worry sweetie."

"You're right, of course darling, I'm just being silly. Anyway, I get to wear that fabulous new blue gown for the first time tonight, just the sight of me in that will win them over."

"Absolutely darling, it'll dazzle em."

The new blue gown in question was the most gorgeous concoction of ice-blue coloured silk, covered in sparkling clear crystal droplets, with edgings of darker blue ostrich feathers around the neck and on the cuffs of the diaphanous sleeves. Under the spotlights it would be a sensation. Jake thought it was the most beautiful gown he had ever had, and that was saying something considering all the previous ones he'd worn over the years. While Jake was being got ready, both he and Ricci were listening to the magical comedy genius of Bobby Scott. He had them rolling in the aisles with his infectious brand of humour.

Jake commented to Ricci, "We couldn't have got anyone better than our friend Bobby," and Ricci agreed with him.

Shortly after that Ricci said, "Right darling," taking a step back to look at the full effect now Jake was dressed, "that's you done gal, I can't do any more with you, you look incredible."

Jake was admiring his alter ego in the full-length mirror on the wall as Jim came in to tell him to break a leg and go out there and enjoy this whole unique experience, but the first thing he said was, "Wow beautiful lady," and he gave a loud wolf whistle. "I just want to say one more thing before you go out on stage and shine like the star you are, and that is, you always own whatever stage you're on with your wonderful presence, but just remember darling, you *literally* own this one!"

"Darling Jim, thank you, you always know exactly the right thing to say."

Ricci went to Jim and gave him a small box. He unwrapped it, opened the box to find a pair of gold cufflinks in it. He looked at Ricci and gave him a kiss and said, "Thank you Ricci, they're fabulous, I'll treasure them."

"Miss Rusty L'amour on stage please," the intercom called, "Miss Rusty Lamour on stage please."

The applause was thunderous as she ambled onto the tiny stage after Bobby gave her his thrilling introduction. She walked over to the piano, looked at Trevor her pianist and said in her trademark butch cockney style voice, "Ow ar ya mate." Rusty had to pause then for a long time to allow her audience to subside from laughing before she could then adopt her feminine persona and fully become the legendary Rusty L'amour. She caroused, romanced and captivated her opening night audience into complete submission. They all knew who she was when they paid to come through the doors, but they had never seen her like this; she was stupendous, she had conquered their hearts.

Chapter 45

Next year would be the tenth anniversary of Rusty's Place and Jake and Jim were already planning to have the best party ever to mark its success, their success. They had worked hard and it had paid off, both in a financial sense and the fact that the club was now firmly established as one of the best London nightspots, if not *the* best. Anyone who thought they were anyone, came to see and be seen here. For nearly a decade the club had played host to the rich, the famous, as well as the infamous, the aristocrat and the royal. It was the place to rub shoulders with the elite, but above all else, you came to see Rusty L'amour. The club had taken precedence over everything to ensure that it had the best possible chance of succeeding. Jake had given *Goodbye Mrs McGiver* every consideration, but in the end he had decided not to commit himself to it again; for one thing it held too many painful associations. He thought the people offering him the part understood, anyway, he didn't really care whether they did or not, Jim certainly did, and that was the main thing as far as Jake was concerned. The role was eventually given to the well-known actress Stella Thornton, and it was a roaring success, Jake was thrilled for her, even sending her a bouquet on her opening night with his good wishes for a long run. Turning the part down meant that Jake would be able to concentrate more on the club, helping Jim as much as he could.

Christmas was fast approaching and their advance bookings were unprecedented; it was going to be their busiest time ever.

Jake and Ricci had been shopping for decorations at the same company that supplied Harvey Nichols, the garlands they had chosen were of the highest quality in classic shimmering gold, and the large baubles were also in a gold shade with a red satin bow on the top of them. That was it, simple, classic and tasteful, they didn't want to go tacky and put Merry Christmas signs everywhere, the ambience would be festive enough. They would stick with plain white tablecloths as they always looked so smart, and to complement them, on each table there would be a small gold floral arrangement with a red faux candle lamp – perfect. They were going to be open on Christmas Eve before taking a well-earned break over the rest of the holiday until New Year's Eve when they would be open for business once again. Jake and Jim loved Christmas and were so looking forward to spending a quiet time together relaxing at home doing absolutely nothing. They had talked it over and Jim had asked their chef Marco to come and stay at their home to cook for them over Christmas, as Jim knew he would otherwise be on his own, all his family being in Salerno. He had been only too pleased to accept, as Jim had told him privately to forget they were his employers – "Over the holiday we are your friends, we will share Christmas together."

The club was jam-packed on Christmas Eve, and the customers were intent on merrymaking and having a good time. The champagne was flowing like water, especially the Cristal, so as far as Jim and Jake were concerned the tills were ringing Christmas bells.

When it came time for Jake to do his act, he had a surprise up his sleeve for them all. Bobby introduced him in his own inimitable way.

"Ladies and gentlemen, please welcome on stage the one

and only Miss Rusty L'amour."

The applause began, then as Rusty appeared the whole place was in uproar. Jake was dressed in a red outfit with white fur trim as Mother Christmas, the short figure-hugging coat revealing his gorgeous shapely legs. Once the audience had calmed down sufficiently he began to sing a song he had written especially for the occasion, and he sang it in a sexy, breathy, coquettish, enticing way, singling out men in the audience to flirt with.

I've got something that you really want this Christmas,
Something that you truly truly do
If you've been a very very good boy
Mama Santa's gonna give it all to you

When Jake had finished the song, he felt the wave of love and admiration flowing out from his audience. Everyone was on their feet clapping, whooping and whistling, asking for more. The evening was a complete success. What a way to start Christmas, he was on such a high, feeling good that he had pleased the crowd, getting their festivities off to a good start. He hoped they would remember his performance; Jake wouldn't forget it in a hurry.

By the time, the club had cleared of customers, the staff had finished all their jobs, Rusty had been dismantled and Ricci had put her back on the shelf until the next time. Jake became Jake again.

All the bouquets, gifts of chocolates, etc. had been dispersed and shared among the female staff, apart from the enormous heart-shaped box of luxury chocs from Harrods that Jake wanted to take home along with the biggest bunch of roses he'd ever been given.

Ricci went home in a taxi, very happy, because Jake and

Jim had given him two bottles of Cristal and a cash bonus for all his hard work. Jake, Jim and Marco did their final routine checks around the place, making sure that all equipment was turned off, all the doors were locked, ash trays emptied carefully, the staff making sure nothing was smouldering and likely to cause a fire. They finally gathered their things together. Marco had several large bags that Jim helped him to carry out, they switched off the lights, Jim locked up and they went home. It was two thirty in the morning and even though the three of them were all shattered, they were in a wonderful mood and looking forward to a lovely Christmas.

It seemed strange to Jake to be using a taxi, but he and Jim had made the decision earlier in the year that keeping a chauffeur and a limousine was an extravagant expense they didn't need, considering the amount of times they used it. So they had sadly dispensed with Dennis's services, but they had done so in the best and most generous way they could think of. They gifted Dennis his uniform, along with the Daimler that so loved driving, so that he could start his own business, giving him a glowing reference besides. Jake remembered when they'd told Dennis they were letting him go, he was heartbroken to leave their employment; he was proud of working for his celebrity employer, but when they presented him with the Daimler and its logbook, and told him to set up his own chauffeur-driven private hire business, he broke down and cried. He was overwhelmed, he couldn't believe their kindness and generosity.

Jim said to him, "We know who to call now Dennis when we need a limousine and a driver we can trust. Let us have one of your business cards when you've set up, OK?"

Dennis, still overcome, hugged them both, thanking them

from the bottom of his heart. Jake and Jim watched him proudly get into his very own Daimler and drive off into the distance. They would never forget the look on his face.

It was good to be home. They quickly showed Marco around their home, especially the kitchen, then they took him to his ensuite room and said goodnight. Jake and Jim retired to bed not long afterwards.

Jim was woken up abruptly by the telephone at around five o'clock, it was their landlord letting him know that the fire brigade had informed him the club premises were on fire and that it was very serious. They were fighting to save it.

He said in a very stern voice, "You had better get down here."

After he had put the phone down, he woke Jake who was still sound asleep. "It's bad news, I'm afraid love," Jim said, shocked.

Jake saw the dreadful look on his face, and asked, "What Jim, what's happened?"

"Our landlord just telephoned to say that Rusty's is on fire, the fire brigade is there. We'd better get down there to see what the damage is."

"Oh my god, no, however could that have happened? Did they say how serious it was?"

"He said they were trying to save it."

"Oh bloody hell, that sounds really bad, doesn't it?"

"Yes Jake, I think we need to prepare ourselves for the worst. C'mon, let's get dressed, I'll drive us."

Both in shock, they dressed. Jake suddenly thought of Marco and hurriedly scrawled a note to tell him where they had gone.

As Jim turned into Tavistock Square, nothing could have

prepared him or Jake for the sight that met their eyes. There were two fire engines in the street, with firemen and hoses everywhere. They could see the club was seriously ablaze, flames were leaping high out of the building and the air was thick with acrid smoke. Instinctively they left the car and began to walk mesmerised towards the blazing building. They were suddenly halted by a fireman telling them to keep back.

"But it's our club," Jake said, sounding very feeble.

"I'm sorry about that sir, but you must keep back, it's very dangerous."

Jim put his arm around Jake's shoulders, partly to give him support, partly to stop him from going any further. There were tears in his eyes as he exclaimed poignantly, "I think we've lost it Jake, I think it's gone."

Jake felt his knees buckle from under him. He would have fallen to the ground if Jim hadn't been holding onto him.

Jake wailed, "No, no, our lovely club gone!"

Jim noticed the landlord walking quickly towards them. He had a furious look on his face and started shouting at them. "What the hell did you do? This is all your fault, you've obviously done something wrong."

Jim stood up to him straightaway, saying, "It's not our fault, I suggest you try to calm down and be careful what accusations you throw around. You'd better wait until they tell us what the cause of the fire was."

"Calm down, calm down, I'm fucking ruined, you'll pay for this, you wait and see."

He wheeled around and stormed off. Jim was relieved, he thought for one moment the man was going to get violent, and they would end up having a fight. He was obviously in shock like they were. They just stood there in a complete daze holding on to one another.

Jake spoke through his tears. "All our hard work gone up in smoke, it's just too awful, Jim."

"At least no one has been hurt, we could have been in there, or it could have been full of customers, we can be thankful for that."

"Yes, I suppose you're right, but even so, whatever are we going to do now?"

"Everything will be alright love, let's just wait until they tell us what caused it, we'll take it from there, eh?"

"How is everything going to be alright Jim? All my beautiful gowns have been destroyed along with everything else. I don't know how I'll get over this."

Jim hugged Jake even tighter. "You will love, we both will, we'll do it together."

A large crowd had gathered now, and press and camera crews had arrived. Suddenly a reporter thrust a microphone at them as someone was filming them. He asked them how the fire had started. Jake buried his face in Jim's coat.

Jim just said, "We have no idea, but it looks as though we have lost everything. We don't know any more than that, please don't ask us any more questions at the moment."

The reporter ignored what Jim had said and continued, now angling the microphone towards Jake, "Do you think Rusty's Place will ever re-open again?"

Jim glared at him and snarled, "Are you mad? How the hell do you think we can answer such a stupid question as that at this time? Go away and leave us alone."

Thankfully he did just that and decided to get the cameraman to pan around the crowd.

Jim thought that Jake should sit down so they walked over

to a bench and they sat down huddling close together. Jim had been thinking. He said to Jake, "I think the best thing we can do love is go home, there's nothing we can do here at the moment. We can come back if and when we need to, there's no point torturing ourselves watching this lot. What do you say?"

"You're right, Jim, let's go home."

They walked back to the car, got in and drove away.

Chapter 46

It was eight thirty when they arrived back home. Marco was in the kitchen busy preparing for lunch. He came in to greet them, looking very concerned as he could see from their tear-stained blackened faces that they had both been crying. He asked if they were alright and how bad the fire at the club was. When Jim told him the extent of it, and that he thought it had all gone, he hugged them both and said that he was very, very sorry. Of course, it impacted on him as well, as he was now unemployed. He had really loved his job and he knew he wouldn't ever find two nicer people to work for. He told them that Ricci had telephoned and that he would be ringing back and said he would make them coffee.

"Would you like me to cook you some breakfast?"

Jake waved his hand and replied, "No thank you, Marco, I really couldn't eat anything at the moment. I must go and take a shower."

"Well you might feel like something afterwards, eh?"

"Yes, possibly, thank you Marco."

Jim thought it best that they should all eat something. He said, "Have you had breakfast yet, Marco?"

"No I haven't Jim, I was waiting for you both to come home."

"In that case, while Jake's upstairs showering, I'll take a shower in the downstairs bathroom and then I think we should all sit down to eat breakfast together, if you don't mind cooking Marco?"

"No, not at all Jim, of course not, no trouble at all. I'll go and make a start."

"Thank you so much, Marco, I know the fire has put a dampener on Christmas. We don't feel much like celebrating, but I think we should try to keep things as normal as possible."

"Yes I agree. Well, you don't have to worry about any domestic arrangements regarding food, I will take care of everything, if you let me know what time you want to eat lunch."

"Let's say about two, shall we?"

"OK, very good."

Marco went off to the kitchen and Jim went to have a shower.

Jake was upstairs getting undressed. He put some of the clothes he was wearing into the laundry bin, the rest would have to go to the dry-cleaners, they reeked of smoke. He saw his blackened face in the mirror and he just broke down and cried, he felt so desolate. This was the beginning of a natural grieving process he would experience and have to go through because of his irrevocable loss. Jim, Marco, Ricci, and anyone else connected to the club, would experience the same to a greater or lesser degree. After he had showered and dressed, he went back downstairs. When he smelt breakfast cooking, he had to admit that he did feel hungry. The telephone rang so he answered it.

"Hello."

A tearful Ricci answered with gushing emotion and concern for his two friends.

"Darling, I'm so dreadfully sorry, I couldn't believe it when I saw it on the television. I haven't been able to stop crying. How are you, and how is Jim? You must both be devastated, poor love."

"I don't really know how I'm feeling Ricci, I'm just numb at the moment. We went to see it, it was so horrendous."

Their conversation went on for a good ten minutes until Jake began crying again. He thanked Ricci for ringing and said he would call him in a few days.

Christmas celebrations were practically a non-event. They all went through the motions of observing certain traditions, but they were tainted and seemed unreal, it was like there had been a death in the family. They somehow got through Christmas Day and Boxing Day, Marco had been marvellous, looking after them as though he was their own son.

The day after New Year's Day, when a lot of businesses returned to work, Jim telephoned their insurance company and informed them of the fire. They were very efficient and told him that they would investigate and complete an assessment as quickly as they could. They would contact the Fire Service to obtain a report on their findings. They came back to Jim two days later to let him know that the Chief Fire Officer had informed them that the cause of the fire had been located in a fuse box. It stated that recent wiring work had not been carried out properly and they had discovered that the fuse box had not been earthed. This meant that the electrical company that had carried out the work would be liable. They would be sending Jim a letter explaining everything to him. They asked Jim to locate all the relevant paperwork, i.e. certificates signing off as safe, any work that had been carried out. It was an enormous relief to Jim that he had kept all such paperwork in his study at home and not in the office at the club. Meanwhile, they received a letter from their landlord's solicitors informing them that he was taking proceedings against them as a result of the fire. Jake and Jim contacted their solicitors and put the matter in their hands.

It was all such a worrying, stressful time, that seemed to drag on forever, well into February of the new year, but eventually the whole business was sorted out successfully in Jim and Jake's favour; the insurance company paid them out. This awful period was over and they could begin to put it behind them. They both hoped that the coming year would prove to be a better one for them, once they had received compensation for the fire. So much seemed to be going on domestically, it seemed to be a time of changes. Pru, who had been at pains to point out that it was the most awful timing, had given in her notice and announced that she was going to get married. Jake and Jim on the one hand were saddened that she was leaving, but absolutely delighted at the news she was getting married. Jake joked that he wanted to be matron of honour so that he could buy a new outfit, and everyone laughed out loud. Several days after they had been told Pru's news, Jake spoke to Jim about an idea he had. "Jim, I've been thinking. Do you think in the light of Pru leaving us and getting married, that Marco might like her job?"

"Well I never, I don't believe it, you must be telepathic Jake, I've been thinking exactly the same thing. We will have to ask him, discreetly of course, so that Pru doesn't feel we can't wait for her go. I don't know if Marco would want a live-in position or not, but we will certainly ask him. I think he would be perfect and he's such nice guy."

"Yes he is, he's genuine, I don't know what we would have done without him over Christmas. He worked so hard to make it as good as it could be for us, under the circumstances. Let's call him and ask him to come over and see us."

Chapter 47

The decision to employ Marco was one of their best. He had made himself practically indispensable, he was so good at his job and he had such a wonderful uplifting personality. Jake had nicknamed him Happy Larry because he never seemed to be moody or down in the dumps, he was always cheerful and he seemed to hold them in high regard. Marco had been thinking of moving out of his rented flat in Richmond sometime in the new year as it was far too expensive; he thought he could get somewhere much better for the same money or less. So when Jim and Jake called him saying they would like to see him to discuss something with him, he was intrigued. When they offered him a job as their live-in housekeeper he was over the moon. When he learned how much they were going to pay him for the privilege, he was even more pleased, and he had a self-contained flat as part of the bargain as well; he couldn't believe his luck. He recalled how he hugged and kissed them in gratitude. Jake and Jim were so impressed with his work, and, as good as Pru had been, they had to admit Marco was better. One surprising thing, they had never even considered whether Marco could be gay, it hadn't really crossed their minds, but it turned out he was. Shortly after he moved in, he confided in them both, he said it was the main reason he had left Salerno and moved to Britain. Jake and Jim were delighted, they didn't have to be on their guard like they did when Pru worked for them and the three of them became great friends. It became evident during a three-way chat that Marco was looking for a long term partner. He said he didn't like just having one-night stands, he wanted to share his life permanently with someone. Jake thought of introducing someone he knew to him.

One weekend during the summer, Ricci and Toby had been invited to stay. Jake had also invited someone else, having first spoken to Ricci to get his opinion, and asking Ricci to sound him out; it was their mutual friend Michael from Burmans. Nothing had been said to either Marco or Michael about their matchmaking, it was just a matter of providing an opportunity for two young single guys to meet, and then watch to see what happens, perhaps occasionally engineering situations that would leave them together on their own. It was an interesting experiment and to everyone's delight it appeared to have worked. Jim said he had seen them in the garden together kissing passionately. When he told the others, they all agreed that they hoped it was the start of something big, but only time would tell.

During Sunday lunch, the conversation turned to the possibility of a new venture for Jake and Jim to get involved in. Several ideas were bandied around, quite a lot of them were silly pie in the sky ideas, but Ricci came up with one that Jake and Jim thought was worth serious thought.

"Why don't you set up a theatrical academy, a sort of school for drag? You could teach people all aspects of stagecraft."

"Great, yes, and you could teach the students how to do make-up, wig dressing, wardrobe, etc."

"Oh you want me to help?" Ricci asked, surprised and excited. "I would love it."

"Of course, how could we do it without you love?"

Jake's face screwed up in deep thought lines, then he announced, in a loud voice, "I've got it, why don't we call it

The Hartnell-Wiggins Theatrical Academy? Sounds good, doesn't it?"

Jim, who hadn't really had much to say, suddenly exclaimed, "I think we're on to a winner, you've definitely got something there."

Jake went on, "I think it would have to be residential, rather than just a day school, we would have to look for a suitable building."

"Better still," Jim said, wide-eyed with enthusiasm and excitement, "why not build our own state-of-the-art premises right here in the grounds? We've certainly got enough land, providing we can get planning permission of course."

"Jim, that would be wonderful, can we really do it?"

"Of course we can Jake, why not?"

Jake pronounced, "Here we go again love," then standing up and stretching his arms up and out in a flamboyant stage gesture that Rusty L'amour would use, he grandly declared,

"What are we waiting for darling?
Let's get this show on the road."

Epilogue

Jake could not believe he and Jim were sitting at a table right next to the stage of 'The Talk Of The Town" in what was the old Hippodrome Theatre, waiting for his heroine Dusty Springfield to appear on stage. Jim had booked the tickets as a surprise present for Jake's birthday. They had arranged for an enormous bouquet of red roses to be delivered to her dressing room with a note attached from Jake to say that his dream had finally come true, he was in the audience about to watch her performance.

The theatre manager came to their table to hand Jake a note. After he'd read it, he was so excited Dusty had invited them to come backstage to her dressing room after the performance, he felt as if he were in a dream and gone to heaven. It proved to be the most memorable evening of his life. He had finally got to meet the person he had adulated and adored for so many years. He was not disappointed, she was everything he had imagined she would be, charming, gracious, kind and lovely. When he extended an invitation for her to come and see him at the club, she said she would be delighted to as soon as she was able. Unfortunately, it never happened due to the dreadful fire that destroyed Rusty's Place. Hers had been one of the treasured notes of condolence he had received after it had happened.

On opening the newspaper one day, it came as a shock to read that Terry the ex-bus conductor turned house burglar had been arrested again, but for aggravated burglary this time. He had unfortunately progressed to using extreme violence on an elderly couple living in Hampstead, tying them both up and gagging them; they must have been absolutely terrified. As a result of the attack, sadly the lady victim died. Because he had form, Terry was arrested and identified by the lady's husband. He was brought to trial and convicted of murder, and he was quite rightly given a life sentence.

Jake thought to himself how fortunate he was that he had never become personally involved with such a lowlife as him, he could have ruined his life.

As it was, his life was wonderful, planning permission for the theatrical academy had been granted and they could now go ahead and start building. It was going to take a lot of hard work bringing the dream to fruition, but this was going to be Jake and Jim's greatest achievement yet. It would mean they were creating a legacy that would continue long after they'd gone. It would enable lots of other would-be drag artistes/performers to achieve their ambitions.

They opened a bottle of champagne, as they looked back on all the events that had happened since they met all those years ago at Ricci and Toby's party. They both realised how lucky they'd been.

Jim held Jake in his arms, kissed him and said, "You and I are two of life's survivors, Jake. I'm so lucky to have you, I will always love and adore you." He raised his glass, "Here's to our new venture the Hartnell-Wiggins Theatrical Academy."

Jake chinked glasses. "I love you too, darling, more than words can say. Here's to us and our new exciting venture!"

Darling Jake is the sequel to *Jake* by the same author.

In 1946, Vera Evans is ostracised and thrown out by her family because she is pregnant. The stigma of illegitimacy dictates that she enters a charitable nursing home for unmarried women to have her baby. The home hides a dark secret that Vera wants to run from and with the help of a newfound friend she escapes its sinister confines and gives birth to a boy, whom she calls Jake.

When eleven-year-old Jake, a gentle, nature-loving country boy goes missing in the depth of winter, in a small rural community, a large-scale police search is launched. This captivating story describes the anguish of his parents and the subsequent arrest of Jake's father, who is suspected by the police of having something to do with his disappearance, possible murder.

The extensive search for Jake in a wild rural location heightens everyone's fears for the safety of the boy.

What has happened to Jake?

Is He Alive, Or Is He Dead?

www.amazon.co.uk/Jake-Keith-Bond-ebook

Printed in Great Britain
by Amazon